DESCENDING SOULS

JOHN DONEY

To order additional copies of this book, contact:
Xlibris Corporation
0-800-644-6988
www.XlibrisPublishing.co.uk
Orders@XlibrisPublishing.co.uk
302111

CHAPTER ONE

T he pain surged through his body; cold air filled his lungs. He coughed and spluttered as he remembered how to breathe again. With each breath, he felt the pain burn through his body. The breaths were deep and fast as the rain pounded down upon him. He ran his fingers against his chest, feeling them sink into the deep cut at the centre. The warm flesh cupped his fingers up to the finger nails.

He forced himself to sit up, removing his fingers from the wound and placing them on the wet ground. He felt intense pain as the damaged muscles in his chest moved against each other due to the gaping wound. The cut was so deep that the muscles felt like they may fall from his body. He cupped the injury with his hands as he leaned forward. Each movement caused him to scream. He looked down, slowly removing his hands as blood poured from the wound. He saw the scar and followed its outline with his fingers. For an instant, the pain didn't exist, the rain didn't exist—just his scar, an upside-down triangle with a straight line entering the top and passing through the point at the bottom. The cut was so deep that it had torn through several muscles. Every time he moved, the pain increased. Agony surged through him, and he wished it was over.

Why wasn't it over?

He glanced around and saw no one. The alley was long, and the rain poured. As he attempted to get up, the pain increased. Through gritted teeth, he fought back his cries as the blood continued to flow from his wound. His insides felt as if they were moving on their own in ways only they chose. He discovered another wound. Agony flared from it. He ran his finger around the rim of the small circle and then slipped his finger inside. The hole in his chest seemed endless. He couldn't hold back his agony, and his screams went unheard. He lay back on the wet ground, which had an inch of water covering it. The rain flowed over his body, and the blood from beneath him was carried down the alley on the current. The large hole that the bullet had exited from began to heal. He felt the flesh pull itself together. The pain at first was excruciating, his agony heard by no one.

Then it stopped. He sat up and looked at his chest, feeling the pain ease. He ran his fingers across the wound to feel the gaps closing. The torrential rain washed away the last of the blood; his scars had gone. He remained kneeling on the ground as the rain, heavier now, continued to wash away the pain.

It always got busy when the weather was like this. The city of Alterson was large, with an ever-growing population. Rev. Daniel Jones had seen the city go through bad times. His church had survived the recession of 2010, and he had watched as a fire burnt through higher Alterson five years later. He'd tried to help rehome its victims, watching the city as it gradually raised itself from the ashes in the years that followed. However, never had he seen things like this.

The heavy raindrops sounded like an army marching along the slated roof of the church. Their continuous steps echoed over the chatting of the hall's new residents—something else they'd grown used to, like the smell of dampness and body odour. The torrential rain had been continuous for nearly a week. The first people who had entered his church had left from Balcoon Street after their ground floors had flooded. It hadn't been the first time the ground floors of their houses had flooded during the heavy rains of winter; however, it was the first time their houses had gone under the river's current.

'You'll have to start building an ark soon, Rev!' Boris bellowed, startling Reverend Jones from his thoughts. Since Balcoon Street, many streets had been evacuated and the people brought to his church hall; others were taken to the county hall on the other side of the city. The church had been stripped of its glory by these winds and torrents. Whereas the church used to bathe in glory from its stained glass windows as the sun gleamed through, it was now shadowed in darkness, as boards protected the windows. The only light in the hall was from the dimly glowing bulbs.

Reverend Jones felt uncomfortable in the church hall now. Even he felt it silly, but he felt the gods weren't watching as closely as before. He used to feel comforted when he saw the colours of the windows dance along the grey brick walls. He pulled himself from his thoughts as he cast Boris a grin.

Boris was one of the men from Newcastle Street. His home was flooded during the first few days, shortly after the flood on Balcoon. Boris Ludvig was an ageing man who had lived in Alterson all his later life after moving from Russia in the Nineties. He had often helped at the church, and today was no different, for he was rushing around handing out hot cups of tea to all those who needed them. He had been in the church when his house flooded three days ago, but the knowledge barely slowed him. He looked at it as a case of whatever will be will be. Reverend Jones liked Boris. He was a kind man, and with the way things were going, Jones knew he needed people like him.

A number of families in the church had lost everything. One family had been rescued from their upstairs bedroom windows after the bottom floors of their house had flooded. He had been talking to their mother, Susan, that morning. She was devastated. All their family photos of deceased relatives and the children growing up, everything from their past, had washed out to the river. The only reassuring thing was the fact that they were all alive. They were lucky. The floods had taken a number of lives.

Ms Lully was a good friend of Jones's, and she had drowned in her downstairs bedroom. She was old and unable to make the stairs to save herself because the water came so fast. All Jones could do was pray that the Lord would have mercy on these people. He glanced around at all the sleeping bags and people that filled his church. Lord have mercy on them all.

He had made his way from the alley, the elements freezing his body. Goosebumps rode across his skin with each lashing of cold wind, the raindrops reddening it. The city seemed empty as he stumbled through the ghostly streets.

As he approached the city centre, he heard voices. The voices startled him, and panic set in. He glanced around the area and noticed an alleyway between two shops. He ran into it and pressed his back against the cold, wet wall, peering up the main street.

There were several youths laughing as they walked through the rain. One was swinging a bottle in his hand, his other arm wrapped around the girl next to him. The youths were drunk. Their loud voices filled him with fear as they sounded through the empty street. He stepped back further so they couldn't see him. As he watched them pass, their laughter echoed in his head.

'Hello, Susan, how are you now?' Reverend Jones asked, sitting down next to her. She was seated on the floor, her youngest son fast asleep, resting his head on her lap. Susan forced a smile as she stroked her son's blond hair.

'Like I said, we're alive.' Her smile was fading as her eyes welled up. Jones placed a comforting hand on her shoulder.

'I know it's not the same, nor will it ever bring back what you have lost, but I thought it might help you start again.' Jones held out a disposable camera, which Susan took, allowing a single tear to escape. She quickly wiped it away.

'Thank you.' Her smile no longer seemed quite as forced.

He walked down the long, cobbled main street of Alterson, which was layered with several inches of water, deeper still where the drains had overflowed. It seemed familiar, but he had no idea how. *Have I been here before—walked these streets?*

Slowly, he walked along the pavement next to a shop's boarded-up windows. As he passed, he stopped. He looked long and hard at what used to be a toy-store window. The wood seemed to be calling his name. He placed a hand against it and felt sure he heard a soft voice speak: 'Tommy?'

Then there was nothing. He took his hand from the wood, looked at it, and then continued down the street. He rubbed his hands against his arms in an attempt to fight the coldness that had settled in. The torn T-shirt hung from his shoulders, his chest still exposed. His trousers were soaked through and trainers ruined. His long black hair had rat-tailed down his face. His body shivered as he walked away from the main street.

Then the thunder rumbled through the street behind him.

'Hello, Mrs Shannings? Are you okay?' Boris asked as he opened the kitchen door, his smile as warm as ever.

'Apart from the demand on this 'ere boiler, we're fine.'

'Sorry, Ali, but I'm going to add to that demand now.'

'Should've guessed you'd be in here for a reason other than saying hello! How many you need, love?'

'About another six for now. We've just had a family come in from South Court. Their house has been hit by these floods too.'

'South Court! That ain't a good sign! They're quite a way up the hill there. Is it flooded like the others?' Some houses in the lower parts of Alterson had been flooded up to the top levels. One police officer had said that four houses were barely visible, just the peaks of the roofs showing.

'No, it's just beginning at South Court,' Boris responded. 'They've moved everything upstairs in an attempt to save it, but the bottom floors are covered by a couple of inches. It's just a precaution for now. Think they're gonna evacuate the whole estate by tomorrow. Rain's hammering down out there more than ever tonight. Must be an inch more every second—never seen anything like it!' Boris watched as Alison Shannings poured the tea into mugs that were waiting to be filled on a tray. None of the mugs matched, as the church's utilities were stretched to their fullest.

'They're a lot better off than the others. Cheryl, dear of her, is still crying over her poor cat. Poor thing was left to drown.' Ali wiped her brow before continuing. 'Can you do us a favour, Boris love? When you're out there, bring us some cups back.'

'No problem, Ali. Will be back in a jiffy!' Boris scooped up the tray of tea and headed back out the door. Alison refilled the boiler with a big sigh.

What she'd give for her Michael back. He'd be helping her here now. Boris was as good as gold, but she was aching after all these hours in the kitchen—struggling to make enough food and keep the hot drinks going. She had several people to help, but she knew that they had bigger problems than she did. Her house, near the top of Old Oak Hill, was safe.

'Ali, how are you doing in here? Would you like a rest?'

Ali blinked hard, pulling her attention away from the grey boiler in front of her. Catching a glimpse of Rev. Daniel Jones in the mirror, she turned to face him. 'No, Daniel, I'm fine. Plenty of life in this ole dog yet!' It was a lie, but she knew Daniel Jones was feeling the same. He had been awake since it all began, since the first homeless man came looking for shelter eight days ago. She had seen him take small naps in the pews, but he hadn't left the church once.

'If you need a break, though, just say. Susan has offered again to help if you need sandwiches made.'

'She's a good one, ain't she? I had little Jenny helping in here earlier as well. Dear of her. Don't think she'd ever made a sandwich before.'

A smile crept across Jones's face at the fondness in Ali's voice. 'She's a good girl. I was talking to her father earlier. Her mum has made a full recovery now. They're keeping her in the hospital again tonight to watch over her. They say that her vitals are a lot better now. Remember, if you want a break, just say.'

'Thanks, Daniel. I've got Boris 'ere at the minute, and we're coping. He just said we got another family in. It's getting pretty full in 'ere now, ain't it! What's the hospital like?'

'They're still completely full. They're going to send a couple of doctors here to check over us later . . . , just to be safe. Bethel is looking rather weak, and I'm beginning to get concerned.'

'Did you manage to get hold of her son?'

'Not yet, but even if I could, he couldn't get here anyway. Several trees are down on the outskirts of town. They're barricading the main roads coming in. Also, the train track heading in from the south is flooded. They said that they're expecting a break in the weather within the next couple of days, but how much worse will it get by then?'

'That's a question that I'd rather not ask right now!'

He looked down the hill to see the water levelled with the upstairs windows of the houses. Several cars floated upon its current and stopped as they pressed against a roof of somebody's former home. On the outskirts of the newly made river, close to the top of the hill, several police officers stood around their cars. Draped in waterproofs, they faced the elements in the line of duty. He looked around once more and then made his way towards the other side of the city.

The streets broadened into a large car park beside the Westside Shopping Centre, which he wandered through. Thunder rolled along the clouds above him, coldness riding the air around him. He hoped for some shelter and warmth. Rubbing his body, he glanced ahead.

The flash was so bright that it temporarily blinded him, the sound deafening. Its impact sent him flying back to the ground. He sat up and realised that a lightning bolt had struck a clothes bank. The metal bin had disintegrated, and its contents were scattered around the car park.

He ran across and grabbed several garments. He slipped his torn T-shirt from him, tearing the remaining bit of fabric holding the front together. Dropping to the clothes on the ground, he struggled to put on a black T-shirt against his wet skin, followed by another shirt. Next to him, he saw a long black coat, which he pulled on. Despite the layers of clothes, he still felt cold, and the rain still poured down upon him, the dry clothes soon becoming damp.

He wrapped the long coat tightly around his body as the rain began to soak through the layers. He walked out the entrance of the car park and made his way along the main road. The road was now a small river, the water just above the pavement height, and manholes were overflowing. At the end of the road, he saw an old warehouse with shattered windows.

Entering, he glanced around the large room. Small pools of water filled the centre of the concrete forecourt. He watched the rain dance along the surface puddles before noticing the broken skylight.

In the corner of the room, something moved; rustling amongst the debris, it caught his attention. As concern struck him, a small rodent scurried from the pile of rubbish and through a crack in the dividing wall. He watched the mouse with relief as it vanished into the darkness. Hesitantly, he glanced around the level he was standing on, unable to see the next.

He walked towards some steps connected to the dividing wall; they led to the next level. From the third step, he scanned the second floor of the warehouse. Some rotting carpets lay on the floor, offcuts from the stores' glory days. Several carpet tubes lay across the back wall, damp and rotting.

He sat on the top step and pulled the wet coat tighter to him, hoping his body warmth would help dry the heavy fabric. He sighed as a shiver ran down his spine. Shivering, he watched the rain drip into the puddles in the centre of the showroom.

'Bethel?' Jones crouched down next to her. 'Bethel?' he repeated, gently touching her shoulder. There was still no response. Jones readjusted himself so he was kneeling in front of her.

'Bethel? Are you okay?' The words went unheeded. Jones reached for her hand that dangled from under the blanket. Her hand was frozen. Discreetly, he checked for her pulse. There was none. Bethel was now another casualty of these storms.

The wind howled through the warehouse, sending the debris of leaves and papers into large whirlwinds. As he huddled in the corner, a newspaper blew against his legs. He reached down to remove it, but as he did, something made him want to look. The cover showed the symbol that had been carved into his chest, telling the story of the murders in Alterson's main street as they had attempted to assassinate the police chief. The story gave several names of the innocent victims from the drive-by attack. One name felt familiar: Claire Hearst. An image overcame him: the long blonde hair, her large green eyes, red lips . . . Then, as quickly as it came, it was gone.

'Thomas Atkins . . . , I need your help.' He raised his eyes from the paper and saw a hollow form standing before him. His eyes froze open, although he wanted them to close. 'I'm Harry Roberts, and I need you to help me with my daughter.' The words were faint, as was his form. Tommy could clearly see his features and make out his long face, his flat nose, and his eyes deep in their sockets, but he could also see through to the wall behind. The man's slim body almost seemed to float as he stood before him.

'You're a ghost . . . !' Tommy exclaimed as he pulled the coat tighter, crumpling the paper within it. The words trailed into silence. As Harry began to speak again, Tommy's screams drowned out his frail voice. Tommy continued to scream and push himself further into the corner of the room, pulling his head under the collar of the coat.

Despite the explosion occurring outside, the sound echoed through the church.

'What was that?' Jones asked, bursting into the kitchen.

'It was outside. I just saw a flash! I think it was lightnin',' Ali said, glancing as far as she could from the small kitchen window, the cascade of rainwater falling down and blurring her view.

'I'll go check.' Jones swung his coat on and headed towards the church doors. Several people had already left and headed towards the flames that lit the ground.

A lightning bolt had hit a headstone of the Benovolt family, a large statue of an angel with its wings closed. The statue had been blown from the stand and now lay on the grass behind it. Reverend Jones, Boris, and several other people stood looking down at the flames that burned continuously on the wet grass. The flames were burning in the shape of open wings. Other than the two closed wings broken from the statue, there was no other damage. The destruction seemed deliberate. Jones looked at the others and then back at the angel wings burning on the ground.

'We'd best go back in,' Jones said, breaking the silence. 'I know they say lightning doesn't strike twice, but I don't want us taking any chances.' As they headed towards the church, Jones grabbed Boris's arm, holding him back from the crowd. 'I need your help in a minute, Boris. We need to move Bethel into the back room. Just before this, I found out she's passed.' Boris gave a silent nod as Jones looked back at the burning wings. The rain continued to pound down heavier than before, but the flames danced unchanged.

CHAPTER TWO

CHAPTER TWO

CHAPTER TWO

T he sun warmed Tommy's cheek as it shone through the broken skylight of the old carpet warehouse. He sat up and looked around. That *thing* had gone. He wiped his hands over his face, smiling at the warmth, and then looked up at the overpowering light. The brightness caused him to turn his head away, and he looked to the ground once more.

Again, he saw the newspapers next to him, almost as if they had been placed there. He picked them up, glancing at the story of the drive-by shooting. It was only as he began to read it that he realised that he could. He had no knowledge of who he was, but somehow, he knew what all the words on the page meant. Claire Hearst wasn't the only one to die that day, but it was the only name that stood out to him. He ran a finger over her face from a memorial photo they had published a few days later, wishing he could remember more.

'I'm sorry, Dr Harrow, but I may have had you come out under false pretences. A lot has happened here since we spoke. Unfortunately, Bethel has passed away. However, as you're here, I would like you to take a look at little Timmy. He's only six, and he's come down with quite a fever.' Reverend Jones made his request as he and the doctor entered the church hall.

'I'll make a call in a minute and see if they'll collect Bethel. Until then, however, point me in the direction of the young Timothy.'

Dr Barry Harrow had been a doctor in the city for close to twenty-four years and was known and respected by a number of people, patients, and professionals alike. He approached Timothy and knelt down next to him with his reassuring smile.

'So how are you feeling, Timmy?' he asked, placing his hand on Timothy's forehead. 'You're quite warm, aren't you?'

'I don't feel very well. I felt strange after I spoke to Bethel yesterday,' Timmy informed him as Harrow frowned, reaching around in his bag for his stethoscope.

'He also couldn't remember much for a couple of hours,' Timothy's mum interjected.

'Did he collapse? Faint?'

'No, his memory just seems to have vanished. It was shortly after that that he began to burn up and break into these sweats.'

Dr Harrow acknowledged Susan's words as he checked her son's heartbeat and chest. Timothy jumped slightly as the cold metal of the stethoscope touched him. Harrow gave a chuckle and an apology as he listened.

'His heartbeat and breathing seem fine. He must have caught some type of chill. There's a lot of that going on lately, given how the weather's been. Also, everyone being cooped up in this room together will make germs and viruses more contagious—especially if Bethel was already ill. I wouldn't worry. He should be fine, but if he doesn't improve, feel free to contact me again.' Dr Harrow placed the stethoscope back in his bag and scruffed up Timmy's blond hair. 'You'll be alright, kid.'

The city was beginning to fill up as Tommy made his way down the main street. As he passed an elderly couple, he had a strange feeling come over him. Someone young feared for them. He could hear the words saying where they lived and that they were in danger. The girl loved her grandparents. Tommy paused and watched them walk away. For a moment, he wanted to stop them and tell them. It was then that he realised they'd never even seen him.

Who was the voice?

The pavements were drying; the drains seemed to have cleared, and some shops had reopened. People now rushed to buy food as the city's weeklong standstill had come to an end. The forecast had predicted some of the highest temperatures in decades for the next week, with no sign of any rain. The rain had vanished as quickly as it had appeared.

Tommy stood by the boarded-up toy store once again, looking at the chipboard. Something drew him to this place . . . , that window. He felt someone—someone who loved him. She had been there. As he touched the boards, he could almost hear her voice as she said his name:

'Tommy.'

He stepped back and shook away the thoughts before walking towards Alterson Park. He walked down to the riverside and sat on the wooden bench, watching people as they walked by. The bench had been underwater seven hours ago. Now the river behind him rushed along, nearly six feet below the park, as was normal, carrying the floods back to the sea.

'Daniel, I've just been up to see Bethel. I don't think she passed away yesterday. The discolouration of her skin, deflation of her eyes . . . , I'd say she passed away nearly a week ago.' Jones turned to him with a puzzled look as he set down the kettle. Dr Harrow had closed the door to the kitchen as he entered so no one else could hear the news.

'How's that possible? She was talking to us yesterday morning. She wasn't making much sense, granted, but like I said, she wasn't well.' Reverend Jones's words were accompanied by the clanging of the spoon as he stirred their cups of tea.

'I don't personally know. Medically, I wouldn't have said that was possible.' Dr Harrow took the cup from Jones as he continued, 'Once we get her to the hospital, we'll run a proper post-mortem to be sure of the cause of death,' he paused as he took a sip of the tea. 'That's a good brew there.'

'I've checked on Susan and Timothy,' he continued. 'He seems to have had some strange symptoms, but everything seems to be fine now. He should be okay, but keep him monitored the best you can.'

'I will, Barry. You know that. Although I've just had Officer Samuels pop in, doing his daily check. Apparently, some people will be able to go home quicker than expected. The houses are being pumped as we speak. The floods have dropped as quickly as they rose.'

'It's been an incredibly strange week. I mean, have you ever known temperatures like these in November? To be honest, I don't even think the summer was this hot!'

'That's true. Talking about strange things, did you hear about the lightning hitting the Benovolt angel last night?'

'Only what I heard said around here today,' the doctor responded. 'Care to enlighten me?'

'Well, you've probably heard everything. It's been the most talked about thing here since. The lightning bolt hit the angel statue of the family grave. It fell backwards, breaking the closed wings off, and for nearly four hours, in that heavy rain, two extended wings burned on the grass. They went out as the last of the rain fell in the early hours of this morning.'

Harrow gave another look of confusion as he sipped at his tea after gently blowing on it.

'You want to know something even stranger?' the reverend continued. 'Look out there now. The grass where the flames were isn't even damaged.'

'That surely can't be possible?'

'Exactly what I thought, and for the life of me, I can't work out how or why. Guess it's just another one of those strange things that's happened this week. Samuels was saying that there were three reports of lightning last night. The one here. One outside that Night Arts Centre, that nightclub that the gang frequents—apparently, it blew apart some of those big, glass recycling bins they have lined up in the alley. The other one hit the Westside Centre shoppers' car park and blew apart a clothes bin. It sounds as if it was all planned, doesn't it?'

Dr Harrow frowned as he took in the information. 'It's probably they were the only lightning bolts that connected or caused damage people have found. In all honesty, though, I can understand the others . . . , but not the flaming angel here, especially when it was the last one. Maybe it was his way of answering all your prayers! One thing all the people out there have said in unison is how much you've been trying to help and how much time you've spent praying for it. You're a special man, Daniel. Maybe you've been noticed now.'

For a moment, a silence dropped over them as they exchanged smiles and drank their tea.

'I don't think it works like that.' Jones laughed as he placed the cup back on the draining board.

CHAPTER THREE

Samuels walked along the corridor on the second floor of the Alterson Police Station. As he did, he glanced out of the windows that overlooked one of the main roads that led into the city. It was busy for the first time in over a week. The main food stores had reopened that morning, selling limited fresh products they had managed to get delivered that morning other than the basic canned food they'd been left with in the previous days. Their staff had been more than halved too during the week, with only the nearby staff appearing for work. Despite the heat beaming down and the floods vanishing overnight, the routes into the city were limited, with several trees down and train lines damaged.

The fresh products had been announced on various local radio stations and TV programmes, so the race to get them was on. Samuels almost chuckled as he thought about how the Christmas rush was happening a month early this year!

He had been working in the flooded areas most of that morning, and there had been a lot of progress made. They had originally thought it would take a number of weeks for the tides to drop to a normal level, let alone pump all the water from the houses. The water levels had dropped within a matter of hours early that morning. Between two and five, the river had dropped to a new low, and the streets had drained themselves.

No one had ever seen anything like it. This was the third, and worst, time Samuels had worked on a flood in Balcoon Street. Both times, it had taken longer to flood the houses and much longer to clear than this. No one could understand it, but they were all grateful. Of course, despite having their houses drained, it didn't make much difference to the people, as their lives had been partly destroyed. All the memories they cherished were now reduced to a soggy mess. His heart went out to them.

As he entered the small locker room, he saw Marie Hoskins seated at one of the three benches that lined the centre between the rows of grey lockers. She held a sandwich in one hand, and her other flicked through the pages of *Heat* magazine, which rested on the bench in front of her.

'Working out what's hot and what's not, eh?' Samuels asked as he opened his locker.

Marie looked up with a smile. 'Something like that. Got your usual comics today?'

Samuels returned her smile as he pulled his bag from the locker. 'I read a comic here once and never live it down.'

'Don't worry; I won't bring it up again. So how's things down at Balcoon Street? Can you see the front doors yet?'

'Houses are being cleared as we speak. Completely drained a couple already this morning. No idea where all the water went. Last night, it was running over the houses, with cars as sailboats, and this morning, the rivers were at their normal height, if not lower. Weirdest thing ever!'

'Hey, every year's got to be known for something; 2019, the year of the weirdest weather!' Marie exclaimed as she poured a cup of coffee from her flask.

'You know they have machines that'll make that for you in the other room? It saves you making it in the mornings.' Marie gave him a sarcastic smile.

'If you're saying that this year will be remembered for the weather it would make a refreshing change from the years being remembered as something the Rivals did,' Samuels said. '2014, when the Rivals gang outnumbered police. 2016, the first murders of the Rivals gang. Need I continue?'

'I've only just been transferred here, remember. I don't know much about them. All I've been told is to watch how I go about arresting them, and that I'll know them by the symbol.'

'Yeah. There's a lot of people that'll tell you that kind of shit. It'll come down to whether you're a real cop or one of "their" cops. Sometimes, they'll try to slip you cash under a table. Other times, they tend to scare you into it. Personally, they don't scare me. They want to come at me with force, I'll have no trouble pulling the trigger on them. They were the ones who took my son from me.'

'I also heard that from the chief. He said I could learn a lot from you. Not many know this, but a friend of mine got hooked on their drugs, and she overdosed on a batch last year. Cocaine. I came here 'cause I wanted to cut them down to size so it doesn't happen to anyone else.' Marie sat upright, sipping her coffee.

Samuels could see that same mixture of upset and anger about her, the same emotions he felt when he thought of them and how they took his son from him. 'It's not that easy, unfortunately. They've been around for a number of years, as you've probably researched. Made loads of money during the recession about ten years back. They were selling illegally imported cigarettes and alcohol back then at a real low price. They could undercut every shop on the high street. Once that market was established, they moved on to the drugs, and Tony Boswell and his building industries covered it all up. He had so many companies working for him that he could cover almost everything up. He knew the recession would protect him on that front. He had bought so many companies in Alterson that the only way to check that they weren't linked to the black market trading would be to temporarily close them all down and check them over. At one count, it worked out that we'd have to close down nearly forty companies. Unemployment was at the highest ever. No one could agree to it or find enough evidence.

'The symbol soon became the "in" thing amongst the clubbers, and slowly, they formed a gang that outnumbered us. It wasn't until five years in that the murders became frequent. At first, we believed that they were planned by the key members that we have on file here. They were some of the first people Tony Boswell employed. We haven't been able to trace the members for the past few years. They seem to have dropped off the radar when it comes to crime scenes. Murders aren't quite so frequent, but we've also had many copycat killers using the symbol to cover up other murders. No one can really find a way to take them down. There never seems to be enough evidence! It just becomes a losing battle.' As Samuels explained, he could sense that his voice was becoming emotional, which he tried to cover up with a shrug of his shoulders.

'We'll find some. I guess we just have to sort out the current crisis first!' Marie announced.

Samuels smiled. He could feel how worked up he was getting, and he knew it must have been showing. He gave a nod and changed the subject.

'They reckon most of the people will be able to return home this evening to see their properties,' he said as he unwrapped a sandwich from its cling film and took a large bite. 'Hate that saying, though: "see their properties". They used to be *homes*. It's almost as if they lost that title. I was in some this morning. Hardly anything is salvageable.'

'It must be devastating to lose everything like that.' Marie stood up. She picked up her flask, screwed the lid on, and placed it back into her locker, followed by her magazine. 'Best be heading back out there now. I'm with the clean-up crew in the city centre. They're hoping to have all damaged areas reopened by the weekend.'

'They'll have to go some. They only have forty-eight hours. Good luck to 'em!'

CHAPTER FOUR

'Fuckin' old fag!' Ian screamed as he threw a boot into the homeless man's ribs. He accepted the attack without resistance. He was old and outnumbered, and he was use to the young people of today, those bearing the symbol particularly.

'Go on, Chris, nail him!' Ian's voice was arrogant. He stood there in his jeans and shell suit top, single stud in his left ear, calling the shots. He knew Chris wouldn't do it. He, like many of the others, wanted to be part of Ian's gang because other kids thought he was cool. He was just out of school and had been given a job trafficking drugs for Ben Williams at Alterson College. Everybody knew the respect that would gain someone, Ian especially.

Ben Williams was one of the most trusted and highest positioned people within the Rivals gang. He knew his job and made sure only the right people knew him. Ben had been good friends with Ian's cousin for about eight years, and Ian worshiped his cousin for it. His cousin was Gavin Wallace, commonly known to his friends as Squawk. He was one of the biggest dealers on the club and pub circuit in the city. That's what Ian wanted to be doing one day, working and selling next to his cousin, a family business. Who needed to stack shelves when you could make easy money for one night's work?

'What ya waitin' for? He ain't gonna fight back! He's some homeless fuckin' drunk that don't mean shit to anyone!'

Chris stepped forth and gave a light kick into the whimpering man's ribs. Ian let out a sigh and shook his head.

'Fuckin' pussy,' Ian said, pulling Chris back, waving in his other friend. 'Craig, you got more balls than sissy Chrissy, right?' As Ian looked at him, Craig's confidence grew visibly.

'Yeah, 'course I have!' As he finished the words, his kick gave an echoing thud into the homeless man's ribs, causing him to cry out.

'That's more like it! You gonna have a real crack, Chris?' Both boys looked to Chris.

Chris had just turned sixteen. He had been bullied by some members of Ian's group and felt if he became a member, he'd be accepted and be one of the bullies, no longer the bullied. As he watched the homeless man reach out for his hat, he recalled himself being on the floor and reaching out for his books.

Just before the man gripped the rim of his hat, Ian's foot stamped on it, and his fingers cracked, causing his whimpers to become louder cries. He begged them to leave him alone, which the youths mistook for a request for another attack. Chris stepped away and watched from a distance as Ian and Craig threw a number of kicks into the man. Amongst their own cries of hate and the homeless man's pleas for mercy, they never saw the dark figure creep up behind them.

Ian felt the hand on the back of his neck seconds before he was thrown backwards to the ground. Craig stopped kicking and looked at the tall figure, the long black hair shadowing his face, the long coat and black clothes ... The seventeen-year-old was clearly full of fear.

'Oy! You fuckin' startin'?' Thomas Atkins turned to face Ian, who was still on the ground.

'Neither of us are. Go home,' the words were said calmly and coldly as Ian struggled to his feet.

'Who the fuck do you think you are? Do you know who I am?' Ian demanded as he rolled his sleeve up to show the Rivals symbol, an upside-down triangle with a line through the centre.

'A troubled kid. That's all you are. Don't let that scar damage your soul. You're still young.'

'Scar! That's my crest! Who I am, what I believe!' Ian worked himself up again, this time pulling a knife from his pocket. With the press of a button, the blade exposed itself.

'Is that what you believe?' Thomas asked, waving a hand towards the homeless man. 'You believe you proved how tough you are by attacking someone who can't fight back?'

'Fuck you! I'll fuckin' kill you!' Ian stepped forward, swinging the blade back and forth. One swing sliced Tommy's cheek. The crimson liquid ran from the cut. Before he could connect again, Tommy grabbed Ian's wrist and pulled the blade from it with his other hand. Without taking his eyes from Ian, Tommy threw the knife into the river behind them. As he released Ian's wrist, Ian fell back to the grass next to the pathway.

From the roadside, a couple watched. Craig had just run past them, and Chris was slowly walking to the homeless man. Ian watched his friend flee and looked at Tommy again.

'I'm gonna tell my cousin on you, ya know. I swear he'll fuckin' kill ya for this!' Tommy remained silent and nodded. Ian struggled up and maintained eye contact with Tommy. 'You're one fucked-up Gothic faggot, ain't ya!' Ian walked backwards, keeping his abuse and guard up until he felt a safe enough distance to turn around and run. As he fled the scene, he pushed between the couple that had approached them.

Thomas Atkins knelt down next to the old man and helped him sit up. His beard was dirty, stained with the years of rough living on the streets. His face was wrinkled, his blue eyes filled with wisdom. Just above his right eye, he had a small cut, and the back of his head felt swollen. As the homeless man sat upright, Chris placed the hat back on his head. He looked at Tommy and gave a nod, accompanied with a nervous smile, which Tommy returned. Chris's smile became more confident, and he slowly stepped back from Tommy and the victim before fleeing the scene.

Tommy took the man's hand in his and thought back to what he was feeling earlier as he'd approached them. The thoughts were there again, this time stronger. A blonde woman handing out flyers, tears in her eyes. Years of sorrow flowed through Tommy, and the homeless man's eyes opened wide. He said only one word: 'Daphne!' Tommy released the man's hand and ran his hand over his cheek; the knife wound had healed and the thoughts faded. He had no idea what had happened, but the old man began to struggle up as the couple stood over them.

As they offered to help, Tommy stepped back. He glanced at the man as he struggled to all fours.

'You made me remember!' the homeless man said as he pulled himself up with the help of the suited man. 'I lost my tablets; I stopped taking them. I need to find her, my daughter.'

'Do you know where she is?' the woman asked. She was of medium build and was wearing a navy suit with the jacket done up. Her smile was warming and her appearance friendly as she reached forth, placing a hand on Tommy's arm. Tommy shook his head and stepped away from her.

'How'd you do that, sir?' the homeless guy asked, and Tommy shrugged, shaking his head.

'I . . . I don't know. I . . . I just kind of did. Take care of him. I have to go!' Before anyone could say anything else, Tommy hurried away from the area.

As he ran through the park, along its windy path, he knocked into an older man. They both stumbled, and as Tommy went to apologise, he felt something run through him, something different, something he couldn't understand. So many images flashed before him. Images of angels and flames—and people that looked different. Something wasn't right. They stopped and observed each other. Tommy looked at his stocky build and greying hair. In turn, he looked over Tommy. Whatever was there, Tommy knew they both could see it. Tommy said sorry before he continued to run down the path, barely hearing the words 'I'm sorry too, my friend' as Boris said them.

CHAPTER FIVE

CHAPTER FIVE

'You must feel like some of the unlucky ones being left here tonight,' Reverend Jones announced as he sat in the pew next to Susan.

'No, we're fine. You've been amazing these last few days. I honestly don't know how we would have coped without you.'

'I'm just doing my duty. I can't rebuild your memories or resurrect Bethel, but I can put a roof over your heads and give you some blankets and an ear to bend,' Jones said, forcing a smile.

'Bethel meant a lot to you, didn't she?'

'She's been coming here for years. In all honesty, she was here before I was. I can't help feeling partly responsible. She was a dear soul.'

'It wasn't your fault, Daniel. If you want to blame anything, blame this weather. It's taken many good people.' Susan placed a hand on Reverend Jones's shoulder and gave it a reassuring rub.

'They certainly have taken a number of good men and women from us this time round. I was talking to Officer Samuels this morning. Last night, two firemen were lost to the floods. Somebody had ended up in the water at South Walk Gardens, and the current was carrying him to the main river. The firemen went across in a boat, but with the torrents we were having last night, they got washed under with the current. Both firemen on-board drowned, as well as the guy they were trying to save. They died putting everyone else first—and you people call me amazing. Those people are the amazing ones. They've been out there every minute of every day during this ordeal, and they saved numerous lives with barely a thought for their own safety. They all deserve medals for what they've done.'

'Don't sell yourself short there. You think about how many people have passed through here these last few days. I doubt you've had a full night's sleep all week. You're more than just a roof, some blankets, and an ear to bend. You made us all into a temporary family. You've given us food, love, and shelter . . . , and, some of us, a lot more.' Susan's response caused Reverend Jones to blush as he glanced around the dark grey walls of the church.

'Thank you, Susan. May I just say, though, if you continue to preach like that, I'm expecting you to start here on Sundays.' Reverend Jones stood up with a large smile on his face, and Susan laughed. 'May I just ask, Susan, what else did I give you besides food, love, and shelter?'

'A disposable camera!' She waved the camera in the air.

'That I did.' Jones laughed as he headed down the aisle of the empty church.

Tommy sat in the warehouse, rubbing his hands together as he looked at them. *How did that happen? What was it?*

He had been uneasy since he had passed the images on to the homeless guy. His body had tingled, and he had felt his insides change to a certain extent. The scar from the knife had healed. *How?*

Knowing he felt something different inside, he wondered if the pain he felt from the alley was just the beginning. He could only pray. He didn't want that pain back. There were so many questions about himself that he wanted answered, but the only questions he could find answers to were those about the symbol he had felt on his chest, the one he believed the Rivals had put there.

Somehow, more papers had arrived in the warehouse. It was as if someone had been secretly planting them in the warehouse for him to find. There were numerous stories from different papers about the drive-by shooting. There were various other stories of gang murders and arrests—how members of the council were rumoured to be linked to them. The only thing the people of authority and the drug pushers had in common was one businessman: a man who was both admired as a hero of the city for his work in rebuilding the main street after the city's fire in 2015 and also despised due to links with some of the Rivals members. He was rich and swayed powerful figures in his favour. His name was Tony Boswell.

Chapter Six

Again, the sun awoke Thomas Atkins from his sleep. Squinting from its brightness, he shifted on the concrete floor, the newspapers rustling on his chest from the article he'd spent the last night reading.

Mary Watson, a local councillor who had sworn to clear up the city's streets, had been run down in the car park as she left her office in the county hall. She had challenged the links between Ben Williams and Tony Boswell. Despite the coincidence, however, there was not enough evidence to link this murder to Tony Boswell or the Rivals gang. The report read that the surveillance tapes from that evening had been stolen. Her funeral coverage was on the front cover of a second paper; she'd had a turnout of over five hundred people. Inside the paper, another page expressed people's views, stating that they wouldn't give up the fight against the gangs.

Tommy sat up, closing the newspapers and stacking them on the pile he had made next to him. As he glanced up at the lower level of the warehouse, he saw several other newspapers blowing around. He checked his pile and realised that all the papers were new ones. He struggled to his feet and went to collect them.

Reading the dates on the six papers, his brow furrowed when he saw that they continued from the previous days. Someone must have been placing them there.

'Hi, Ali. How are you?' Boris asked as he entered the church, taking off his hat.

'Oh, hello, Boris,' Alison greeted as she glanced back at him. She was rolling up some of the sleeping bags that cluttered the floor, stacking them on the seats. 'I'm feeling a lot better now that this weather's cleared up. It's sweltering out there, isn't it? Only God knows how you can keep that old coat on.' Alison's face was full of joy as she straightened her back, her hands on her hips.

'I can't really. I just keep thinking the weather will change as quickly for the worse as it did for the better!' Boris slid out of his grey detective coat. 'Has everyone gone home now?' he added as he laid his coat over one of the wooden benches that lined the church.

'Yeah, Susan and little Timmy were the last. They were helping here with the clean up until Daniel had to go to the hospital. He dropped them off on the way.'

'Was that to do with Michael Johns?'

'How on earth did you know that?'

'I was in the park when they found him. A young couple saw him. He was in a bad state. He'd been beaten up. He was saying something about his daughter and medication. Think he'd had a couple of bottles too many.' Boris sniggered as he made a drinking gesture.

'Don't think so. That sounds just like what had happened. His daughter . . . Daphne something . . . rang here. I'm not even sure we had his name right. He remembers everything, though. Apparently, he's a wealthy man who's gonna see Jones and this 'ere church good. He had some illness; think he was on antidepressants or something.' Alison had continued to pile up the folded sleeping bags as she spoke, and Boris followed her, gathering up the sheets.

The sheets and tidying were all that remained. Some of Reverend Jones's friends had come early that morning and removed the boards from the windows, and now the church seemed to dance as the colours from the windows once again filled the hall. All the temporary light bulbs were rolled up in the corner, awaiting collection from a local company.

'So this guy Johns was on about—the healer or something—he actually solved his illness?'

'Listen to what I'm saying, love. He's still got the condition, whatever it is. Manic depression or something that sounded like that. This guy—"the healer," as you call him—helped him remember it all. Or maybe one of the knocks the guy took to the head helped him remember. Who knows? Can you give us a hand to fold this?' Alison scooped up a large sheet in her hands.

As she turned, Boris raised a candlestick holder. Before Alison could yell, before she could even release the sheet, the metal holder connected with her head, rendering her unconscious.

With a smile and a slight chuckle, Boris looked around the empty church.

'Looks like it was the candlestick holder, but I'm not sure if this would classify as a study or a library.'

CHAPTER SEVEN

CHAPTER SEVEN

CHAPTER SEVEN

As she regained consciousness, the pain became present. Her head was pounding. She slowly opened her eyes, and as the blurry images cleared, she realised that she was upside down.

The blood rushing to her head was making her dizzy. In front of her, she could see Boris's black boots. Her eyes rose along his figure, looking over his light blue jeans, scruffy grey jumper, and then into his face. She blinked hard as she focused on his eyes. Inside each pupil was a little red dot.

She swallowed hard but had to struggle to do so. When she tried to move her hands, she screamed. The pain soared through her hands and feet. She realised what was holding her to the wooden door; he had nailed her upside down to it.

'Sorry about this inconvenience. I don't mean to leave you hanging around,' Boris paused and screwed his face up. 'Oh god, that was cheesy! I've been standing here trying to work out what to say when you came to, and that's all I came up with. Isn't that lame!'

'What? Why?' Her questions were covered by her fear, her voice high pitched. 'Oh god. Let me down, please!'

'Okay, because I like you, I'll answer all those questions. Also, just so you know, if I were about seventy-three thousand years younger, I'd definitely try to get a piece of you! I bet you were really hot in your day.' Boris sniggered as he paced back and forth in front of Alison. Her tears rolled from her eyes down to her hairline. 'Let me begin with the question *what*. Well, I'm actually called Nemon. I'm pretty old in comparison to you. Like I said, if I were seventy-three thousand years younger, I'd consider you mating material, even though then I'd be about three or four hundred years older than you.

'I'm basically your average possession demon, although I dislike that name. I much prefer *body occupier*; it sounds more dignified. I've survived for years, body leaping. I've recently been a cop, an old lady, a little boy, and then this old fellow, Boris. Just so you know, when I'm in here, so is Boris. Man, he's pissed about this. He can't help you; he's kind of my prisoner. He's locked up in the back of my mind. Well, actually, to be a little more precise, it's his mind.'

'You're a demon, and you walked into God's home!' Alison's voice was struggling and weak, but her anger and disgust shone through.

With a wave of Boris's hand, Nemon continued, 'Okay, yeah. I'm on holy ground, but sometimes we need to be. The church, though, that was great. I was welcomed. How many former prisoners of hell are welcomed into God's house by one of his worshippers? Let me explain how this happened. About a week and a half ago, I was having a whale of a time possessing this cop. He used to be one of those goody two-shoe ones, always upholding the law. Then I got in there and started living the life. The gangs round here are pretty good material for future possessors. Some are real evil. For about seven months, I was making good money taking these kids' drugs and selling it on, threatening to arrest them if they didn't hand them over. It was going well—even got a couple of those younger female addicts to sleep with me for some. Those young ones have some stamina, you know. They can go for hours. Well, it's not like they had a choice. Anyway, this was going well, and then one of the gang members, one of the higher-up guys, felt the need to put a bullet in my chest. That then stopped the cop's heart beating. You know the minute it happens. Their skin becomes heavier. When a human dies, he becomes dead weight. It's called that for a reason.

'You can possess a dead body because the outside isn't affected. By that, I mean it doesn't rot like a normal dead body. However, inside is a different story. I'm dead, so I don't use any of the inner organs to breathe. So once the body is dead, the insides begin to rot. Outside, the skin that I'm wearing is fine, but inside, the smell is hard to describe. Rotting flesh is truly as vile as the films and stories make it out to be.

'Still in the cop's body, I'm sent into rescue old Bethel. Thinking that her body is still okay, I body hop to it. I can't explain to you how much of a relief it was to get away from that smell. However, during my aim of escaping in that body, loads of water rushes in as I open the door. Poor old Bethel drowns, and I'm now left in the next dead body. What a dilemma! I can't jump back to the cop 'cause his body is now cold and beginning to decay, floating around above me, so I have to swim to the surface in this old lady and try to explain it.

'When I get up top, I'm greeted by two firemen in a rubber dinghy. They pull me in, and I pretend they bring me to. Male demon here so not so keen on taking mouth-to-mouth from a guy, but needs must when the devil drives and all that! They then think they save me, and I say that this brave policeman pushed me from my house. Where is he? The panicking begins, and ten minutes later, they discover the dead body. I also overhear them say they're going to bring me to the church, and of course, I read some of Bethel's mind before she drank too much water, so I knew I'd be welcomed with opened arms. I also knew from her mind that I needed to look for some personal things in this church.

'Then, a couple of days and the rain hasn't stopped. The only people who kept speaking to me were the reverend and the kid. So I temporarily possessed the kid. Kids' bodies aren't strong enough to hold someone of my age and wisdom. He'd overload and possibly die, and I'd be forced out. Being a demon, the last thing you want to do is be trapped without a body 'cause after a matter of minutes, you get called back to the inferno and punished for cocking up. So because the kid liked Boris and spent some time following him round like a puppy dog, I saw Boris as a happy substitute. So that's *what* I am, and I'm guessing I've also answered *how* for you too. Despite you not asking, mind.'

Nemon knelt down and looked at Alison's face. With a sigh, he began tapping her cheek. Alison's eyes opened once more. 'You know, lady, if you're going to ask questions, you could at least stay conscious for the answers. Anyway, now I'll explain why you're upside down on a church door. You'll like this one. You see, I need you here for my answers 'cause God—your God, that is, you know, Jesus's dad—brought someone back on his side. In doing so, he had to send him from above, so he made it rain. Somewhere, and I'm guessing close by, someone or something has returned in this everlasting battle. So what do you think about God killing all your friends?' Nemon's malicious smile filled Boris's face.

'My God wouldn't do it. This is your kind's work.' Alison's voice was weak, her body riddled with pain, but she found the strength to argue, to stay conscious. She couldn't tell if the pain or loss of blood was making her dizzy. She didn't even know what to make of the demon in front of her, but she knew she couldn't believe him.

'Trust me, this is yours. This is also why you'll lose. He's a pussy! Look at us—when we send our warriors into battle, we raise numerous warriors at a time. We smash a hole through the ground, causing an earthquake, a tidal wave. Hell, I came out through a volcano in the early days; there must have been a thousand of us at that time. Each of these ways causes you humans loads of pain and death, so much so that none of you notices us come out of the ground. We're what you fear, what you tell stories about to scare your kids. And you can never see us amongst you. All those deaths this last week were accidental. The reason we're winning is because your God cares, and we don't. I was one of the first he expelled from his pearly gates. Sooner or later, we'll break through those gates and he'll pay,' Nemon stated, gripping one hand against Alison's cheeks, squeezing them inwards, her lips goldfished. She closed her eyes as she began to pray.

'Our Father, who art in heaven, hallowed be thy Name. Thy kingdom come. Thy will be done, on earth as it is in heaven.' Nemon released his hold as Alison's words grew clearer and stronger. Boris stood up, annoyed.

'Why do you humans continue to sing that shit when you're at death's door?' Boris yelled. 'You think you're judged on words. You're judged on who you were, what you've done. How you honoured thy neighbour and all that bullshit. It isn't just about words.' He dropped to his knees in front of her, his thick fingers squeezing her cheeks again, harder. Alison struggled to recite the Lord's Prayer once more. 'For fuck's sake!' Nemon said, releasing her face as her reciting continued. His anger was bubbling through his veins. 'You're all the fun of the fair, aren't you!' Nemon sighed as he shook his head, Alison's words drilling into his brain. 'I'm sorry, but I need to know why he was brought back here in Alterson.' As Nemon said the words, he reached behind him and gripped the handle that stuck out from the back of his belt.

He looked her in the eyes. Even now, he couldn't understand how some people could give compassion to such dumb creatures. The Lord's Prayer continued to be recited right up to the point he placed the knife against her throat. Her eyes flicked open as she felt the cold blade against her. She released several tears as the prayers became fainter, only to be replaced by sobs. The second he pulled the blade across her throat, all sound stopped and the blood flowed freely from the wound. It drained down over her face and dripped to the floor, pooling around her body.

Nemon took a cloth from his pocket, wiped the blood from the bronze knife, and looked at the engraving on the handle. The language was so old that not even he could remember it. Nemon had been around long enough to see languages created, mastered, and forgotten. This one, however, was created before humans, forged in the fires from the hell in which he'd been banished as time itself began.

As he watched the blood begin to flow from the deep cut across Alison's throat, he held his hand above the pool of blood and placed the blade in the palm of his other hand. While reciting the Lord's Prayer backwards, he pulled the knife quickly from his hand, cursing his pain as the black blood seeped from the deep cut. As it mixed with the pool of Alison's blood, steam rose from it and the two colours blended into one.

As the black blood swirled around the pool, it began to form images: the alleyway and the lightning bolt that brought the character to life; the symbol and wounds clearly showed on his body; the image of the man walking through the city in the rain; fighting the gang members and saving the homeless man in the park; his face from when they knocked into each other; the image of Thomas Atkins was clear; then there was the landscape of the church Alison was sacrificed against. With that, the black vanished from the blood as it began to seep through the crack between the gravel pathway and granite step of the back of the church.

Nemon stood up and looked at Alison's body. Feeling the scar on his hand heal, he smiled as the pain was relieved. Next time, it wouldn't matter from where he sent the message back to his masters; the holy ground had released the information of God's soldier in their battle. Nemon now knew whom he had to drain.

'Oh, well. From now on, I'm called Boris, then. I think he'd say sorry for having to do this!' With the words, Boris rammed the knife into Alison's abdomen and pulled the knife down, cutting through various organs and her cardigan. Small amounts of blood left in her body seeped from the deep wound that exposed her insides. Boris removed the knife and then inserted it again, pulling it across the width of her body before removing it once more. Then he cut two more lines, completing the symbol. Once satisfied with the Rivals scar on her body, he left and went around to the front of the church. He placed the knife safely under a headstone on the outskirts of the cemetery. Another sentence in a foreign, forgotten language, and the grass moved like fingers gripping the blade before pulling the blade under the surface. While doing this, he constantly observed the area. If this plan worked, he couldn't get caught.

Slowly, he walked into the chapel. For a moment, he looked at the large wooden crucifix in front of the altar. It must have been the first thing they put back as the people left. Boris glanced around once more, smiling towards the bell tower, where the single bell would ring on Sundays. If only the people of Alterson knew the real value of that bell tower, what power it could possess.

Casting the thoughts to the back of his mind and remembering the task at hand, he paced his way to the kitchen. Using Boris's memory, he pulled open the right drawer and grabbed the sharpest knife. He walked into the church's hall, gripping the knife tightly. Despite it being Boris's body, Nemon still felt the pain when Boris was injured. With a glance at the bell tower and then back at the doors, he made several light cuts on his arms and hands. He then made two deep ones in his leg and one final wound into the side of his stomach, making sure not to hit any vital organs.

As he dropped to the floor, he looked to the bell tower with a smile. He'd finally found it.

CHAPTER EIGHT

Tommy felt something was telling him to head out into the city; something was driving him. Someone was feeling scared but not for himself. He was younger than the person who was scared. They feared the people with him would kill him one day.

As Tommy walked down a side alley, he could sense the emotions getting stronger. As he arrived at a dead end, he rested against a wall, placing his palms and forehead against its coldness. The feelings became overpowering; someone else's emotions rode through his veins. He was there. He could sense him. Tommy stepped away from the wall as he heard the voices.

'You got it, then?'

'No, I told you I can't afford it. Please don't steal anything. It's my mum and dad's. They worked hard for everything. They'll never forgive me.'

'Then you'll have to tell her why we did it, won't ya? Admit it's all your fault! I explained to you in simple terms. Ya don't give us the money or something worthwhile, then I don't protect your property! How many houses on your street been burgled this month, eh?' There were two voices intimidating the youth. Tommy could also feel the youth's fear.

Tommy stepped back and ran towards the wall. Gripping the top with his hands, he swung over and landed next to the teenager. He was young and scared, only about fourteen. In front of him were his adversaries, both in their mid-twenties and bearing the symbol of the Rivals on their forearms. One was wearing army trousers and a white tank top, with scruffy-looking hair just long enough to reach his eyes. The second was stronger—his muscles filling the sleeves of his T-shirt. He had black jeans and spiky brown hair. In his hand, he gripped a knife, the blade pointing towards the youth. In the youth's hand was a mobile phone; his other was squeezed tightly together, holding something that must have been precious to him. It caused his knuckles to glow white.

The silence lasted a few moments. Maybe it was the shock of the entrance that startled them. Maybe they had heard of that morning's incident. However, the silence didn't continue. Before any words were spoken, the blade was quickly jolted in and out of Tommy's chest. He fell back to the wall and slid down to the ground. 'See what I'll do to you if ya don't give me them rings?' The thief's confidence had grown as he saw the tears roll down the boy's cheeks. 'What ya fucking waiting for? We could just go rob your mum now, ya know! Take her TV, DVD player, all her jewellery. You know the rules. Pay me for their protection. Now give me them rings!' With hesitation, the boy loosened his grip, his hand still held close to his side.

The youth hadn't taken his eyes off Tommy's body. The thief sighed and reached forward to take them, and as he did so, Tommy's hand darted up and grabbed his wrist tightly. The thief looked at him and attempted to break free, slicing the flesh on Tommy's wrist. Crimson liquid ran from the wound, but the grip remained tightened. He slashed at the wound several more times. The cuts were deep but to no avail. Tommy's grip wouldn't loosen. The youth closed his fist once again, concealing the rings. The thief's friend threw several punches into Tommy's face. One split his eyebrow open, and blood seeped from the wound as Tommy stared out from under his long hair.

'You have a phone. Call the police and ask for Officer John Samuels,' Tommy said as the thief stabbed the knife into Tommy's shoulder. It remained there, the blade digging into his flesh, yet the grip still remained. The thief struggled, pulling against Tommy like a disobedient toddler trying to flee his mother.

The second man went to grab the boy and stop the phone call, but with one quick movement, Tommy kicked him to the ground, knocking the wind out of him. 'You should run now. Tell your boss and his friends that justice will be served. Mary Watson's dream shall not be broken.' The second man got up and watched as the kid dialled the police. He looked at the blood dripping from Tommy's wrist. The cuts were deep, and the blood flowed quickly, despite Tommy keeping the firm grip. The knife stood upright in Tommy's shoulder.

'Sorry, man!' he said, shaking his head as his friend looked on, still in Tommy's grasp. As Tommy watched the second man flee the area, he delivered a hard punch to the thief, sending him to the ground. His jaw had dropped to one side, and it looked broken as he fell unconscious. Tommy removed the knife from his shoulder and then turned to the boy and smiled.

'You know who they are, don't you? What's his name?' Tommy asked, pointing to the fallen man.

'Matthew Rodderson. His brother bullies me. He comes to my house and tells me what they'd steal, makes me tell my mum he's my friend.'

'Don't let him in any more,' Tommy stated, holding one hand out to the boy, his bloody one behind his back. Hesitantly, he shook it. As he did, he smiled. Tommy felt the pain in his chest cease as the emotions left him.

'My parents didn't care if we were robbed, did they? They just didn't want them to hurt me.' The boys words were full of joy. 'How'd you know that, mister?'

'Parents fear for their children more than the loss of possessions,' Tommy replied as he stepped over the fallen man and walked out of the small entrance and on to Boston Street. The blood was now drying on his skin, and the wounds were healing. 'Your parents love you. Go home to them and tell them everything,' Tommy added glancing back over his shoulder. The boy nodded and gave a wary wave as Tommy continued down Boston Street.

As Tommy passed the end of the street, a police car swung into view. As the car turned the corner, Tommy saw Samuels for the first time in what seemed like forever. As Samuels caught a glimpse of Tommy, his brow furrowed. He knew Tommy, and he'd clearly recognised him. After a few seconds, Tommy fled the scene, and Samuels approached the scared teenager.

CHAPTER NINE

Reverend Jones walked into the church, carrying the brown envelope containing the money that had brought him so much joy. Michael Johns was a very distinguished man. Before forgetting his medication, after his wife passed away, he had successfully run a chain of hotels throughout England. His daughter had continued to do so in his absence. He was so thankful for all the help Reverend Jones and his helpers had given him that he had handed him a reward for his work. When Reverend Jones tried to refuse, Michael Johns forced it into his hands, saying that it was a gift. He was grateful for the church's help and knew that Jones had never wanted anything in return. Jones smiled as he looked at the crucifix he had replaced that morning. The sun reflected proudly from the tarnished wood, and the window's colours covered his walls again. His church once again was filled with warmth.

As he walked up the central aisle, he heard Boris's moan. He turned to the side and saw him gripping his wounds. Blood was seeping between his fingers, and his jeans were stained from the cuts in his leg.

'Boris!' Jones exclaimed, dropping to his knees in front of him, trying to see the wounds. Boris pushed him away with a cough, pointing towards the doors.

'Outside! They took her outside!'

'Who? Ali?' Jones's face showed the shock he was in, and he momentarily looked forth and back, unsure of what to do.

'There were four of 'em. They knocked me down and took her out there. Find her!' Jones nodded and pulled his mobile phone from his pocket, dialling Officer Samuels's personal number as he ran from the church into the cemetery. The sun was now setting, and its red glow filled the air. As the phone rang, Jones saw the trails in the gravel where Alison had been dragged. As he approached the corner, Samuels answered.

'Jones? Are you all right?' The question lingered as Jones stood face-to-face with Alison's mangled body.

'No, no, I'm not, John. Please come here. Hurry.' With those words, he dropped the phone and raised a hand to his mouth, trying unsuccessfully to cup the escaping vomit. With deep breaths, he raised his head again, and as he did so, he felt the bile claw its way up his throat. Again, he vomited.

Squawk stood up from his old-fashioned sofa as he heard the loud banging on his door. He stepped over Fiona's legs before she coiled them under herself. He left the small front room where he'd been with his friends and started down the short hallway of his flat to the door. The knocking never stopped.

'For fuck's sake, I'm coming!' The banging continued. As the door opened, a man burst in, pulling the door from Squawk's grip, slamming it closed behind him. Still not speaking, he flipped the latch on. From the front-room doorway, three people glanced down the hall at the fear-stricken man. Sweat was running down his face and dripping from his chin. His hair was wet and stuck against his forehead.

'You better have a fuckin' good reason for bustin' in here like that!'

'I do, I do,' he stated, swallowing deep breaths.

Squawk shook his head, leaning cross-armed against the wall. 'I'm waitin' here, ya know?'

'He got up! Rodderson stabbed him in the chest . . ., and he got up! There's no way he could have got up!'

Squawk had a smile creeping across his face as he heard the man's ranting. 'What the fuck have you been taking?'

Rodderson's friend, Adam, shook his head from side to side, cancelling out Squawk's question. 'We were collecting from one of them kids he stalks on Ridge Street—same as he always does—and this Goth just jumped the wall. Rodderson shoved the knife right into his heart, and he got up. We couldn't stop him. He cut his arm up to fuck too, and he wouldn't let go! I hit him loads of times, and he didn't flinch! They called Samuels and said something about Mary Watson!'

'Mary Watson? She's been dead twelve months or more. She was one of Molks's hits. He ran her down as she left work. She apparently had some evidence of a meeting between Ben and the bosses. You say he got up from a stabbing?' The man nodded, his eyes wide open and beads of sweat dropping from his short hair. 'That ain't even possible. He was probably drugged up on something and is bleeding out in a ditch now.' Squawk glanced back to the others.

'What he look like?' Shaun asked from the doorway.

'A Goth! Long hair, dressed in black! He's not normal. He, R . . . R . . . Rodderson, stabbed him, and he just got up!'

'Fuckin' shut up, would you? God. If Rodderson really did stab him in the heart, he wouldn't have got up. Rodderson obviously thought he did but missed everything and grazed him.'

'Squawk, hold on, man,' Shaun said, walking towards them. 'When Ben was dropping the gear off earlier, he said something about a Goth attacking your cousin in the park 'cause of the symbol. What if he's some descendant from Mary . . . , wanting revenge? Maybe he had some type of stab-proof vest on or something like that. If he was covered, who knows what he was wearing to protect himself.'

Squawk nodded. 'It would make sense,' he pondered aloud. 'The knife would even feel like it went into his flesh. It probably just touched it enough to bleed.'

'No, not what happened!' Adam, Rodderson's mate, exclaimed, waving his hands from side to side. 'No protection—went right in and out. Whole blade was covered in blood.'

'You're doing my fuckin' nut in now. Who the fuck are you, anyway? I only ever saw you round here, licking Rodderson's ass. How do I know you didn't do it? For all I know, you could have mugged Rodderson and called the cops and made up all this shit to cover it! I think you should fuck off now, don't you?' Squawk grabbed the man by his shirt with one hand, pulling him forward from the door. With the other, he reached behind Adam and undid the safety catch.

'But he may be out there.' Adam panicked as his eyes darted from Squawk to the others. Shaun was now beside him with a grin that spread the width of his face.

'What have you been taking tonight, mate? You're all over the place. Go and sleep it off before Squawk loses it with you.' Shaun laughed as he walked back towards the front room, taking the blonde-haired girl under one arm and placing a kiss on her lips.

Squawk pulled the man towards him, allowing him to open the door. Smiling at the fear in Adam's eyes, he shoved him outside, into the hallway of the building.

'Now, seriously, fuck off before I hurt you, all right?' Squawk watched as the man glanced around the stairwells before running down them. Seeing Barry rush across the car park below, Squawk closed the door with a giggle to himself. 'What a fuck-up!' he exclaimed as he re-entered the living room to Shaun and their friends.

'Do you reckon there's any connections between that guy and the one that confronted Ian this morning?' Shaun asked as Fiona sat on the sofa, pulling his arm around her.

'If it is, Ben's gonna gut him for it!' Sonia, Squawk's girlfriend, added.

'Fuck knows,' Squawk stated. 'I'll talk to Ben in the morning. He's got a few things he's sorting out tonight. He's seeing Boswell and working out how this gear is coming in for the weekend. Can't chance the usual lorries because the filth's directing the traffic in 'cause of all the devastation on the roads. No one's been out for a couple of weeks, so this weekend will be pumping. We should clear a couple of grand easy, so no one wants to miss this market.'

Rapid made three white lines on the table. With a rolled-up twenty, he snorted an entire line before leaning back in the chair with a deep breath. Rapid had been friends with Squawk and Ben for years. He started with them smuggling cannabis into Alterson in his car's fuel tank. No police checked there. Eventually, they invited him into their group, and he began selling in the pubs and clubs under Squawk's supervision. Then, as time went on, he became almost a bodyguard to Squawk and his mates. He had even pulled the trigger on a couple of targets. That pay was good. Tony had given him enough to live happily and post some home to his sister to get her through university. His family lived in Oxford and had no idea what he was doing for a living in Alterson. They believed he was working as a clerical assistant for a small law firm. He was glad they never knew what he'd done for the money, but the people he'd taken the lives of, he felt deserved it.

'That was a good one. Did you see his face? Sonia, did you get it?' Squawk asked as Sonia nodded, turning the video camera towards Squawk as he leaned forth, picking up the tightly rolled note. Just like Rapid, in one easy motion, he inhaled a line of powder.

Sonia held the camera on her partner for a while as he remained in the pose where he'd finished the line. She'd always loved his smile and returned it with her own, just like now. She had loved Squawk from afar for a long time, jealous of his previous girlfriend and chain of one-night stands. Despite being one of the one-night stands, they eventually became frequent lovers, and then nearly three months ago, they slotted into the roles of boyfriend and girlfriend. She loved everything he gave her: the love, the drugs, and the lifestyle. She felt lucky to have met him.

She turned the camera towards Shaun and Fiona, who were close together on the corner of the worn sofa. Fiona had her leg hooked around her boyfriend, holding him closer to her as she pulled his body over hers. She planted some heavy kisses on him before realising the camera was filming them. She smiled with a wave to Sonia and the camera, causing Sonia to laugh.

'See the love birds! You get quite horny on his stuff, don't ya?'

'It's not the drugs. It's just having a great boyfriend!' Fiona announced, kissing him once more,

'Your great boyfriend has a line set up.'

Fiona smiled and then lowered her leg, allowing Shaun to slide away and sit up on the sofa. After a mouthful of beer, he leaned forward and scooped up the rolled up twenty. With the camera closely following him, he snorted up the line and sat back with a deep sigh.

'Now that was good shit!' he exclaimed as Rapid laughed, pulling another sachet from his bag. He flicked the packet, holding it in two fingers in their direction, and tore the plastic open. Sonia filmed him tipping the substance out and then scanned around the room before pausing the camera over the table.

On the table in front of them were several used syringes from earlier. The five friends were intoxicated, and only the video recording would remind them of their good night.

The police car swung into the church's entrance, flooding the cemetery with a sea of blue lights. John Samuels swung from the driver's seat, running towards the church, closely followed by Marie Hoskins, both gripping their guns. Without hesitation, Samuels burst into the church and saw Reverend Jones wrapping one of the white sheets around Boris's leg. The sheet next to him was already dyed crimson. Samuels stopped and lowered the gun, looking at the situation.

'Daniel, what's happened?'

'They got attacked by four people. Boris is here, but Alison Shannings is at the back of the church.' Daniel's eyes looked down to Boris, and the colour fled his face.

'Is she . . . ?' Samuels allowed the question to trail off. A silence fell as Daniel Jones nodded.

'We'll go and call it in,' Marie softly said, scuttering from the church hall.

'It's not pretty. They've ritually sacrificed her,' Jones added. Samuels looked at him for a long moment, unsure if he'd heard him right.

'They've crucified her?' Samuels looked at Jones for a form of confirmation; he couldn't believe that would happen. As Reverend Jones nodded, Samuels felt his throat grow dry. 'Do we know who?'

'They've left the symbol on her. Nothing like before. I've never seen anything like this.' A tear escaped Daniel's eye as he spoke. Boris remained silent. He'd been looking to the ground since their arrival. Samuels was concerned about whether he was even conscious.

'There's an ambulance on its way,' Marie called from the doorway. 'I'll head around back.'

'Wait, Marie. I'll come with you.' Marie followed the instructions and remained in the tall doorway of the church. 'I'll talk to you both again in a minute. We'll check the area.' Jones nodded as Samuels turned and left the hall.

Marie and Samuels walked side by side along the church, listening to the gravel crunch under their feet. 'Daniel said this scene's going to be horrific,' Samuels warned as they turned the corner.

No words could have prepared them. From the deep cut in her stomach, some intestines had begun to slip out and were now dangling from the wound. Her face was still covered in crimson, her eyes wide open and staring at them.

Samuels stepped towards Alison's side, avoiding the vomit on the floor. He knelt down next to Alison's body, reached forward, and closed her eyes. In doing so, he heard something. Lowering his head to her mouth, he faintly heard the word once more; with the last of the air in Alison's lungs, the word 'Nemon' escaped. Samuels paused for a moment and then looked back at Marie.

'Are you okay?'

'I think so. I've always prepared myself for these situations, always thought I'd be excited to be involved in a murder case. Sorry.' She shook her head as if to clear it. 'Given the depth of the cuts and the positioning of the body, I believe it to be a replica killing of the Rivals gang,' she reported, stepping forward and placing her shoe into the pile of sick. She glanced down and momentarily closed her eyes as Samuels fought back a giggle. 'There's vomit, which may mean the murderer regretted his actions.'

'Marie, are you sure you're okay? I think the sick is probably Daniel's, from when he saw the body.'

'I don't know. Do you mind if I go and sit down for a minute.'

'Yeah, of course, you can. If you can call it in to the station, they'll need to take photos of the scene, check for any evidence,' Samuels informed her, waving his hand in the air.

Marie nodded and slowly backed away. The sight of Alison was making her feel nauseated, but she couldn't turn away. It was the first dead body she'd seen; it was also worse than any case photos she'd worked with in the past. She swallowed hard and then turned the corner, the victim away from her view. She looked to the night sky as the stars sparkled, taking a deep breath. Her eyes felt watery, and she was light-headed. Steadying herself with the help of the church wall, she walked to the car to report to the station.

CHAPTER TEN

CHAPTER TEN

It had been a long night in the cemetery. The sun was now rising, forcing the darkness to retreat. Several of the headstones cast their long shadows across the green lawns. Samuels sat on the bonnet of the police car, sipping from the mug of coffee that Reverend Jones had made him. Marie was talking to a couple of forensic photographers.

In the gentle breeze, police tape flapped from the church entrance. The sun was already warm within its early minutes of daily life, giving birth to another scorcher. Around the graveyard, several men went through the motions, although there seemed to be no evidence around.

Samuels and Marie had been there the entire night. Both were about to leave work when Samuels received Reverend Jones's call. Throughout the night, a number of people had been phoned, and all had responded within moments of their call. Due to the seriousness, they had called in a number of forensics after having Boris collected by an ambulance. It had been around one in the morning when the first forensic arrived. The reporters had appeared before that. They must have been listening in on their own scanners. Police had since forced most away by taping off the whole cemetery.

Nathan Riley approached Samuels, still wearing his white disposable gloves. His tie was tucked into his pale blue shirt.

'Do you wear that tie to bed or just put it on the minute you swing out of it?'

Samuels asked. Samuels had removed his tie in the earlier hours of the morning.

Nathan gave a smirk, disregarding the question. 'We've checked everything we can here. I need to get her back to the lab so we can examine her further. The only helpful advice I can currently give you is the fact that the murder weapon is different to the one used to stab Boris Ludvig. It was about eight inches with a rough edge.'

'We suspected that, given how Boris had said they took her out of the church after leaving the knife in him,' Samuels explained, receiving an annoyed look from Nathan.

'Also, the item they used to knock her unconscious was blunt and swung downwards towards her, which means the attacker would have to be taller than her. I'll hopefully have more evidence for you by this evening.' Samuels nodded. 'Um, I may need another favour, well, permission . . . You see, with the way she's positioned, I would prefer to take her as she is. Um. Would it be possible to remove the door and get permission to take it to the lab?'

'That can be arranged. Is that the best way?'

'If we don't, I fear that by moving her, things may become dislodged and possibly even fall . . .'

'Okay. Just remove the door, and please, don't finish that sentence!' Samuels interrupted. Nathan gave a nod before scurrying away. Samuels glanced back towards the church, where Reverend Jones sat on the step, leaning forward and holding his mug of tea with both hands. *Poor guy. After everything he's done, still he has more thrown at him!*

Samuels finished the last mouthful from his mug and walked across to Daniel. Samuel's shadow covered him, stealing the sunlight. After a moment in the shade, Jones looked up with a forced smile. He was looking weak; little colour had returned to his cheeks.

Samuels nodded and then asked, 'How are you doing?'

Jones shrugged. 'How am I meant to be doing in these situations?'

'What you're doing now. If you didn't sit there, wondering if you could have done something different, I'd be worried. I know you cared for her a lot. She was a good lady.'

'That she was, John, that she was. After everything that's happened, how could God have taken her like that? After everything she's done for so many . . .'

Samuels leaned back against the wall, unsure of how to console his friend.

'You shouldn't blame God for this. He never put Alison on that door. That was a human—barely, mind you, but all the same, he was a human. One that will be very sorry when I get hold of him.'

'I know I shouldn't think it, John, but when you do . . . ,' Jones paused for a second. Then he said, 'Kill the bastard.' Samuels was taken back for a moment as Jones's words sunk in. He hadn't slept properly for close to a week and had just lost one of his best friends; then he saw another go off to hospital with multiple stab wounds. Hesitantly, Samuels accepted the words as grief and nodded.

'He'll pay for it, trust me.'

'Tony, we may have a problem with this guy. If it was just Rodderson's mate, I wouldn't have bothered you with it. But my cousin seems to think it's the same guy that attacked him in the park yesterday.' Squawk was arguing as Tony waved a hand, dismissing the statement for a second time.

'Sounds to me like some prick who thinks he's a hero. Spread word around and make sure that next time they stab him in the face. Bigger things are going down. You know that. I've got a boat coming in from Okerton this evening from Valentino, and we've got enough gear on-board to sell the city three times over this weekend. With all the cops directing traffic in and assuring the debris clear ups, we've only got the harbour master down on the docks. It'll be plain sailing.'

'What's the shipment?' Ben asked as Squawk shook his head in disapproval.

'It's fashion,' Tony emphasised. 'Bought about three thousand garments for Friendz Trendz—easy cover-up. No one will suspect it,' Tony paused as he noticed that Squawk's attention was elsewhere. 'For fuck's sake, Squawk, stop shaking your head at me. Think it through. Your cousin was confronted as he beat the shit out of a homeless man. He's a kid. He took a swing and then ran away. Rodderson's lot is just street scum picking off houses to buy our gear that we sell to them. I understand that you want a piece of this guy because he threatened your cousin, and should he come near any of you, we'll deal with him, but he's one man thinking he's an army. He can pick at these little people for as long as he wants. He fucks with any of us, kill him.' The words were cold and forceful. Squawk nodded in agreement as Ben smiled.

'Now, with that out of the way, what time will the delivery be made?' Ben asked, sitting down at the long desk in Tony Boswell's office.

'It's arriving as we speak. It'll be locked up in warehouse twenty-three. Our usual colleagues will be there on the security watch for you to collect it. I don't want anything to go wrong tonight. I'm guessing everyone will be out in force—customers and what limited filth they have available. I'm trusting you guys here 'cause I've been called to London to meet up with Hayden Richards. He said he needs us to start doing some runs with some new clients that are based there. They sound like pricks, but if the price is right, it may be some good business. Also, with me being out of town, the blue scum won't be able to link myself and any problems you guys may cause. Keep it as sensible as you can and watch what twats you surround yourself with. We all know how out there some people can be. Hayden has already mentioned that some of our associates are nervous dealing with us. One said, we think we run the city. If only they knew the truth: we pretty much do!'

'I ain't going to leave him, Mum. He loves me!' Fiona cried as she stormed out of the kitchen and into the hallway. Her mum, Rebecca, hastily followed.

'He does not! Can't you see that? All he's doing is using you.'

'How, Mum? You don't know nothing about him!' Fiona exclaimed as she stopped and turned to face her mother.

'I know enough. I've seen his tattoos! I know what that symbol on his arm means. He's one of those gang members. It was in the paper.'

Fiona shook her head in anger. 'They aren't like that paper makes out. They only fight when they're intimidated. They don't even like violence.'

'Yeah, what about their drug habits? I know that's true, and I know you do it with them,' her mum accused as Fiona looked away angrily before quickly looking back.

'Well, I don't, and neither does Shaun.'

'No? Then explain this!' Rebecca demanded, tossing several syringes on the floor.

Fiona instantly dropped to her knees, scraping them up. As she gathered the discarded needles into one hand, she continued yelling, now in a higher pitch, 'You went into my room! I don't believe you! Where do you get off?'

'You're lucky, Fiona. If your dad was alive, he'd . . . ,' Rebecca started, but Fiona cut in.

'Yeah, well he's not, and even if he was, what good would he be? He'd be too busy with work or down the pub.'

'Shut up, you ungrateful . . . ,' Rebecca said, raising her hand as if to hit her. Before she moved towards her only daughter, she froze. It felt as if time stood still around them.

'Go on, Mum, do it! Fucking hit me like he would,' Fiona dared as her mum lowered her hand with a tear in her eye. Silence dropped between them for a moment.

'Please don't see him any more,' Fiona's mum softly pleaded as Fiona silently shook her head, ignoring the tears she saw falling from her mother's eyes.

'Mum, understand, please! I can't leave him. I love him . . . ,' Fiona's words trailed off as a silence fell over them once more.

'I can't stop you falling in love, but I can stop you from falling as deeply as I did with your father. I forbid you from seeing him while you live under my roof,' Rebecca stated with a firm voice.

'How dare you, Mum!' she snarled. 'If that's my choice, then I choose Shaun over you any day. Unlike you, despite how much you annoy him, he'd never make me choose. I'll be out from under your roof by this evening.' Fiona stormed upstairs to her room, still clutching the syringes as tightly as the addiction did her.

As she entered the bedroom, she threw the syringes on the bed before slamming the door. She looked at the door and then kicked it several times, each one echoing around the room. As she felt her tears escape her eyes and flow over her cheeks, she looked around the room, feeling the love that surrounded her. She was wondering what the future might bring if she went with Shaun. She raised her hands and hid her face within her palms as she sat resting her back against the door in tears, tears of love that's lost along with the strength she now lacked.

'You know what I said earlier, John? That was anger talking. I don't want you to become them. You know that, don't you?' Reverend Jones asked as they listened to the kettle whistle to a boil.

'Yeah, I do. Personally, I sometimes wonder if the justice system works. There're so many technicalities criminals use now. Plead insanity and get counselling . . . Lawyers try to justify crimes—even knowing that what their client did was the worst thing possible. There's no justice here any more. If I hit or hurt a criminal capturing him, he has a right to sue me.'

'Samuels, if I've learned anything in my life, it's that at the end, these people will get their punishment. Hell will be the worst prison. Nothing we can do to them here can ever touch that. That's one thing I'm sure of,' Jones stated, pouring out the boiling water, drowning his tea bag, watching as it floated to the surface to be fished out.

CHAPTER ELEVEN

CHAPTER ELEVEN

CHAPTER ELEVEN

T he light shone so brightly that Tommy could barely read the typed words on the paper. This paper was from four years ago and told the story of the city's fire. It had started at the south end of the city in a high-priced residential area. There were a number of photos of the burning inferno that scorched the city for nearly forty-eight hours. The photos were almost as dramatic as the images of the burning of the London Bridge. There was no cause given for the fire. No evidence could be collected from the destruction that took nine lives—those of two firemen and seven residents—one of which was a local judge, Barry Olsen, who believed Tony Boswell to be an untrustworthy man. As always, they had a page of local people's views in the *Alterson Scroll*. Many believed that Tony Boswell, who at that point owned a number of shops on Alterson's main street and two pubs on the outskirts, caused the fire to assassinate that one judge. When questioned, Tony Boswell had a secure alibi, as he was in Brighton with a local councillor called Kaz Sanders.

'Tommy?' The voice was faint. Tommy lowered the paper and looked up to see the frail form that had approached him on the first night he had arrived in the warehouse. He folded the paper and stood up to look the translucent form up and down.

'Who are you?' Tommy asked, still taking in his hollow-like appearance. 'Are you not going to scream and hide this time?'

'No. Things are different now. I've experienced things, learned more.'

'You're scratching the surface. All these papers you're reading will only begin to explain how complex everything is becoming. Are you willing to help?'

'I'm talking to you. Consider that the beginning of my help.'

'Thank you,' he said, nodding. 'I'm Harry Roberts. I came back from the other side. Like you, but not the same.' Tommy's face showed his confusion without words. 'You were chosen. Sent back by the gods, the powers that be. Myself, I couldn't leave things the way they were. My family is unhappy because of them.'

'Because of who? The gangs?'

'Yes and no. My daughter, Fiona, is in love with one of the men. He's not a good man. Since being here, I've observed him doing things, bad things. He's unfaithful to her. He has a string of women. He's beaten men for money. He's threatened my daughter.' Harry's voice was growing fainter as he looked away, his anger evident in his voice.

'Why not stop him—confront him like you have me?'

'I can't. Only people like you can see me, the dead. I'm not like you. As you can see, I don't have form. I'm just a spirit that graces the world. I was allowed back due to my choices to observe.'

'What if I said I'd help?'

'I'd be grateful.'

'You called me Tommy earlier . . . and Thomas Atkins the first night you approached me. I've heard that name before. I'm assuming its mine?'

Harry's frail form nodded. 'It was yours before you passed.' There was a silence that lasted seconds but seemed an eternity.

'How did it happen?' Tommy asked. 'My passing.'

'I don't know. Like you can sense emotions, spirits can sense souls. That's what you are. You're a body reformed due to their good soul for a purpose. There's something different about you, though. Someone's holding you, caring for you.'

'That voice . . . , the female voice I've heard whisper my name,' Tommy exclaimed as he looked to the sun. 'I don't know who she is. How can I find out?' He looked back to the warehouse, his eyes taking a few moments to adjust.

'I'm sorry, but I don't have your answers. I don't know how or why you were selected over the others. I just know you're here.' Again the silence.

'I'll help your daughter.' Despite Harry's face being faint, Tommy could see the relief.

'I really appreciate this, Squawk!' Fiona said as she dropped her rucksack in the flat's hallway.

'You two were lucky ya rung when you did. I was only just leavin' Boswells. We've got shed loads of gear coming in tonight. Is there much more luggage?' Squawk asked as he watched Shaun drop two suitcases behind her.

'Only one, but I'll get it.'

Squawk nodded and stepped past Fiona, grabbing one of the cases.'Come on. I'll show you to the room. Excuse the state of the front room. I still ain't had a chance to tidy from last night yet. I don't know about you, but this morning, I was pretty rough. Thought Tony would have gone mental 'cause I was wasted, but I just about scraped through the meeting!' Squawk swung open the door to the small room at the back of his flat. It contained an old double bed.

'I was all right until my mum started kickin' off. I could have done without that this morning.'

'I expect she'll come 'round. All mums do at some point,' Squawk said, setting down the case, allowing Fiona into the room. She slipped her backpack from her shoulders on to the bed and scanned the small room. She looked at the bed and then the wardrobe, which only had one door attached to it. She turned to Squawk and forced a smile.

'Here ya go,' Shaun said, slipping the case into the room.

'I'll leave you guys to it for a bit. I need to lie down. My head is banging still,' Squawk said as he passed by Shaun, heading towards his own room. Shaun patted him on the back as he passed with a nod. He knew Squawk was allowing them some time to talk; Squawk knew how hard moving away from your parents was.

As Squawk left the room, Shaun closed the door, walked over, and hugged Fiona. He didn't speak, but just allowed her to place her head against his chest and cry. He felt his T-shirt dampen under the tears.

'It'll be all right. We know her life revolves around you. Give her a couple of days, and she'll call.' Shaun said, trying to comfort his girlfriend, but in the back of his mind, he was hoping Rebecca would never call again. He had often tolerated Rebecca, but he knew she disliked him, and the feeling was mutual.

'I'll be all right. It's just weird. She's all I've known. With the way our lives have been, all we've had was each other. When I entered this room, the first thing I thought was how much smaller it was compared to my bedroom back home. That's what this is now, though, isn't it! My new bedroom, my new home.' Shaun didn't reply; he just smiled as Fiona pulled in tighter to him. 'We'll be all right. We have each other, and I know you'll love me more than she ever did!' Fiona added, feeling her tears well up again.

Squawk closed his bedroom door with a large yawn, turning towards his bed. His headache seemed to be getting more intense with each movement. He couldn't remember much from the previous night, but he remembered glancing at the clock around six o'clock after the sun had begun to rise. He had only had a few hours' sleep before his meeting with Boswell.

Sonia lay asleep on his bed with the covers draped over her and the floor. Squawk sat on the edge of the exposed bed and softly stroked his partner's leg. He smiled as he felt her soft skin as she moved slightly under his touch. She turned to face her lover, sliding up and causing the sheet to drop, exposing her naked breasts. He gave her a smile that she returned, hugging into the pillow.

Sonia truly loved Squawk, his short stubbly scalp, his blue eyes. She even liked the feel of his chin as his beard began to form. As she thought of his features, she bit her bottom lip briefly.

'What's the time? I'm still feeling a bit rough.'

'It's about two. Fiona's arrived. She's with Shaun in the other room. She's staying here for a while,' Squawk informed her, pulling his T-shirt over his head.

'Why's that?' Sonia said, adjusting herself so she was resting up against the headboard. 'I've lost count of how many times she said she'd never leave home 'cause she has it so easy!' Sonia tucked her long brown hair behind her ears and reached for her cigarettes on the bedside table.

'Turns out it wasn't her decision to make. Her mum found her stash and banned her from seeing Shaun. When she said she'd keep seein' him, she was told to go.'

There was a slight smile on Sonia's face as she held the cigarette between her lips, sparking up her lighter. 'Fucking hell,' she exclaimed! 'Alice was thrown from Wonderland!' She dragged deeply as the cigarette began to glow.

'Hey, cut her a break. It ain't easy leavin' home on those kind of terms. Not everyone has a boyfriend like me to slip into the bed of!' Squawk sniggered as he slid his jeans down. He smiled to her as he lay down on the bed next to her. Sonia held out the cigarette, and Squawk took a big drag, held it in his lungs, and then exhaled.

Sonia looked his body up and down. He was well formed; you could clearly see every muscle and even count the six-pack of his midsection. Every time she saw him take his shirt off, she felt an urge to run her fingers over the rippling muscles.

After taking another deep drag of the cigarette, he offered it back. Sonia shook her head, declining as she ran her hand up and down his exposed torso. She turned to him with a smile as she slipped her hand into his boxer shorts, feeling his excitement build. Still holding him in her hand, she slid her body closer, allowing her body to touch his, feeling her warmth against his skin as she began to kiss his neck. He placed the cigarette in the ashtray and met her lips. Their kisses grew heavy, and soon, she pushed the sheet from them, pushing his boxer shorts down with one hand before she pulled her naked body on to him with the need of feeling him inside her.

'Samuels. Go ahead.'

'Hi, John. We've been examining the body, and we've found some flecks of what we believe is ash inside the wounds,' Nathan reported. 'Mainly upon the throat laceration.'

'What do you mean, *ash*?'

'Like you'd get after a bonfire. I've got Louise running tests on it to see if there is anything specific about it that could help us. There have been a number of bits found. It must have been on the knife. It's going to sound strange, but look around the outskirts for any small fires that may have been.'

'Do you really think they'd have had a bonfire in a cemetery before carrying out a murder in the church?' Samuels replied as he watched the men around the cemetery continuing their search. 'Besides, detectives and forensics have been checking this place with a fine-tooth comb all morning. They'd see something like that straight away.'

'The reason I mention the fires, John, is that the ash couldn't have stayed on the blade that long. Ash would have fallen off quite quickly. It would also mean the knife would have been exposed while approaching the scene. If it had been placed back in the sheath, the ash would have become dislodged from the knife teeth. Maybe the blade was buried in the ash beforehand and collected on the way. Given the tone of the murder, they may have even done this as part of the ritual in the cemetery.'

'I'll take all that on-board as we continue the search. I'll tell the boys in a minute. What can you tell me about the blade?'

'Not much different to what I said this morning. The blade was about eight inches with a severed edge. The teeth, I suppose, would be a couple of centimetres apart, possibly the type of knife used when gutting a fish. The laceration across the throat had been done so uniquely; it's like nothing I've ever seen before. When it comes to the stomach, it appears that the cuts were done in two directions. The flesh was cut downwards continuously, then occasionally the knife doubled back along the wound. I can tell this because of the damage to the intestines.'

'Nathan, I don't need to know about that at the minute. All I need to know is that we're looking for bonfire ash and a fishing knife of eight inches.'

'Okay, John. I'm sorry. I know you knew this person. Just so you know, she was murdered with the one cut across the throat. That's where the ash was thickest, proving it to be the first cut. She wouldn't have felt the other injuries.'

'That is a very small amount of comfort. But even if I didn't know her, Nath, I still feel you enjoy your job a little too much. Give me a call if you find out anything else.'

Nathan agreed, and Samuels dropped the phone before approaching Marie Hoskins and two other officers who were sipping from mugs of tea.

CHAPTER TWELVE

CHAPTER TWELVE

CHAPTER TWELVE

Squawk sat up, knocking over his cup of tea as the phone startled him. Swearing briefly, he glanced at the caller ID and answered, 'You alright, Ben?'

'Yeah. We've collected our delivery; it's looking pretty sweet. It's in the trunk of my car. We'll swing by at about seven to collect you.'

Squawk glanced at his watch: five thirty. 'Alright, mate. I'll get my shit together. Fiona moved in this morning, and I was totally shit-faced last night—only just recovering.'

'Busy day, then. I thought you weren't entirely with it this morning. Tony never noticed, though, so you're all right.' He could hear Ben's faint laughs behind the phone but chose to ignore them.

'Cool. I'm gonna get some food and then shower. Hoping Sonia doesn't hear the water. She'd probably want to join me! I swear the girl's sex mad. All fucking night she was . . . ,' he paused to search for the word. 'Well, just that: fuckin'!'

'Lucky thing, ain't ya? She's better than that last bitch you were dating. Fucking hell, she'd scare the dogs off your lawn!'

'I warned you about talking of her like that,' Squawk snapped, the light-hearted tone changing.

'Sorry, man. You know how Claire and I never got along. Did you ever hear anything after she left?'

'No, not a thing. Thanks for the pretend concern, though.'

'At least I care enough to pretend! Sorry, man. Look, I better get the odds and ends here tied up. See ya in a couple of hours, yeah?'

'Yeah. Speak then!' Squawk terminated the call. He placed the phone against his lips as he thought about Claire for a moment, and then he dropped it on the sofa next to him, knelt forward, and stood the cup upright. As he stood up, he saw the spare room door open, and Fiona leaned against the door frame.

'You alright?' she asked.

'Yeah, fine. Just had a memory moment, ya know?'

'Claire was nice. She just didn't like your career choices.'

'That's the understatement of the year!'

'She was worried she'd lose you to the pigs. Long-distance relationships don't work at the best of times. Even worse when one's in jail!'

Squawk laughed as he picked up the plates from the chair and walked towards the kitchen, followed by Fiona.

'Sonia's lovely, though, isn't she?' Fiona said.

'She's great. I haven't felt the way I do with her since Claire. Do you know what's weird, though? A minute ago I could barely remember Claire—still can't remember her face that well.'

'That's because of Sonia. Perhaps she shagged that memory from your mind last night!' Fiona laughed as she picked up the tea towel, twirling it around in front of her.

'Heard the whole conversation between Ben and me, eh?'

Fiona's smile filled her face for the first time since she'd said goodbye to her mum. She whipped him with the towel as he returned the smile. 'Can I help tonight?'

Squawk glanced at her as he rinsed off the plates. 'What do you mean?'

'At the club. I could help you sell. Maybe even help you make some money to cover me staying here.'

'I don't know? What would Shaun say about it?'

'He wouldn't mind. It'll make me feel better anyway. I'll get all tarted up and everything.'

'All right. I'll give you some pointers, but if there's any trouble, you come and tell me straight away. There's some right fuck-ups out there!'

'Are you sure?' Samuels asked as he pulled up outside the hospital.

'Yes. I'm fine. How many times do I need to tell you that, John? I'm going to see Boris, check how he is, then head home,' Reverend Jones stated, placing a hand on the door handle.

'I'm willing to wait to drop you back. You've had a really long week.'

Jones smiled at his gesture and declined the lift home, opening the door. 'John, your week has been equally as bad, if not worse. I've been talking and socialising with people. You've been saving them.'

Samuels smiled and gave the stubborn reverend a nod as the door closed. Samuels wound the window down and called after Jones, 'If you need me, just give me a call!'

The streets were filling with people as Tommy entered the main street. Everywhere was now dry, and people wandered through the town with T-shirts or short-sleeved shirts on. A group of girls passed Tommy, their outfits leaving little to the imagination. Even with the sun retiring to the moon, the heat still rode the air.

As Tommy passed the central toy store, he glanced at the window that had previously been boarded up. He heard the voice say his name again. As he glanced at his reflection, he saw a face looking over his shoulder. Her blonde hair flowed down her shoulders, her eyes were green, and her red lips formed a large smile. Before Tommy turned, the image vanished as quickly as a blink of an eye. Unsure of what he'd seen, he continued down the main street, glancing behind every so often in case she reappeared. *Is it another spirit? Is it an echo from my past?*

There were other things going through his mind. He had no idea how to interact with people. *Would it be like the reading and come back instinctively?* Harry had given him the description of his daughter, and after seeing the many newspaper articles, he had a good grasp of the men that dealt within the Night Arts Centre. He could sense mixed emotions in the air, but nothing like previously. There were some fears of their symbol, but none seemed to draw him to them. For the first time since his return, Tommy was dependent on himself.

CHAPTER THIRTEEN

CHAPTER THIRTEEN
CHAPTER THIRTEEN

The music to the club seemed deafening as Tommy entered. The clubbers that jumped and moved on the dance floor clearly appreciated its fast beat, their glow sticks floating amongst a sea of lasers that danced around the club's walls and ceiling, flashing strobes giving them temporary silhouettes. As the DJ called out, there was an outbreak of cheers, and the tune changed from a base sound to some form of high-pitched synthesizer.

Tommy glanced around, leaning against the railing overlooking the sunken dance floor. Satisfied the members he was searching for weren't there, he made his way through the packed club towards the bar. As he approached, two men turned and knocked into him, spilling some of their newly bought drinks. One mumbled something as Tommy looked away. Tommy looked around the club again as the barman approached. He leaned across the grey bar, awaiting Tommy's order. Tommy declined, explaining that he was looking for someone, and with a roll of his eyes, the bartender turned to the next customer.

The bar, like the club, was hectic. A number of people leaned across, notes in hand, awaiting service. Amongst these people, several sat sipping drinks. They almost seemed out of place in comparison.

Next to Tommy, seated at the bar, was a medium-built brunette who had glanced towards him a couple of times already, as if to build up the confidence to speak. When she realised her glances had been detected, she forced a smile, which Tommy returned. Something about her had caught his attention, and Tommy kept looking back.

Is she from my past? Was she the voice I heard? As the thoughts circled his mind, he realised he was staring and tried to divert his attention. As he did so, the woman looked at her drink, her grin growing.

'I'm sorry. You just looked familiar,' Tommy said, trying to make his glances seem less obvious. As she looked up, Tommy noticed how her smile brightened her face. Her pale skin and green eyes seemed completed by her lightly coloured lips.

Before Tommy could reply, someone tapped him on the shoulder. The brunette turned her attention back to her drink. As she saw the girl, her smile faded. Tommy turned around to see a slim-figured blonde. Her make-up was applied thickly, although her smile gave her face all the attractiveness it needed.

'The bartender told me you were looking for your someone,' she stated, emphasising *someone* as she bobbed up and down on the spot. Tommy took in her appearance. Her slim form was hugged by a tight, red low-cut top that exposed her cleavage. A small amount of her midsection showed before a short skirt flowed freely, covering her thighs and ending just above her knees. A small matching black bag hung from her shoulder.

'I'm sorry. What do you mean?' Tommy asked, noticing the similarities to her appearance and the description Harry Roberts had given him.

'I mean, you wanna get high?' she asked with a raise of her eyebrows.

'Are you Fiona?'

Fiona nodded, her smile filled with confidence. 'Yeah, guess Squawk told ya to look for me. I'm new at this, so you'll have to bear with me a bit. Not sure who the regulars are yet. So how much ya want?' Fiona cautiously showed an envelope in the palm of her hand; it had the Rivals symbol on it.

'Do I want to get high?' There was a moment's silence as Fiona's rhythmic dance continued. 'The higher you get, the farther you have to fall.'

Fiona looked puzzled as her dancing slowed down. She quickly slid the sachet back into her small bag. 'What the fuck! You ask for me, then you don't want it. This ain't like the cheap shit those wannabe peddlers are pushing down the pubs. This is the good shit that'll really blow your mind!' Fiona sneered as she turned to walk away.

Tommy quickly reached out and grabbed her arm tightly. She swung back towards him and stared into his eyes. 'All the drugs in this world can't save you from yourself. Only you can do that.'

Fiona's anger grew as she pulled her arm from his grasp. 'Don't you ever touch me!' she snarled as Tommy maintained eye contact. 'Fucking Gothic prick,' she mumbled as she forced her way through the crowd, back to Squawk and her friends at the other end of the bar. Tommy took a deep breath, registering the faces that now looked at him, before turning back to the bar.

'You're right, you know, that nothing in this world can save us.' The brunette's words were softly said as she looked back at him.

'Some things can save us, but acceptance is always the hardest part.'

The brunette smiled genuinely as she extended her hand. 'I'm Amber Johnson.'

Tommy accepted her hand and shook it. 'Thomas Atkins.' Amber had a glow to her, with chin-length hair that seemed to hug her face. She was wearing a light blue shirt and black trousers, nursing a pale green drink in her right hand, the orange swizzle stick resting against the side.

'So, who are you waiting for?' she questioned with a smile.

'She's been and gone now.'

'The blonde? The men always love the blondes.'

'Her father asked me to look out for her tonight. Who are you waiting for?'

'No one. My mate is a no-show. Don't suppose you need a drinking buddy?'

Her words fell on deaf ears, for Tommy was now standing, observing Fiona at the other end of the bar with several men, one of whom was Squawk. Tommy recognised Squawk from the papers that had appeared in the warehouse. He had been arrested for possession and dealing of narcotics, but somehow, the charges and drugs vanished overnight, and he was released.

The dim lights hanging over the bar lit up their features. Tommy could see the anger in Squawk's glare, and their eyes locked. The club was fairly dark, and soon, Squawk stepped back into the shadows, heading towards Tommy through the sea of people. During his march down the bar, he tapped a few other people on the shoulders, instructing them to follow.

'Amber, I'm terribly sorry, but I'm not who or even what you think I am. I'm completely different, and right now, it's important that you don't know me.' As Tommy finished the rushed sentence, the larger of the three men with Squawk grabbed him with both hands. He gripped the sides of the trench coat just above chest level. He lifted Tommy with ease and slammed his back against the wall, the impact briefly knocking the wind out of him.

Amber heeded his words, more out of instinct than Tommy's commands. She looked down at her drink, afraid to look up. Several people nearby didn't share the same views and stood with their eyes glued to the unravelling carnage.

Tommy got the air back in his lungs and swallowed deeply. He stared into the man's bloodshot eyes. His hair was scruffy and dyed blond, its dark roots showing. His left eyebrow had a silver stud in it, and he hadn't shaved for a few days. His face was familiar and had been centrally placed in many of the newspaper articles. He was Ben Williams, one of the well-known members of the Rivals gang.

'Where'd you get Fiona's name from, you fucking faggot!' Ben screeched with a mix of beer breath and saliva. Accompanying his words, Ben slammed Tommy against the wall once more. There was a gap at the end of the bar now, as a number of people had stepped away, likely recognising Ben and the others and not wanting to be involved in the situation. Several doormen were approaching the scene, stopping during their approach as Squawk spoke to them. The bartender leaned across the bar and yelled at Ben, saying that he had to take it outside, that the cops were going to be called. Ben met his glare, although the bartender appeared not to be intimidated and stood his ground.

'We all need to talk, and I feel it would be wiser to do it outside, don't you?' Tommy calmly suggested as Ben's attention turned back from the bartender.

'Too fucking right we need to talk!' Ben snapped, releasing his grip. They locked stares for a moment longer, and then Ben stepped aside, allowing Tommy to pass. Ben followed just a few footsteps behind as the crowd parted for them to get to the club's entrance. The four men who had approached Tommy followed him out, along with Fiona and Sonia.

As they entered the small alleyway to the left of the club's entrance, Ben shoved Tommy to the ground. Knelt on all fours, Tommy glanced around. This was where he'd returned. This was the alleyway in which he had awoken to the pain burning through his chest. That scar—the same one that was showing on Ben's arm.

'Right. Let's start again. What's your name?' Ben asked as Tommy got back to his feet.

He glanced at the six people and the surrounding area as a chill seemed to blow through. Tommy smiled as the cold brushed against his face. 'What's in a name? Is it not just something to put on your gravestone or for people to remember you by after your death?'

Ben quickly stepped forward, grabbing Tommy by the throat. They locked stares, the smile not shifting from Tommy's face. Even as Ben squeezed tighter, the smile remained. In anger, Ben pushed Tommy back; Tommy stumbled and then fell on to his back. Tommy instantly got on all fours. Pain echoed through him as he felt the force of Ben's boot against his ribs. The impact flipped Tommy over on to his back again.

'Ben!' Fiona shouted, diverting Ben's attention towards her. He grinned slightly as he shook his head at Fiona. As they exchanged stares, Tommy quickly got back to his feet. Ben turned to Tommy, surprised at how quickly he'd gotten up from the attack.

'Fine. Don't tell me your fucking name, but tell me this: how do you know Fiona's?'

'Sorry, Ben, I don't feel that's any of your concern.'

Ben swung around with a roundhouse kick that connected with Tommy's jaw, sending him spinning to the ground.

'Ben!' Fiona screeched once again.

Ben sighed heavily, turning back towards her, his anger bubbling. 'Fiona, will you stop yelling! That's his job,' Ben snapped, pointing to Tommy, who again was getting back to his feet. Ben calmly continued, his tone lower, 'Look, Fiona, you're new here, and this is the only way smartasses like him can learn.'

As Ben turned his attention back to Tommy, he realised that Tommy was already back on his feet. His lip was split, and blood edged its way down his chin, but still, there was a slight smile on Tommy's face. A look of confusion filled Ben's, followed by a brief moment of concern.

'It's you, ain't it? The fuck-up Rodderson's mate was on about. I'm gonna kick the shit outta you for what you did to Squawk's cousin!' There was a slight sound of excitement in Ben's voice as he clenched his fists.

'That's your theory on life, isn't it, Ben? Violence solves everything. It doesn't, you know.' Ben shook his head with a chuckle as Tommy looked past him to Fiona. 'Fiona, your mum's worried about you as is your father.'

Fiona's face grew red with anger. 'My dad's dead, you fuck-up. He's burning in the fires of hell, which is where you belong!' she exploded as she ran back towards the club, closely followed by Sonia, who encouraged Ben as she chased after her friend. Everyone looked on in shock for a moment before Ben quickly swung around with another roundhouse kick. This time, Tommy ducked under the kick and swept out his other leg, causing Ben to fall to the ground. As Squawk and two others walked towards Tommy, fists clenched, the alleyway filled with blue lights and the wailing of a police car.

'Pigs!' Squawk hollered as all the men scattered in different directions. Tommy watched as Ben ran past him with a glare.

Tommy stood alone in the spotlight of the police car's headlights. Officer Samuels stepped out. He pointed his gun at Tommy, both hands grasping it. 'Freeze.'

'Are we out for a Sunday drive, Officer Samuels?'

Samuels ignored the remarks as he walked around the car door, his arms still extended. He lowered one arm and removed a pair of handcuffs from his belt, dangling them to his side with one hand. 'You're under arrest,' Samuels stated as he cautiously edged his way towards Tommy.

Slowly Tommy shook his head, and again, the chill blew through the alleyway.

'Are the bones of your intent sharp enough to penetrate the lies of your justice?' The question echoed through the alley as the officer stopped like a deer in the sights of a hunter's gun, unsure whether to attack or run.

'What do you mean by that?'

'Exactly what you thought. Why do these things happen? Let me tell you something. In life, things happen—wrong place, wrong time. You can't change these things no matter what you do to prevent them. However, you can control what happens after. Tim needs justice, just like Fiona Roberts needs guidance.' Tommy watched as Samuels lowered his gun and handcuffs. 'I'm not here to hurt you, Officer Samuels. I'm here to help. You had a young boy call you yesterday, and you arrested a man who was planning to rob his family. They need to be stopped, and I only trust you to do it. I'm going now, but we'll speak again soon.'

Samuels remained silent, giving just a slight nod of his head. As Tommy approached, he could sense Samuels's fear, and he knew the man was afraid that he was doing the wrong thing in letting him pass.

'I'm not going to break the law, but I am going to allow you to enforce it,' Tommy added. Samuels slipped the gun back in the holster and allowed Tommy to walk past into the maze of people that had formed at the entrance of the club. Amber stood amongst those looking on in amazement and confusion.

Reverend Jones sat bolt upright in his bed. The thin bed sheet stuck to his chest against his cold sweat. His breathing was heavy. The dream had felt so real. He peeled the sheet from him and swung around on to the edge of his bed, reaching for the glass of water. He took a large mouthful and swallowed, trying to moisten his dry throat. The horrific images he had witnessed couldn't be real. He had to know, though, if the books were there, the nightmare had to be true. If the angel had shown him correctly . . .

'Ben. Did you feel that?' Squawk asked, slightly uneasy.

'Feel what? That the fuckin' filth saved that freak from a good kick-in?'

'No. That there was something different about him? Something familiar? We've seen him before!'

Ben stopped walking and turned to Squawk, his smile slightly crooked. 'What you mean?'

'I don't know, mate. He just reminds me of someone, but I can't place who.'

'Look at it this way. He's claimed to be linked with Mary Watson and Harry, Fiona's old man. There's only one thing in common: They're both dead, so unless we have something like *The Sixth Sense* going on, I think he's Captain Fruit Loop, all right. He may look familiar 'cause he's been stalking us or something. He had to know who Fiona was—could have followed her from her house to yours. Maybe even from there to here. One thing that's for sure is I'm gonna teach him a sturdy lesson next time.' Ben stormed past the bouncers and back into the Night Arts Centre.

Squawk glanced towards the alleyway, Tommy's face still etched into his mind.

Jones stood face-to-face with the angel that once again stood over the Benovolt family graves. He and Boris had struggled to place it back there that morning as the people began to leave. Daniel had felt it disrespectful to leave the angel on the ground.

For a moment, he stood in silence. The gentle breeze made the cellophane of some freshly laid flowers rustle, and out of the corner of his eye, he saw the police tape flickering. With a deep breath, he placed his hands on the shoulders of the angel and pushed it back. As it fell, he looked towards its base. A small granite square remained. Jones dropped to his knees and grabbed the granite. With all his strength, he pulled, managing to get his fingers underneath, gripping it better. With one more heave, he lifted it away from the grave, exposing a hole.

The thin layer of cement that surfaced the grave was cracked, with a number of weeds growing through it. Where the granite had been placed, three metal handles remained. They had been supporting the stone above the hole. Hesitantly, he slipped his fingers around the rusting metal and, with a tight grip, pulled the metal grid upwards, with the damaged concrete base cracking and sliding down the large metal grid as he did so. As he turned the metal frame to one side, he saw that the pit was a deep hollow. The smells of mature leather and stale water were overpowering.

At the bottom of the shallow grave, he saw the books—just like the images of his nightmare. Laid across them was a large hollow golden cross. The appearance was like that of guttering around a house, and inside the guttering was water. He knew from the dream that the water had been blessed within the church shortly after the Benovolt family had been laid to rest. He also knew the books would explain the dream—the demons, ghosts, and ghouls, which, for years, he had convinced himself weren't real.

With a lump in his throat and his heart beating fast, Reverend Jones stepped down into the shallow grave, collecting the first book, its leather spine worn with age and the pages faded. He opened the cover to see the dignified handwriting of Raymond Benovolt. The top of the page, dated 1872, read, *Hunting of Ghouls: Sherwood Forest, Nottingham.*

Tommy stormed through the warehouse doors and glanced around in the darkness.

'Harry, show yourself!' His voice echoed around the room, causing only mice to stir and make their presence known. 'Harry,' Tommy repeated, turning as he looked around once more. He stopped in the direction of the doorway. Amber Johnson stood peering in from outside. There was an awkward silence as she stepped into the warehouse. Her eyes darted from side to side as she looked for the person to whom Tommy was calling.

'Who's Harry?' she asked. Tommy looked around again as he saw Harry's weak form appearing in the corner.

'He's the dead ghost that told me to talk to his daughter!' Tommy snapped, glancing towards Amber. She remained near the doorway, looking slightly scared, although her intrigue probably stopped her from running.

'Harry, why does your daughter think you're burning in the fires of hell?'

Harry's form became clearer as he approached Tommy. 'It's my burden. I'm forced to watch.' Harry looked towards the floor, seeming disgraced by his words. 'I wasn't a good man, Thomas. I did bad things to them and convinced myself that it was for their own good. Convinced her that she deserved what I'd do to them when I arrived home.'

'Look at me! What did you do to them?' Tommy's words were cold, and Harry looked up.

'I hurt them physically. I would lose my mind and beat her mother. Her face would be bruised and bloody before I'd apologise. She'd always accept it, no matter what I did. She'd say it wasn't healthy to go to bed angry. She was remarkable, and I was pathetic. One day, after a Sunday of drinking, I came home and really lost it. I grabbed a knife from the bread bin and threatened to stab her in front of our daughter. She went to the window to call for help, and I grabbed her by the hair and threw her to the floor. I raised the knife and threatened her again, my back facing the window. Fiona grabbed the dinning room chair and ran at me. I don't blame her. I just wish she'd done it sooner. I was trapped between the chairs legs, and she pushed me back. The window smashed, and I fell from our third-floor flat. My head hit the concrete, and my skull shattered, my brain turning to mush. I died instantly.

'It seemed like an eternity that the thoughts replayed before I saw them again. I was there when Fiona was let off without charges. I was relieved, to say the least. I've watched over them ever since, watched as they grew stronger together. Lived like a mother and daughter really should. They'd smile, laugh, and joke, not live in fear like I made them. I watched Fiona slip into that seedy world, watched it corrupt my innocent daughter. I'm not proud of what I've done or who I was. Deep down, I feel the world would have been a better place if I never existed, but I did. I created something wonderful in that girl, and I don't want that scum to ruin her like I would have.'

Tommy could see his distress. He was genuine. He had repented for his sins, but couldn't forgive himself. Tommy nodded. 'He won't. The gangs won't. They've hurt too many.'

'Is he here?' the feminine voice questioned.

Tommy turned to her, amazed that she hadn't fled at the thought of him talking to an invisible man. She didn't even look dazed by the thought. 'Yes, he's standing in front of me.' Tommy observed her for a second. She appeared more curious than scared. 'You actually believe me, don't you?' She simply nodded. 'What makes you believe me?'

'I had a brother named Oliver. He believed he could . . . Well, I heard him talking to someone once, asking what death felt like. I could guess that he felt he was talking to a ghost. There were some complications at the time, and no one believed him.'

'Ask her what the complications were,' Harry cut in.

Tommy glanced back to him. 'You can hear her?'

Harry nodded. 'I can hear and see her. It just doesn't work the other way around. It's like a one-way mirror.'

'Right. Harry can hear you as well,' Tommy said, which Amber accepted with a nod. 'What were the complications?' he asked her.

'Me. I had been diagnosed with pancreatic cancer. It's a very aggressive form with a low survival rate. Oliver and I were always close, and he took the news hard. Everyone thought he was losing it. As you can imagine, telling people he was talking to ghosts would have been the icing on that cake. However, he swore on my life that he was talking to them. He even said they could help me. He said they had offered him a deal, one he'd be proud to take. When I asked what it was, he refused to tell me, saying that if he breathed a word of it to anyone, it wouldn't come true. He kissed me goodnight on the cheek and hugged me tightly that night. And I'm so glad I returned his hug.

'The next morning, he was late getting up, and we assumed he had overslept. He wasn't one for mornings at the best of times. I went up to his room, and he was in bed. It was the strangest thing you'd ever seen. His body had aged, and his hair greyed overnight. Strands came out in my hand when I ran my hand over it. His skin had stretched and wrinkled. When the doctor came, he said he died of old age. They couldn't believe it was Oliver at first. The post-mortem proved it was him through dental records and fingerprints.' As Amber explained everything, she walked towards the steps in the corner of the room. She sat on the bottom one, placing her arms on her knees, which were level with her shoulders.

'Ask her if there was anything strange in the room—a small fire . . . an amulet?'

Tommy gave Harry a puzzled look and then repeated his question.

Amber looked up, and a tear rolled down her cheek, carrying with it a thin line of mascara.

'The egg cup in the ashtray . . . There were some burnt matches tucked under it and his necklace in it. No one really understood that, but we just assumed he'd had some food during the night. He loved boiled eggs.' A smile briefly flashed over her face, but she shook it away.

'I know what happened!' Harry exclaimed, causing Tommy's attention to turn to him. 'The egg cup would have contained water and his necklace, which would have had a cross on it. With the right incantation, he would have converted the water into holy water. Then boiling it would have created an aurora in which he could speak to the holy powers.' There was a moment where everyone remained quiet. Amber wiped away a tear, smearing the make-up across her cheek.

'How do you know? Who are the holy powers?'

'The same people I faced for my sins. They go by various names. They're the people who can forgive and allow the dead through to the next level, granting them peace. I declined, saying I couldn't forgive myself.'

'Problem with that, Harry, is that Oliver was living.'

'He was chosen . . . , selected. He already had a purpose. He just found a way to fulfil it early. He bargained for it. Traded his mortal life in exchange for his sister's.'

'He could have made that sacrifice for you,' Tommy suggested, turning his attention back to Amber. 'What happened to the tumour?'

'It vanished before the next scan. What kind of sacrifice would it have been?'

'He accepted a life he was destined to have. I don't know what that means.' Tommy looked at Harry, who shrugged.

'All I know is what I overhear,' Harry said. 'In this form, between worlds, you hear things. Not everything out there is good. I've heard of two destiny callings. They are often declined unless they were genuinely destined to be selected. I've been like this for three years, and only two people have been destined for bigger things.'

'What do you mean that not everything out there is good?' Amber frowned as she heard Tommy repeat the words.

'They fight, Thomas,' Harry said. 'They are always defending them. Keeping the balance. Those stories you're told in school—heaven . . . hell . . . They exist, and Earth is between them. It's a battleground. Lately, I heard the number twelve mentioned between them. I also heard that you were coming back to level a playing field. That's all I heard.'

As Tommy turned back to Amber, concern still filled her face. 'Oliver went to a better place,' Tommy said comfortingly, watching Amber's fears almost float away. 'Harry knows. He's heard that he's making things better. Doing his part in the grand scheme of things, creating peace here, so to speak.'

'That's not what I said! I don't know where he is.'

Tommy shot Harry a glance, which Harry accepted as a sign to be silent.

It had taken Reverend Jones nearly two hours to move the books. He had ended up pushing them in the gardener's wheelbarrow, which was stored in the shed behind the church. He had placed the books in the locked storage cupboard at the far end of the church hall, knowing they'd be safe there since he had the only key. He had lost count of the books and hadn't read more than a couple of the titles. Some books were fairly thick in size; others were only a few pages.

It was now three forty in the morning, and Daniel Jones was again on his knees, doing the jigsaw puzzle that he'd created when removing the metal grid. The concrete had been there for some time, and it had weakened and cracked over the years. While lifting the grid, the lumps had separated, and they now seemed impossible to slot back together.

Several of the smaller shards had fallen through and left small holes in its appearance. Jones had attempted to place some of the weeds from the surrounding graves in the holes to cover it up. It didn't look brilliant, but he hoped it was enough for others not to notice. He knew the police were not coming back to the area, as they believed, after thirty-four hours of searching, that the weapon had been carried away by the attackers and no evidence had been left at the scene. He carefully placed the granite base back on the handles of the grid.

Standing up, he looked at his artwork. He felt nervous as he looked at the cracks that showed so obviously, and the angel would be too heavy to lift alone. He stepped back. Then, knowing there was nothing more he could do, he returned the wheelbarrow.

Chapter Fourteen

Akira Mason sat slumped back in the plastic chair. His eyes followed the outskirts of the grey room for what felt like the four hundredth time. He glanced at the table and the empty plastic cup that sat upon it.

'God, I'm bored! Can I have another cup of water?' he called, watching the door in case it opened. He gave a deep sigh, running his hand through his long black hair. He stood up and paced the room; it was small. Within four strides, he'd reached the end. He had come face-to-face with the large blackened glass, which he started making faces at. 'Come on, I know you're watching me! I'm your little guinea pig! Watch your hamster run! Why not just get me a wheel to run around in?'

'I would, but that might register as some form of discrimination these days,' Samuels stated as he walked into the room. 'Why do you think we would want to watch a kid like you'—he looked at his watch—'at seven fifteen in the morning?' Akira followed his movements with his eyes, watching as he sat on the chair next to the table.

'Would you like to sit, Akira?' Akira shrugged and took two large steps towards the seat.

'Do you know why you're here?' Samuels asked as Akira shrugged once more. 'Around thirty-eight hours ago, a woman by the name of Alison Shannings was murdered. Have you ever heard of this person?'

'No. Should I have?'

Samuels held his stare and then looked at the sheet of paper he was carrying. 'Have you ever talked about killing someone and hanging them upside down on the doors of a church?' Akira's eyes darted forth and back. 'Maybe at college when you were threatening a teenage boy called Matthew Kemp?'

'I was only bullshittin' him. Look at me—I'm unique. Usually, I have black eyeliner on, and I even wear black lipstick quite often. They think I'm either a vampire or devil worshipper. They were taking the piss, so I said the kind of shit they'd expect. I didn't kill anyone.'

Samuels smiled as he leaned forward. 'If you were only bullshitting him, you were very convincing. That boy came to us that evening as soon as his last class finished. Three days later, Alison was found nailed to a church door upside down with her stomach cut open. Imagine what the reverend thought when he found her gutted on the backdoor—sacrificed just like you threatened to do to Matthew Kemp four days ago.'

Akira's face drained of confidence, along with colour, as his jaw dropped. 'I can understand how sketchy this looks, but—'

'Sketchy?' Samuels interrupted. 'You predicted it!'

'Okay, bad choice of words. How could I have got her upside down on my own?'

'Another man who was injured, stabbed within the church, said four people dressed in black, stabbed him, then dragged Alison from the church. Who were the people with you?' Akira sat in shock, shaking his head. Samuels stood up, letting out a sigh. 'Is this how we're going to play this out? You sit in silence until the police officers search your house and bring in the evidence?'

'They won't find anything there,' Akira mumbled.

'Why's that? Where did you hide the weapon? We've searched the whole cemetery, and its not there.'

'Listen, I'm an idiot at times, okay! I smoke pot. I threaten people. Hell, I even bit my teacher when she called me a vampire wannabe, but I swear on my life that I never killed another human being—and I never will. It's a look, and yeah, I know how I feel—I want revenge sometimes. I know I say my dad should die for what he's done to my mum, but I'd never be the one to do it. You've got to believe me.'

Samuels observed him for a moment without speaking. He then picked up the sheet of paper and walked to the door. 'We'll see how the search goes before we go any further. I have a couple of other leads to follow up on,' Samuels stated, hearing Akira whimper behind him. He then walked out, locking the door.

Daylight reflected brightly from the white walls of Wilsons Terrace. Tommy walked along the third level to No. 23 and knocked loudly on the door.

Inside, Rebecca scurried along the hallway towards the door, checking that the chain was firmly on as she peered through the spyhole. She saw Tommy standing a step or two back, next to the railings. 'Can I help you?' she asked.

'I don't think so, but I'm helping you. I know how Fiona got mixed up with the wrong people, and I know she's a good kid.'

'Are you one of them?'

'No. I'm someone who's had enough of their ways and is going to help change it.'

'They'll just kill you like they killed the others, so what's the point in trying?'

'Because sometimes it's better to die trying than not to have tried,' Tommy stated, leaning back against the railing.

'You'd still be dead!'

'I like the quiet.'

'Why do you want to help us? Why Fiona?'

'I knew your husband. I know he'd be worried right now. Despite everything, I know how much he loved you. He never forgave himself for all those times he hurt you.'

'I still loved him, you know. After all those times he'd beat me, I still loved him.' She undid the bolt and removed the chain.

As Rebecca opened the door, she saw that Tommy had gone. She glanced around and then slowly closed the door, securing it tightly again.

'We've brought someone in for questioning,' Samuels announced as Reverend Jones opened the door to his apartment.

'Did he do it?'

'I don't think so, but I think there may be a slim chance that he's involved with the people who did,' Samuels explained. A short silence followed, broken as Samuels added, 'Can I ask you a question?' Jones nodded as he led the way to the kitchen. 'You remember when you were talking to Michael Johns . . . and he talked about the guy draped in black . . . and how he knew stuff about him and his family?'

'Yes,' Jones said, pointing to the kettle as he flicked on the switch.

'Please. What did he say about him again?'

Jones pulled two mugs from the rack and placed them on the sideboard. 'Said that when the guy placed a hand on him, he started to remember things.' He dropped the teabags into the cups. 'Said that he saw his daughter searching for him, handing out the flyers.' Jones opened the fridge door, removing the milk. 'It sounds a bit strange, but then again, given the kinds of days we've been having . . . ,' Jones left the words trail off as he poured the milk into the mugs, watching as the teabags struggled to the surface.

'I saw him last night, or at least I think I did. He was strange, but something he said reminded me of Tim. It sent a shiver down my spine. He asked if the bones of my intent were sharp enough to penetrate the lies of my justice. Tim always used to say that the intent of justice and actual justice were two different things. How would he know that? I can understand knowing about my son's murder—it's been in the papers all the time—but those words?' Jones shook his head as he lifted the whistling kettle.

Samuels gave a childish look as Jones poured the tea. 'Maybe angels do exist,' Jones said. 'Think about it: the lightning bolt hitting the statue . . . and the wings being burnt into the ground, then not leaving a mark. A day later, this guy appears and starts saving people from the gangs . . .'

'Billy, that kid he helped, gave a description of him as the guy that stopped the men who were stealing from him. Billy told me that he claimed Mary Watson sent him. Could an angel be here—and on top of that be talking with the ghost of a former councillor? As nice as that sounds, I'd need proof,' Jones paused for a moment, thinking about what he was going to say or whether he should even say it. He'd known John for years; they'd become friends during the passing of his son. Jones thought a moment longer, maybe it would be the proof Samuels needed.

'If I tell you something, it has to be off the record. You'll think I'm insane, but I can assure you I'm not.'

Samuels set down the tea and observed his seriousness. He nodded, and Jones continued.

'Last night, I had this weird dream. I saw a man running, and he was carrying a sword. Its handle was engraved with two snakes, and these creatures were chasing him. They had green skin with little horns or spikes all over them. Then he actually spoke to me. He said it's up to me. It's time for my calling. Then I saw the lightning bolt hit the Benovolt grave again, only this time the statue fell forward and the whole top caved in. The grave was hollow, and in the centre were hundreds of books with a large metal cross over them. There was holy water in it. I saw it being poured from the altar in the church.'

'This sounds like a simple nightmare to me. Well, maybe not simple.'

'That's what I thought, but I had to know. I went there. They were there, just as expected. Finish your tea, and I'll show you.'

Chapter Fifteen

Tommy sat reading through the article on Tim Andrews, son of Officer John Samuels. He was shot after a confrontation with three members from the street gang known as the Rivals. He had left a village pub, The Old Rope House, on the outskirts of Alterson and was shot as he headed home. They had three photos from the CCTV footage of the pub's car park. In these unclear photos, it appeared to be Ben Williams and two others. Below, it gave the names of John Molk and Kama Lorenzo. Due to witnesses saying the three individuals were still in the pub, no further charges arose, and the murder went unsolved. Witnesses had also remarked that Ben Williams was seen making several calls on his mobile during the time.

Tommy set down the papers as he heard footsteps and saw a shadow walk past the whitewashed window. Quickly he scampered to his feet and ran to the wall, putting his back against it.

With an armful of books, Amber entered. 'Did I startle you?' she asked, seeing Tommy against the wall.

'I'm not used to guests. Well, living ones anyway,' Tommy stated, reaching out and offering to take the books. Amber had changed since leaving in the early hours. She had also showered, and her hair seemed to bounce with each footstep she took. She wore tight jeans with a white T-shirt tucked into them, a coffee logo in the top corner. She had her leather jacket over that. As they walked to the steps, she slipped her hand inside the jacket and pulled out a packet of cigarettes.

'You had cancer, and now you smoke?' Tommy remarked as he placed the books down on the top step, reading the cover of the top book: *Resurrecting the Occults*. The edges were coloured by a Celtic design.

'Cut me a break, all right? I just carried those books halfway across town, thinking they might help you. They were Oliver's. I removed them from his room before the coroner came. Didn't want them thinking he worshipped the devil or anything!' Amber joked as she sparked up a cigarette, drawing on it as she did so. Once it was lit and the lighter slipped away, she gripped the Rothman between her thumb and forefinger and exhaled.

'Thanks. They'll be useful. I know practically nothing about any of this.' Tommy moved the top book to one side, reading the title of the next, the biggest of the four books: *Rare Outcomes: The Truth about the Afterlife*. Tommy slid it across, exposing the next: *Mystic History: The Alterson Archives*. Below it was a photo of an angel with its closed wings, its hands in front, praying. Tommy lifted it and read the fourth title: *Myths, Legends, and the Afterlife*. 'There are a lot of books here on the afterlife.'

'His older sister was about to be joining it, remember?'

'Sorry. I didn't think.'

Amber smiled as she exhaled another stream of blue smoke. 'I've got to head off for now, but do you mind if I come back? I've never had anyone to talk to about this stuff, and I can't help but feel I'm meant to be helping in some way.'

'That's fine. You know where I am.'

'Okay. Got to serve coffee for the next six hours, but I'll pop back after. Probably be stinking of coffee, though.' She added as she got up, brushing off her jeans.

As she walked towards the door, Tommy thought to himself about his past.

Did I drink coffee? Right now, he didn't even know what it smelt like.

They stood in the doorway, looking at the large piles of books. 'How many are there?' Samuels asked, picking up one and flicking through the handwritten pages. There had often been rumours of the Benovolt family hunting demons, but nothing was ever proven or admitted by their descendents.

'I don't know. I counted up to about a hundred and seventy, but then concentrated on moving them before daylight.'

'I know I said this was off the record, but this could be evidence in Alison's death. The ritual could be from one of these books. Maybe someone else found them first.' Samuels dropped the book back on to the pile.

'No, something inside me knows. Besides, the cross was filled to the brim with holy water when I started. By the time I'd finished, I'd spilt nearly every drop,' Jones informed him, observing the mound of books.

'Could they have refilled it?'

'John, look at the grave. You can tell someone tampered with it. They wouldn't have been able to have got it right any better than me,' Samuels was agreeing as his phone rang.

'Samuels,' he said, answering it.

'Hi, it's Marie. There's nothing at Akiras to link him to the crime, and despite his drinking alone at the time of death, there was CCTV to put him in the centre of town. He's in no way linked to the crime. Well, at least physically.'

Samuels sighed. 'Great. Back to square one. Release him and tell him to sort his act out from me . . . and to stop smoking cannabis! See you at the station later.' Samuels ended the call.

'Our suspect is innocent,' Samuels told Jones as Jones flicked through another book: *Disposing of a Zombie, the Living Flesh.*

'This stuff seems so far-fetched, yet so realistic. What should I do with it, John?'

Samuels shrugged, running his hand through his short black hair. 'God knows, but I don't think a church is the best place to store this.'

'What if I speak to Larry about using the apartment next to me? I'll take it out under a friend's name and say I'm moving in his stuff.'

Samuels agreed and suggested boxing the books up.

Tommy had flicked through the first half of the *Myths, Legends, and the Afterlife* book when he came across a chapter called 'Coming Back.' It had a number of scenarios, including one about animals: crows, ravens, and rooks. They were birds of death that could carry the dead to and from heaven to extract revenge on the men that caused their unfair deaths. It also said that the first case of this was the raven that flew from Noah's ark and never returned. Legend believes that the raven was so distraught with the number of souls lost in the floods and looking for guidance that it began to carry the souls to their everlasting peace. Hell also had a creature to counter this. It had serpents and spiders that were rumoured to have crawled from the depths of hell to strike vengeance against the living. The biggest belief of which being the black widow spider. It was believed to capture the souls of widows who had committed suicide to escape their lives alone and drag them to hell, where they'd become lost and alone forever more.

It was several pages later, though, that Thomas believed to be his fortune-telling. A soul was a being who refused to accept the fate of his loved ones and pulled a way from heaven's gates, trading his peace to save loved ones left behind from fear, a man or woman who had lost something close to him and refused to let someone loose the same. They had to have had pure lives and been destined for an important role in the afterlife. Something they may loose during the battles. It also referred to feeling the emotions of the lost or damned, but not their own. However, as he read on, he saw listed a number of ways a soul could regain his memories—but they did come at a price.

As Tommy finished reading the page, he realised that he had come to some understanding, but he also knew that the answers gave him more questions. What had he lost, and who was he here to protect? He thought back to the female voice from the window. Was that the person he had lost? Was the image he saw over his shoulder the previous night the person he was meant to protect? Tommy closed the book, picked up the newspaper again, and began reading.

A fire had taken four lives on the east side of town; it was believed the older of the two sons had a drug habit that had brought the fire upon the house.

Daniel Jones finished packing the boxes that Samuels had dropped off previously. As he packed them into the deep boxes, he had counted the books. They were heavy, and he believed he'd need Samuels's help to carry them to the second-floor apartment he had rented from Larry Hodgekins. He had rented it under the name of Simon George, a friend he had many years ago. He also added that Simon only wanted it as a holiday apartment, and that he, Daniel, was to have the keys.

Jones taped up the last box and sat upon it to rest for a moment. There were 666 books within the boxes—each one a different species of demon.

CHAPTER SIXTEEN
CHAPTER SIXTEEN

CHAPTER SIXTEEN

'Where the fuck were you last night?' Fiona shouted as Shaun whistled his way into Squawk's apartment. Squawk and Sonia glanced at each other and got to their feet.

'I was held up. I got to the club and couldn't see you there. Christ, what's up your ass?' A slight grin accompanied the question, which grated against her. Fiona stared at her boyfriend angrily. Shaun's smile stretched across his face as he gave a shrug. 'What?'

'There was a slightly weird guy there last night,' Squawk informed him, trying to defuse the situation as Fiona slumped in a chair, swilling back the remains of her bottle of wine. 'Said he knew Fiona's dad. Ben was going to tear him up, but the filth arrived, and you can guess the outcome. If you had checked your messages, you would have known.'

'Are you okay?' Shaun asked, his voice now sincere as he diverted his attention to Fiona, who forced a smile.

'Fine,' she snapped. 'Why were you held up?'

'Given everything that happened yesterday, you could have at least made sure you were there last night,' Sonia added. Squawk shook his head towards her, but Sonia didn't reply. The look she gave, however, burned right through him.

'I saw Rapid, and he asked if I could drop some gear off at Ashley Terrace.' A silence fell over the room.

Squawk opened his bedroom door and pointed for Sonia to go in; he knew who lived in Ashley Terrace. 'We're going to give you guys some space. Sort it all out, yeah?'

Shaun gave Squawk a nod as they disappeared, closing the door behind them. Fiona hadn't taken her eyes off Shaun since he said where he had been.

'I'm going to guess the door number was seventy-three.'

Shaun just looked at her, his eyes not meeting her gaze and his jaw slightly open. 'Tell me you didn't do it again? Tell me you didn't fuck that whore?'

'Her name is Michelle, and I told you not to speak about her like that. You know what she used to mean to me,' Shaun stated as he approached Fiona. Fiona quickly got up and swung around behind the armchair, placing the chair between them. Shaun stopped in his tracks and exhaled, clearly trying to hide his anger as he glanced away. 'You thought I was going to do it again, didn't you?'

Fiona looked down, not wanting to admit it, not wanting to face that fear he had instilled in her.

'Say it. You thought I was going to hit you again, didn't you?' He shook his head as if it would hide the silence. 'For fuck's sake, that was just a one-time thing. I just lost it, okay? I saw you with that guy. I put two and two together and got seven.'

Fiona shook her head. 'Why'd you go there? You knew I'd be upset. Don't you think I was upset enough yesterday?' There was a whimper in Fiona's voice as tears began to form. She quickly wiped them away, avoiding anyone seeing her moment of weakness.

'I can't give you a good reason. I guess I wanted to get the money in quicker, help out the guys, so to speak. I don't want you going without. You don't have the money your mum would have given you, so I have to make it for you. I love you. Michelle and I have a history—I've never hid that—but that's all it is.'

Fiona stepped back from the chair and leaned against her bedroom door. Shaun had lied to her before, and she hadn't been able to see through the lies. The more she looked at him, the more sincere he seemed. The silence, however, was clearly making Shaun uneasy.

'Okay,' he announced, his tone changed, 'the truth is, I wanted her to know you had moved in here and that I was probably going to as well. I just didn't want her to hear it from anyone else. I know you saw her texts the other week when she was trying to get me back. I just wanted her to know that I love you and that it's you I am going to be with forever. I didn't want her to upset you any more than you had been.'

Fiona smiled and beckoned him to her with a smile, which he accepted. 'You could have told me that—maybe even forewarned me!' She slipped her arms around him, placing them on his back as he took her in his arms. She kissed him, which allowed him to relax. 'I love you too, baby,' Fiona added as the kisses became more passionate. She reached behind her and pushed down the door handle, opening the door. They entered the bedroom, overflowing with passion. The door closed on the living room, and only muffled noises remained. The frail form went unnoticed and unheard in the corner, his anger high and unfelt.

'I know what you just did, you bastard!' Harry's words went unheard as he walked away from the apartment, vanishing into the air.

Tommy stood looking down at the fallen angel. He knelt on the ground and looked at the pieced-together grave. The sun still blazed brightly as the afternoon approached the evening. Even though he couldn't see into the grave, he knew something had changed. He could sense it.

In the book *Mystic History: The Alterson Archives*, Tommy had read about a family of hunters, generations that had hunted, dealt with, and killed demons and monsters. The family had settled in Alterson before official records were kept.

The first real knowledge of the Benovolts in Alterson was in the early eleventh century. Alterson was often attacked by conquering forces. In the early days, Vikings would have entered through the city's outskirts, mooring up on the long beaches. In the eleventh century, the Romans wanted to claim it.

The Benovolts had seen several invasions and in time reacted, saving the commoners by calling upon what they believed at the time to be gods. They watched as many invaders became tormented and slain. Armies had fallen in one night after their victory over the mortal protectors. These victories, or protection, depending on which way you look at it, were linked with the Benovolt family.

When the Romans were invading and stealing land, some areas remained untouchable. A handful of warriors would defeat an entire army in less than a day, reclaim their land, and then rest with barely a mark on them. Once the armies had fallen, Brandeis Benovolt, under instruction of the city's influential people, would summon their protectors. This would then entail a sacrifice on holy ground, where a knife would pierce the heart of a pure soul. Usually, the sacrifice would be a female who was in her early twenties and still a virgin. They felt that as the heart bled out, the demon would awake. These demons remained the city's guardians for nearly thirty years. It was only then, after the attacks from other countries ceased, that the demons became unreasonable.

Brandeis, now in his fifties, decided to face the demons he'd once bargained with. The battle that ensued saw the sacrificial knife they had been using vanish into the night and the demon, which became known later as the ghost of Benovolt, fall back to the third layer of hell.

It was shortly after the confrontation that Brandeis bought the land the church was built on. It was rumoured to be the area he created his family's resting place that the demon fell. He then built the single-bell church, claiming it gave the city protection and would prevent the demons from ever resurfacing in their city. As the years continued, people believed the stories to be no more than myths.

Tommy now stood looking at the jigsawed grave, wondering if any of it had been true, and more importantly, whether he was something they would have hunted. He straightened up and looked at the angel again. Something made him want to touch the headstone, but he didn't. As he heard the footsteps on the gravel path, Tommy quickly diverted his attention.

The man was in his fifties. He had short grey hair and a few days' worth of stubble. His checked-work shirt was tucked into his worn, light blue jeans. He stopped at the pathway in front of Tommy and looked him up and down.

'I've seen you before somewhere, haven't I?'

'I don't think so,' Tommy replied, sensing something from the man. He seemed to be afraid of something. The more Tommy looked at him, the more the fear grew.

The guy smiled and then extended a hand. 'Sorry. You just looked familiar. The name's Boris. I help out here the best I can.' Tommy took the hand, feeling the firm grasp, sensing the man's fear towards him even more.

'I'm Tommy. I'm sorry to ask, but are you afraid of me? I'm getting a strange vibe from you.'

'Sorry again. I was here during the attacks a couple of days ago, and seeing a guy studying a grave when I come back is just a little unnerving,' Boris said, releasing Tommy's hand. Tommy could sense something else, something deeper, something Boris was hiding deep inside. He pushed the thoughts away.

'My turn to apologise. I hadn't heard anything about the attacks. I don't hear much news or anything. I'm a bit of a loner.'

'Friday afternoon, four men attacked Ali and me. She was a dear old lady. They stabbed me and then dragged her outside. They hung her upside down and killed her. Actually, to be more honest, from what Daniel said, they butchered her. John Samuels is trying to track them down, but as they were all masked, he doesn't hold much hope.'

'I'm a great believer in justice. Samuels is the one man on the police force that doesn't ever seem afraid to take those chances,' Tommy proudly said.

'Yeah, he's one of the good guys. Have you seen him? I was told he'd be here.'

'No. I've only been here about ten minutes or so. He may be inside,' Tommy suggested, walking around the grave. Boris looked at the doors and then back at Tommy.

'Going to sound a bit babyish from a fifty-four-year-old man, but I don't suppose you'd be willing to walk in there with me. I haven't been here since the attack. I checked myself out of hospital a couple of hours ago; no one knows yet.'

Tommy agreed with a smile, and they walked towards the door. 'So how come you checked yourself out?'

'I hate the place, the smells. I know they say it's the smell of healing, but to me, it's the smell of death.'

Tommy led the way into the church, pushing open the large wooden doors. The hall was empty except for the wooden seats. As they approached the third row in, there was a large red stain on the floor. Boris stopped.

'That's where I lay, life oozing through my fingers.' Boris pointed to the stain as he said it.

'Do they have any idea who did it?'

'They never do, do they? All I know is what I've been told. They apparently cut that Rivals symbol into her stomach. Police think they did that to throw them off their track, though.' Boris turned towards the cross that watched over the church. 'Only God really knows what happened here that day,' he added, Nemon's demonic smile shining through, unknown to Tommy.

Shaun was thrusting himself deep into Fiona as she moaned with pleasure. Shaun's breathing grew heavy as his own pleasure grew, and as he reached his climax, he said *her* name: *Michelle*. Fiona's moans ceased almost instantly as she heard his old girlfriend's name.

'Get the fuck off me!' Fiona yelled, pushing his chest away from her. Shaun knelt up on the bed between Fiona's legs. She pulled back before swinging her leg around him and lifting herself from the bed.

'Oh, come on. It was a slip of the tongue.' Shaun fought back his chuckle 'We were talking about her earlier. That's all it was.'

'I was talking about some people earlier too, but I didn't call out their names as I went to cum inside someone else!' Fiona pulled her jeans up, screaming at him. 'You did her earlier, didn't you? You weren't dropping anything off, were you? You were there fucking her all over again!'

'Seriously, Fi, think this through. Okay, fine, I said it as a joke. I admit it wasn't very funny, but—'

Fiona walked towards him, pointing her finger as her anger reached boiling point. 'Shut up! Did you have sex with her?' Shaun stood up from the bed, looking down as he grabbed his jeans. He reached inside them and pulled his boxer shorts on, turning his back to her. 'Answer me. Did you sleep with her?'

'Does it even matter what I say? You've already made up your mind,' Shaun stated as he slipped one leg into his jeans. As he went to raise the other leg, Fiona ran at him and pushed him over. Due to his position, he tumbled to the floor.

'How dare you do this to me again! God, I gave up everything for you!' she screamed, still waving her hands and pointing at him.

'You fucking psycho bitch. What the fuck are you doing?' Shaun pulled his jeans up before getting to his feet.

'What am I doing? I'm making a mistake thinking that my pathetic boyfriend actually gave a shit about me! Maybe the question to you should be *who* are you doing?'

'Oh, fuck it. You know anyway. Yeah, I've slept with Michelle. I didn't last night, though. For the record, it was this morning.' His arrogance spread over his face. 'I had just about enough time to get showered and then get here. There was some blonde bimbo that I met at Rapid's party last night. None of the excess baggage you come with. She was fit, one of the nicest bodies I ever got to grab. If you're an eight, she must have been a nine and a half.'

Shaun continued to boast until he was stopped by Fiona's hand slapping him across the face. 'Following in Daddy's footsteps, are we?' With those words, Fiona slapped him twice more before Shaun reached up and caught her wrist. 'Let me show you how it's done.' He swung his free hand around, connecting with her cheek and causing her to cry out. 'Don't go crying over that. That was just to make you realise what you were doing.' This time, he clenched his fist and threw a heavy punch into her face. The impact caused her to drop to her knees, screaming, as she raised her hand to the cut above her eye. As the bedroom door swung open, Shaun quickly released her wrist.

'What the fuck?' Squawk shoved Shaun back a couple of steps as he saw Fiona on the floor, still topless, cupping her face. 'In the front room, Shaun, now,' Squawk ordered.

Shaun raised his hands as if to surrender and then grabbed his T-shirt from the floor, leading the way from Fiona's bedroom. Squawk followed as Sonia dropped to her knees, taking her friend in her arms. Fiona was shaking. She knew this time that Shaun had planned the attack.

'It's not what it seems,' Shaun said, pulling his T-shirt over his head.

'That's funny because it seems you two having sex led to a fistfight where you pretty much decked her!'

'I can see what you're thinking, mate, but it's not like that. You know how I've been a prick at times. Yeah, well, that was one of them—while we were, you know, at it. I thought it would be funny to say Michelle's name. Okay, I know it was a bad joke, but because I said that, she instantly thinks Michelle and I were shagging last night.'

'Shut the fuck up, mate. I know you, and I know you can't just talk when it comes to Michelle. For Christ's sake, with you, it doesn't really come down to talking with any women, does it? You gave me your word that when Fiona moved in, you'd stop playin' around and be committed. You couldn't even for one night. And of all nights, the first one she moved in here, my house. You promised me. I rang you dozens of times. When I realised your phone was switched off, I knew you were doing someone. After that prick last night at the club, I don't need this. Go on. Get out! Just piss off!' Squawk pointed to the front door.

'You're actually going to throw me out?' Shaun asked.

'No, I'm asking you to leave, but if you don't go, I will throw you out. You both need some time to chill until this blows over, and as she lives here, that means it's you that's gotta go. I'll see you in the club later.'

Shaun shook his head and walked out the door, slamming it behind him.

'You sure you don't want a cup?' Boris asked as he sat down on the wooden chair in the corner of the small kitchen, his hands cupping the mug of tea.

'I'm fine.' Tommy had declined the drink because he hadn't actually eaten or had anything to drink since he had returned. He didn't even know if his metabolism would allow him to.

'You're all right if you need to get off. I'm all right now; besides, the Rev will be here in a minute.'

'Okay. There's a lot more to sort before this evening.'

'Going to stop the gangs again, eh?'

Tommy was taken back by the question. 'Sorry? What do you mean?'

'I was wondering if you were going to fight off the gangs beating up the homeless?'

Tommy gave a shrug of his shoulders. 'Don't know what you mean.'

'Yeah ya do, Tommy. I remembered you a few minutes ago, when you talked about Samuels being the one who'd enforce the law. I've seen you around. You actually ran into me when you were running away from the park that morning. You were the guy that helped Michael Johns. He rewarded the church well after he remembered the past. How'd you do it?'

'Right place, right time. I just stopped the kids, and he looked at me as if he remembered something,' Tommy lied.

Boris smiled. Tommy didn't know anything about himself. Nemon grinned more than ever inside his meat suit. He would drain Tommy, and he'd have no idea what was going on.

'I don't know how you did it, but he said you did something. I'm an inquisitive guy, Tommy. I'll find out somehow. Until then, though, you keep helping us.'

Tommy nodded, feeling slightly uneasy as he remembered bumping into Boris that day in the park . . . , those images. He moved from the kitchen doorway into the church hall, each footstep echoing on the white marble floor. As he reached the carpeted section, he looked up at the colourful church, the stained glass windows dancing around the grey pillars. The varnish on the pulpit gleamed, as did the benches.

Did God bring me back?

Tommy shrugged the thoughts away as he glanced at Boris, who now stood smiling in the kitchen's doorway, the mug held in his hand. Something didn't seem right, no matter what he felt before, Boris was hiding something from him. Hesitantly, he cast Boris a smile and slipped out the door and on to the gravel path.

CHAPTER SEVENTEEN

CHAPTER SEVENTEEN

Tommy walked into the warehouse to see Amber sat on the steps, looking through one of the newspapers. As she heard his footsteps, she pulled her attention away from an article.

'Where did you get all these papers?' she asked, closing the one she was reading.

'They just appeared here each day. Some blew in on the wind; others I just found in the corner. I suppose the best way to answer that would be to say that I don't know.'

Amber laughed as she stood up. 'Did the books help?'

'I think so. They answered some questions but also left me with a lot more.'

'He's done it again!' Tommy heard the voice before he saw Harry's form appear in the room.

'Who's done what, Harry?' Tommy asked, directing his attention towards him. Amber giggled as she spun around, looking for his frail form—to no avail.

'Shaun did. He cheated on her and then charmed his way back into her bed.'

Tommy looked away and then back to Harry, raising his hands. 'There's not much I can do. I'm trying to find a way to sort things out, but it's a bit hard at the minute. They all have alibis. They always seem clean when they've been arrested.'

'I know. Thank you for this morning. You set her mind at ease. Rebecca trusts you.'

Tommy nodded. 'Where is your daughter?'

'She's living with a man they call Squawk. There's something personal between you two. He sensed it last night, but no one knew what it was.'

'They killed me. It doesn't get much more personal!'

Amber looked at Tommy for a moment, the reality of the situation back within an instant.

'No, something more. It concerned the powers, the voices I hear. "The past must not be revealed" is what they said.'

There was a silence before Tommy broke it. 'Where does Squawk live?'

'Clements Tower . . . number seventeen A.'

'Go there, and I'll be there soon.'

'Marie, how are you today?' Samuels asked, entering the police station locker room.

'A lot better than I was. Chief said you worked all day yesterday and right into the evening on that case. How'd you do it?'

'Adrenaline, I guess. It helped in some ways that I knew her. It drives me more. Just want to see the bastard who did it actually go down for it,' Samuels stated, pulling his bag from his locker.

'Just seeing her like that shocked me so much. I'd never seen anything like it . . . ,' Marie's words trailed off as Samuels nodded, pulling his flask out.

'The first dead body I saw was a girl in a back alley on New Bridge Street. She had rung up saying she was being chased because she was going to give evidence against Ben Williams. By the time we got there, she was all over the alleyway. They said she had been shot below the chin—and the bullet exited through the top of the skull. The first time you get one of those cases, the images stay with you no matter what. The thing I found the weirdest at the time was how small the entry hole was and how big the exit wound was. The contents of her skull were sprayed all the way up the wall. Other than that, the only scarring on her body was that symbol carved into her shoulder. Like you, I thought I was prepared for it, but after being there, seeing her like that . . . She was twenty-three, had her whole life ahead of her.' Samuels had sat down with his hand on the top of his flask, but he hadn't unscrewed it because of the memories running through his head. He could remember the scene as if it were yesterday.

'I can already say that I'll never forget Alison Shannings. What was the girl called?'

'Karen Olsen.'

Marie placed a hand on Samuel's shoulder as she got up. 'If it's any consolation, I'm glad my first situation like that was with you. You made sure I was okay. Most of the guys here would have either laughed or dumped most of the work on me. We'll find who did it.' Samuels nodded as Marie walked to the door. 'I'm on admin for the next couple of hours if you need me,' she added before leaving.

As she left the room, Samuels listened to the door creak its way closed, then tightened the cap back up and slipped the flask back in his bag. It had been a long time since he had thought about Karen Olsen.

Tommy had left Amber in the warehouse, looking through the books. Part of him felt he shouldn't have allowed her to stay there, but he knew better than to start arguing with her. She, like him, was looking for answers.

Tommy jumped the stairs leading to Squawk's apartment two at a time. He stood outside and listened in. In the next few moments, Harry's form appeared next to him on the balcony.

'It's just Fiona and the other girl. She's hurt; he must have done it.' Harry vanished back into the apartment. Tommy reached forward and turned the handle. The door was unlocked, and he slowly entered into the hallway.

Sonia was the first to see Tommy as he approached the living room. Quickly, she grabbed her mobile to phone her boyfriend. As Fiona saw him, she moved towards the back of the room.

'Don't be afraid,' Tommy said as he entered the room.

'Like fuck we're afraid,' Sonia stated as her phone danced to life.

'Listen to him!' Harry screamed at the top of his voice. As he did so, all the electrics flickered. The lights dimmed and then brightened; the TV flicked off and on again. Everything went quiet as a chill filled the room.

'I have no reason to hurt either of you. You want to phone Squawk or Ben, be my guest,' Tommy stated, standing next to the living room door.

Sonia looked up from her phone. 'What'd you do? Why haven't I got a signal?' Tommy shrugged as Sonia walked towards him. 'I ought to kill you! Who do you think you are?' Tommy remained calm and didn't reply. 'Get out!' Sonia screamed, and Tommy met her anger with a smile.

'I need to talk with Fiona. I gave my word to her mother that if she was hurt, I would try to help. Surprisingly, she's been attacked from her cheating boyfriend again.'

Silence dropped over them as Fiona reached to her eye. Her eye had now blackened, and the small cut on the corner of her eyebrow cleaned. Her cheek was reddened from where Shaun had slapped her. Sonia looked at both Fiona and then Tommy once more.

'How'd you know it was Shaun?' Sonia asked, looking at Tommy before turning back to Fiona. 'Did you call your mum?' Fiona shook her head.

'I told him!' Harry yelled, swinging his hand towards the bottles that sat on a table next to the sofa. As he did so, despite his hand passing through two of them, the third fell to the floor with a thud. Tommy turned to look at Harry, who had just shocked himself. 'Tell them it was me!'

Tommy took a moment to work out his words as the girls looked at each other and the fallen bottle. *They'll think I'm even crazier than I am. I see dead people?*

Tommy gave a nod and then addressed the girls. 'You probably won't believe this, but I've been talking with your dad. We can prove it. Tell me something, Harry, something only she would know.' Fiona's eyes darted between Tommy and the bottle as Sonia looked at her.

'You're not serious, are you? You're actually believing this shit!' Sonia waved her arms around.

'Go on, then. Prove it!' Fiona challenged, ignoring her friend.

'I don't need to hear this shit,' Sonia announced as she stormed out of the flat.

Tommy didn't move as Sonia barged past him. Harry had now walked towards her and stood next to her, a large smile spread across his hollow face. He glanced at Tommy and began a story, which Tommy recited to her.

'When you were six years old, you were beginning to believe fairies didn't exist, after believing they were there throughout your whole life. You went to bed one night after saying you no longer believed they existed. The next morning, you woke up and found a trail of golden flakes from your windowsill to your bed. Next to you was a little cloth bag containing some rainbow candy, which you believed they ate.'

Fiona's face was frozen in a look that Tommy couldn't describe. He worried that she didn't believe him, worried that she too would scream and run from the apartment.

'No one ever knew that. My mum always said I imagined it. I had scraped up all the dust before going downstairs.'

'I did it! I did it! I wanted her to believe,' Harry ecstatically stated.

'He wanted you to have something to believe in, given the way he was towards you and your mother. He knows he isn't a saint, but he wants to make amends.' With Tommy's words, the smile was wiped from Harry's face.

Fiona looked away briefly. 'Ask him why.'

'He can hear you. He can also see you.'

'He can see me? Did he see Shaun do it?'

'No, I didn't. I left when they went in that room,' Harry quickly said. 'I knew he cheated—that's all!'

98

Tommy looked to him with a nod. 'He never saw him hit you. He had told me he saw Shaun cheat while we were at Night Arts Centre last night. He left to get me after the two of you entered your room.' A short silence followed, broken by Harry.

'She believed the fairies would protect her from me when I was angry. I wanted her to feel that protection. I would have never harmed her. Ask her.'

Tommy repeated Harry's words, and Fiona gave a slight smile, accompanied by some tears.

'He always said he couldn't break their spells. He always apologised for what he did to my mum to me and the fairies! He wanted their forgiveness.'

'He's been watching you since he died. He wouldn't go to heaven after paying his dues,' Tommy added as Harry looked to the floor.

'What happened to him?'

Tommy didn't reply; he looked at Harry. He hadn't actually said what had happened afterwards, nor had Tommy asked.

'I lived through what she did. I was forced to endure everything I did to her. I felt every punch, every bruise, and broken bone, the feelings she went through when I broke her heart. The way she'd forgive me every time.'

Tommy repeated the words as Harry finished. Harry was now repenting his actions once more. If spirits could cry, Harry would have been a waterfall. Fiona raised a hand to her mouth and looked in the same direction Tommy was, towards her father.

'You endured it all? Then came back for us?' she asked him as Harry reached out and touched her swollen cheek. She felt a coldness run through her and stepped away.

'He just reached out to your cheek,' Tommy said, and Fiona smiled.

'What should I do?' Fiona asked, looking back to Tommy.

'You need to stop Shaun. Harry said how Shaun has the same actions as he did at his age, the same anger. He knows what will come from all of this. I have a friend that can help,' Tommy said.

Fiona shook her head. 'I'll end it with him. He won't touch me ever again!'

'You know he will. He's good friends with the people you know, your friends. He'll use them to get back with you. I know a policeman that could prosecute him. He's a good man. He won't bring the others into it.'

There was a moment of awkward silence as Fiona weighed the pros and cons. Finally she nodded. 'Just him, though. That's the deal. They'll leave Squawk, Sonia, and all of the others out of it?'

'You have my word,' Tommy promised.

'If Sonia was phoning them, they'll be on the way back here. She'd wait by the entrance of the building. We can get out through the fire escape,' she stated. She walked through Squawk's room and pulled open the large window that led on to the metal ramp, which a ladder joined at the end. She led the way, followed by Tommy, who pulled the window closed as much as he could. The catch that held it in place was on the inside, out of reach.

They clanged their way down the fire escape and ran along the road behind it, into the grass field. Several children were kicking a football around, and in the far right corner, several mothers talked while their children played, oblivious to their presence as they sprinted past into the housing estate behind.

'Where to now?' Fiona asked as she looked around the housing estate, unsure of which way to go.

'I've been staying at the carpet factory on the edge of town. We can go there,' Tommy said.

Fiona nodded and pointed down through the estate. 'There's a shortcut to the city centre that way. We can cut through.'

With Fiona leading the way, they hastily walked between the houses, heading towards the warehouse, frequently checking behind them in case they were being followed.

CHAPTER EIGHTEEN

ight had set in when Fiona and Tommy entered the cold warehouse. Seated on the steps, a hardback book unfolded on her lap, accompanied by a cigarette in her hand, was Amber. As they entered, she looked up, a smile almost creeping on to her face.

'Bringing back dates now, are we?' she asked, standing up.

Tommy introduced her as Fiona looked at both of them. 'This is Fiona, Harry's daughter.'

'Can she see my dad too?'

'No. I can't see him, but I know Tommy can. He's been talking to him about you a lot. I assume you're hiding from the boyfriend?' Amber added, walking across to them.

'This is going to sound really stupid, but do you have one of those mobile phones?' Tommy asked, looking at Amber. With a nod, she removed it from her tight jeans pocket and handed it to Tommy.

'I have free minutes too!' she added with a sarcastic grin directed at Fiona, who nervously returned it.

Tommy flicked the phone open and dialled the police station. Somehow that number had been scratched into his subconscious memory. He awaited an answer and then asked to be put through to Samuels. Tommy explained everything that had happened, and it took little encouragement for Samuels to agree to meet them. Tommy said that Fiona wanted to press charges against her boyfriend, who was associated closely with Squawk and Ben Williams.

As Tommy put down the phone, another set of numbers was running through his head. He typed the eleven digits into the phone, and it went directly to voicemail: 'It's Claire. I can't come to the phone right now, but if you leave your name, number, and a message, I'll get back to you later.'

Tommy turned off the phone without leaving a message. He recognised the voice. It was the same one that had spoken to him through the window when he returned. He now had a name to go with the voice. Tommy realised that the two girls were watching him.

'It was just something that I remembered. I don't know exactly who she was.' There was a longer silence as the girls exchanged looks. Tommy felt pressured to justify the call. 'I couldn't have left a message, could I? How would it go? "Hi, remember me? I'm the guy you watched get buried a while back, but I'm back now. Fancy a drink?"' Tommy gave a false smile as he thought about so many things.

Was I buried or cremated? Does everyone know I died? Am I still missing? Are loved ones searching for me? Is the girl dead as well?

'True! If I had a dead boyfriend phone me from beyond, I'd probably be upset if our reunion conversation was through my answerphone,' Amber joked as she opened the book she had dangling to her side. 'Found a bit in here about resurrection rituals. Not sure if that's relevant to you. Basically, it's not always about raising and controlling the dead as I thought. When I first read that bit, I thought of zombies! The thing that counts you out of this theory is the fact that they remember everything about who they are. They have the same thoughts as when they were alive.'

Fiona walked across and started looking at the books placed on the steps. She was feeling more and more scared as Tommy and Amber discussed the black magic involved in raising a dead loved one. She couldn't understand what was happening. Within forty-eight hours, her whole life had changed. She'd been forced out of her home for a boyfriend she thought would be her happy ending. That boyfriend had now cheated on her and hit her. That alone would be enough for anyone to contend with, but she had agreed to press charges against him, going against her better judgement and the gang she now lived with, because of advice given from a stranger who was talking to her dead dad.

And on top of that, she was sitting in an empty warehouse, listening to the stranger who'd died and come back, discussing how he was brought back. She felt as if she were part of a TV show, some hidden camera spoof. She struggled to cope with the thoughts running around her head and sat down on the second step, placing her palms against her forehead. She wished none of the last forty-eight hours had happened.

Jones had finished reading one of the volumes and placed it on his bed. It had been about a species of demon called Yellow Spines. They were about five feet tall in height but hadn't been seen in nearly four thousand years. The last sighting was by a hunter in South Africa. He had been called to a friend's farm after his cattle had been mutilated.

Yellow Spines ate raw flesh, and with their razor-sharp teeth, they could easily strip it from the bone. The only way to kill these demons was to inject a poison called serillium into their blood. It was created by mixing the blood of their victims and three different flowers. The last one sighted was never killed, although they mated like humans and had never been sighted alone, which meant his partner had probably already been killed. Over time, he would have died.

Daniel Jones glanced at the cover again, then around his quiet room. *Did the Yellow Spines die out?* he pondered silently.

Samuels entered the warehouse, his gun in hand, closely followed by Marie Hoskins. She was armed too, both hands gripping the handle as if in a movie. Samuels saw Tommy, Fiona, and Amber and lowered his gun.

'It was just a precaution,' he stated, feeling slightly uneasy in his amount of distrust. Behind him, Marie still gripped her gun.

Tommy smiled. 'Understandable. Fiona here has a story to tell you, and she needs some form of protection after.'

Marie lowered her gun and hesitantly slipped it back in the holster.

'Tell me what's happened, and I'll see what I can do.'

Fiona explained the way things had happened and the assaults her boyfriend had given her in the past. Samuels intently listened and hung on every word from the minute she said his name, Shaun Matthews. He was one of the gang members who had been brought in and questioned over the murder of Samuel's son, as he was one of the people that Ben Williams had phoned beforehand. In the back of his mind, Samuels knew that if he could get something to stick on Shaun, he'd have the first real conviction. Samuels hoped Shaun was still carrying illegal drugs to make the arrest be about two things.

After looking at Fiona's swollen eye, Samuels soon agreed to the terms. Despite the evidence being strong against Matthews, he was concerned about what his friends would do, so he suggested they put a police car by her mother's house in case they went for her, and he agreed to keep Fiona in protective custody while Shaun was being arrested.

Samuels explained how this wouldn't be easy but could be the start of making things a lot safer for the city. He said that she was being brave making this move and that he'd do everything in his power to help. He even agreed to bring no charges over this case to her other friends and did not intend to arrest anyone else. She accepted, and they went off together in the police car. They were going to drop her off at the station so she could give her statement, and then they'd swing around to Squawk's and arrest Shaun and only Shaun.

As they drove off, Harry broke his silence. 'Are you sure you can trust him?'

Tommy nodded, but Harry still looked worried.

'He's the only police officer I trust. He's even been reported inside the branch for his heavy-handedness in arresting members of the Rivals. He'll do everything he can to protect her,' Tommy reassured him.

'Tommy's right,' Amber excitedly added, looking away from the book of Alterson's history that lay open on her lap. 'He's always been a good guy. He's the only cop I know that has confronted Tony Boswell and lived. He did it in a town meeting once. Everyone was there, and the papers lapped it up. It was like something from the movies!' she paused. 'Sorry. I guess Harry was talking to you.'

'Let's hope he has the power to do it. If not, I'll never forgive him.'

'That's understandable—she is your daughter. I have to ask how you knocked that wine bottle over. Did you make the lights flicker?'

'I don't know. It just happened as I shouted. The lights, that is. I was angry when I tried knocking over the bottles—maybe that's why the bottle fell.' Harry himself seemed unsure of how the things had happened.

'Maybe there's something in the books? Sounds like a scene from the film *Ghost* to me! He learned to move things,' Amber exclaimed, flicking over the next page. Tommy and Harry both turned to look at her.

Jones was now reading the second journal from the box. He felt it was unbelievable. Vampires? He had heard hundreds of stories and even told some to the children's club at the church during their Halloween party. There was no way these creatures were real. As he read on, he realised there may have been some truth.

Vampires weren't the beings of darkness that they were believed to be. He learned that there are two types: the pure bloods, known as the Lamia, and the half-breeds, which are what people refer to as the vampires. Pure bloods, the Lamia, are usually known as the elders. These creatures are usually found in small groups. On average, the Lamia can breed once or twice in their lives, if they are lucky. The strain on their bodies often leaves the mothers' blood stretched too thin, and quite often, they can't regenerate quickly enough and perish after birth. This is the reason Lamia families are usually male dominated. There's rumoured to be nearly two hundred Lamia families left worldwide, but they are still being hunted. Unlike the half-breeds, who feed off any beings, the Lamia are choosier and prefer to capture more distinguished members of society, as their blood has a richer taste. They can be killed by either decapitation or a wooden stake through the heart. The reason the stake works on these beings is that the wood soaks the blood from the heart, preventing it from pumping the fluid around the body. There are stories of Lamia having bled out after an attack, but the Benovolt family had never witnessed it first-hand. Mostly, they had second—or third-hand knowledge of the Lamia. They had only encountered two pure bloods during their hunts.

Half-breeds, average story vampires, are referred to by the Lamia houses as vermin or slaves. They hold no real purpose except to deter hunters from the houses. Unlike the pure bloods, their hearts do not pump the blood through their bodies, so the only real means of death is decapitation. The blood in a half-breed just circulates on its own; the heart holds no real function, as they are already dead. If their blood levels lower past a certain point, 'bloodlust' occurs, and they become desperate to top the level up inside them. They have also been known to drink extra blood before a large battle to cause regeneration in themselves in case they get injured. Half-breeds can regenerate a lot more than pure bloods, as they don't need to process the blood into their bloodstreams like the Lamia do.

The more of the book Jones read, the more confused he became. He closed the unfinished journal and dropped it on top of the previous one. He removed his glasses and rubbed his eyes. As he looked at the box, he reached to the side cabinet and grabbed the glass of water resting there. After swallowing a large mouthful, he reached in the box and pulled out another book. He flipped it open, put his glasses back on, and read the title: *Demonic Possession.*

Samuels sat in the undercover car next to Marie as they watched the block of flats. Samuels had already headed up to Squawk's flat and found nobody home. He had been lucky enough to have found the apartment unlocked. An unofficial search showed nothing that he could use against them. Whatever they'd been taking or selling from the apartment was on them at that time. Since then, they waited.

It was now nearly midnight, and soon, the pubs would shut. They had ordered a squad car to be placed outside Rebecca Roberts's house, and it too was in place. There was also another car at the Matthews's household. Unfortunately, no one really knew where Shaun would lay his head that night, so it was just a matter of waiting and hoping.

CHAPTER NINETEEN

Samuels leaned towards the window as he heard several voices approaching from the street. He tapped Marie who was already observing them in the mirror, adjusting it to get a better view. There were four people, one of which was Shaun.

Samuels instantly recognised Shaun and two of the others. One was Squawk, and the other was a member called Joe Molk. They had nicknamed him Monkey Man—partly because of his surname and also because he could get into nearly anywhere. Samuels and several other officers knew he had once stolen some evidence from within the station, but they had no proof. The building had been locked as usual. All that had been opened was a small window in the upstairs toilets. Upsettingly, there was no evidence of its entry being forced, nor could anyone believe someone would have broken in at that height.

Samuels waited for them to start ascending the staircase that led towards the flat, and then he turned to Marie with a nod and swung open the car door. He ran at the stairs, gun in hand, closely followed by Marie.

'Hold it right there!' Samuels yelled, pointing the gun at the four men. They stopped halfway up the first flight and turned towards the two officers.

'What you want?' Molk snapped.

'We have a warrant for the arrest of Shaun Matthews,' Marie announced, holding up the warrant, which did nothing but raise a smile from the men.

'I'd appreciate your cooperation, but I'm not expecting it,' Samuels stated, holding out a pair of handcuffs. Shaun shrugged and walked towards them, his hands in the air.

When standing level, Samuels forced Shaun to turn around so his back was facing the officers. 'Put your hands behind your back,' Samuels ordered as Shaun followed the instructions, his smile invisible to Samuels but obvious to his friends, who casually looked on.

Samuels read him his rights as Marie held the three men at gunpoint. They remained on the first flight of steps. They casually smiled and joked as Shaun was placed in the backseat and the doors locked. Samuels looked back at the three men; nothing about the situation had phased them. It had seemed too easy. They'd never accept an arrest like that in the past, at least not without an argument or some abuse. It made Samuels uncomfortable. It was as Samuels called to Marie that they heard the next set of voices approaching.

'There's something here about spirits and poltergeists abilities,' Amber stated, holding both Tommy's and Harry's attention. She ran her finger along each line as she approached the bottom of the first page. She flicked the page, and the motion continued. 'The ability to move objects and control environments,' she read, glancing up before continuing the reading of the book. 'With poltergeists, this is a way of communicating with loved ones, as they have no means of contact through words. Hold on . . .'. Amber's finger followed several more lines before she spoke again.

'When enraged or near the person they swore to protect, they can be empowered with emotional strength or charges. These can cause them to temporarily have the power to control weapons or to even move or hold objects. There has also been some cases where a spirit has been able to temporarily possess a living being. It is unsure how these abilities are obtained, but it often occurs before it is their time to pass over to the light.' Amber stopped reading and looked at Tommy. 'Harry's going to be leaving you.'

'Not until my daughter is safe! I won't leave!' Harry stubbornly added as Tommy turned to him.

'But that's what's happening, Harry. Once Shaun goes to jail, she is safe from him. That was what you requested. The other thing you wanted was to be forgiven by her, and she did that earlier. You don't have to punish yourself any more.'

'How will I know if she's safe after I . . . you know . . . move on?'

'You won't. Fate takes over. Whatever she's destined to be, she'll be,' Amber said, her finger still running along the lines she was reading. Both Harry and Tommy exchanged looks before turning back to Amber.

'You heard him?' Tommy asked.

Amber's finger stopped following the page, and she glanced around the room, still unable to see Harry Roberts. She nodded.

'A while ago, when he explained the bottle and electrics, did you hear him then?'

Still without words, Amber nodded.

Six people approached Marie and Samuels. 'Come on, Marie. We need to get back to the station,' Samuels said loudly, extending his gun as Marie walked backwards towards the car. As she did, the voices began to yell. Samuels tried to ignore them and watch the three men that remained on the stairs. Slowly, they took a couple of steps down, and Samuels could feel his arms begin to shake.

'Stay right there!' he bellowed as two of the men laughed. Marie wanted to lower her gun and run. Even though Samuels was marking the men, she was afraid to turn her back. She knew how these men acted; she knew they'd happily put a bullet or knife in her back if she turned. The two men on the steps reached the bottom and then raised their hands again.

'John, why'd you have to arrest Shaun and not us? Let's face it: I've got the stash in my pocket.' Squawk said, shaking his hips so the bulged pocket showed.

'Because we're not here for drugs now. We'll be back when this guy gives you up to save his own bacon. By the way, it's Officer Samuels to you, Parrot.'

'The name's Squawk, filth!'

A bottle smashed next to Marie's ankles, and Samuels swung the gun around. That instant, the unknown man with Squawk darted forward. With no time to react to his attack, Marie fell to the ground, screaming, dropping her gun as she raised her hand to the wound. Samuels swung the gun back and squeezed the trigger twice. The wild bullets tore through the man's stomach and shoulder, the impact sending him crashing to the ground, shouting in pain. Samuels ran to Marie, his gun extended. The two men remained on the steps, their hands held high and their arrogance now gone. They had never seen the police open fire without warning before. The men walking up the road slowed their pace as they watched their friend gripping his wounds as he rolled around on the ground.

Samuels struggled to help Marie to her feet. The knife was deep in her shoulder. As they went towards the car, Samuels had no choice but to lower his gun as he struggled with Marie. Several bottles flew at them, one hitting Samuels in the head but not breaking. He got Marie into the passenger seat and then ran to his side of the car as another bottle smashed against the roof; a fragment of glass ricocheted off, cutting Samuels's forehead as he swung himself into the car. He ignored Shaun's laughs in the backseat as he turned the ignition, sparking the car to life. He slammed his foot down on the accelerator, and the car sped off from the scene. Behind them, he heard a number of jeers, but he was concerned about Marie, as he could see her slipping towards unconsciousness, her blood running from the wound. Looking at her from the driver's seat, he could see that the top of her uniform was slightly ripped, appearing as if the knife had been stabbed into her and then pulled down.

Squawk walked into his flat and closed the door. They had all gone their separate ways after the incident, leaving Stuart Anderton to bleed out on the road. Off and on, between his holidays in jail, Anderton had been a friend of Shaun's for years. He had been prosecuted for a number of things, including an attack on an off-duty officer, but never, until this day, had he stabbed a police officer. Even worse still, he wasn't provoked or instructed to.

That was one of the reasons Squawk hated him. He was always unpredictable. Squawk often believed that he would turn against them, given half the chance. One line too many was all it would take. In some ways, Squawk was relieved to see him shot down in the street; he already believed that, one day, they would have to do the same to him. As much as Squawk tried, he couldn't understand the reason for the attack against Marie that night. His only theory was that in his drunken state, he believed he had been helping Shaun.

Squawk pulled some cans of beer from the fridge before walking across to his bedroom. There was something he'd been meaning to do since that morning. Pulling back the ring pull, he raised the can to his lips and swallowed down half the can before pulling the shoebox from under his bed. Flicking through the old photos, he saw her: Claire Hearst.

They had been high school sweethearts, together for about six years, until she couldn't handle his choices any more. She had pleaded with him to get help and get himself away from the drugs. The problem was that he had gone too far. It was no longer for fun, as he had often claimed. It had become a necessity. He'd wake up and need a hit just to get through that day. The mornings were always the worst. As he was selling drugs, he always had a supply; he'd have one line every morning before facing the day. As the day went on, he'd often spark up a spliff; sometimes, he'd even do another line secretly at lunch. Then, of course, you'd need another to get him in the mood before going out to sell. There would always be someone to charge that little extra to cover up what he'd kept for himself—someone who didn't know the price of the wrap he'd requested.

He wiped away a tear as he looked at her face in the photo. They were standing cheek to cheek as Claire had held the camera above them to take their photo. He was upset how he'd somehow managed to forget her smile, her green eyes. She was an innocent time in his life.

He did try to give it all up for her once—went two days without taking anything. He began feeling withdrawal symptoms. It felt as if he had insects crawling under his skin, and he had strange feelings in his stomach. He'd have to run to the toilet, unsure if he was going to be sick or shit. He hated it, but she was worth it.

He'd had a visit from Ben and Tony during the second day, and they said he'd have to sell for them or they'd eliminate the problem. Being a good dealer wasn't the kind of job where you could hand in your notice when you thought a better job had come along. To them, it was a lifelong deal. He knew what their threats meant. If he stopped selling, they would take Claire from him. To them, she was the problem. He had no choice.

That night, he came home and set five lines out on the table. As Claire walked in, glowing because of her love for him and how proud she was of him, he leaned forward and snorted the drugs up as he'd planned. She saw him and screamed like never before, telling him how he had let them both down. She couldn't forgive him. He finalised the relationship by saying the drugs meant more to him than she ever could. He said whatever it took, and she eventually said they were over.

All he could do was sit there while she packed up all her belongings, looking at the pure white powder in front of him. She placed her boxes next to the door and said she'd have a friend collect them later. After she left, he'd cried until he felt sick and his body ached.

Squawk tried to overdose that night. It started with the intention of feeling better, but several lines later, he felt more depressed, more desperate for an answer. Soon, he had injected as much as he could. He had lost the ability to fill the needle, and he couldn't see to create a straight line. He sat there in his chair, nothing around him making sense except his intentions. His choices had been the wrong ones, and he'd lost everything.

The doorbell rang, and he had ignored it. Once the door opened, the tall figure came in, his hair covering his face. The hands seemed massive as they moved his head from side to side. Before Squawk remembered anything else, he was in the hospital, vomiting up everything, a tube down his throat. His life was saved. The next few days, he saw Ben and various other friends of his. Shaun had sat with him for a couple of days, saying how things could only get better.

Despite what he felt then, he began to enjoy his lifestyle. He met new girls. For a while, they would be faceless to him, as he'd only picture Claire, although soon he settled into a new pattern of selecting the girls on their looks. One-night stands followed. Sex in toilets and alleyways . . . He was enjoying that lifestyle. He embraced the addiction he had. Now they even filmed their evenings for the sake of their own memories.

Somehow, though, at that moment, Claire was clearer in his mind than ever before. He never knew what happened to her. He never knew who the mystery man was that night, and no one within his circle of friends knew either.

'What happened to you, babe?' Squawk asked aloud, giving the photos one last look as he placed them back into the box.

'He got her killed!'

Squawk swung around to see a middle-aged man standing in the corner of his room. He had clearly entered through the window above the fire escape. Squawk jumped to his feet, scooping up the knife on his bedside table and pointing it towards the fifty-four-year-old man. His attire was smart but casual; he was wearing a work shirt tucked into blue jeans. He smiled, running his hand along his stubble.

'Who the fuck are you?'

'The name's Boris. The long-haired guy you're trying to fight got Claire killed. Personal grudge against you, really,' Boris casually stated. 'You know how you were in on the mayor assassination a number of months after you two broke up?' Squawk nodded, the knife still hovering in front of him. 'He convinced her to take a walk downtown with him that night. He was aiming to phone you as they walked around outside the restaurant. He believed you wouldn't allow the assassination attempt to happen in case you had her killed. Drive-bys are messy things. He didn't get to make the call, though. When he was outside the restaurant, the car sped by, bullets flying. They tore through her stomach. He stood there watching her die for a while before running off. He left her there, choking to death on her own blood, all in an attempt to save his mum's friend.'

The silence seemed to echo around the room. Squawk glanced down at the box before dropping the knife and looking back at Boris.

'I know you're wondering what I want from the descendent of Mary Watson, but its all quite simple, really. I want him dead. Let's just say he's a thorn in my side too. I'll get him alone soon, and then you can sweep in with your friends and finish him.'

'Who are you? How'd you know him?' Squawk asked.

'Let's just say that I used to wear suits, and he's the reason that all I have now is this kind of attire.' Boris flowed a hand over himself. 'I told you the name is Boris, and that's all you're getting.'

'How do I know you're not going to double-cross me after I give you my number?'

'Because you're not stupid, and you need my help. Besides, I know your number. I took it off your phone earlier. The idea of a mobile is to keep it on you at all times. Your missus tried calling you, by the way. She couldn't get through straight away, though. Tommy was here then too. I think he followed her, but I lost them.' Boris threw the phone on to the bed behind Squawk.

'You know his name. What is it?'

Boris gave a snigger before stepping through the window. 'Thomas Atkins. I couldn't find him in any of the databases. Watch it—he's friends with Samuels. I think they're working together. It was your roommate who filed the charges. She ran off with him,' Boris added as he started along the metal fire escape.

Squawk listened to Boris's footsteps growing fainter and then picked up his phone, listening to Sonia's voicemail. She said that Tommy had started talking to Fiona about her father, how she needed to press charges against Shaun for what he'd done. She said she had told him to get out, but he wouldn't listen. Then came her screams. Squawk lowered the phone as the screams continued. Then there was silence. Some muffled sounds were followed by a male voice. 'Stupid bitch shouldn't have got in my way.' As the words ended, the phone went to the voicemail options. Squawk hung up, cutting off the robotic voice. He glanced around the room, wondering what had happened. *What had he done with Sonia? Was she safe?*

He rubbed his face, moaning into his hands, his anger bubbling. Quickly, he raised his phone and punched in some numbers, listened for Ben's voice, and then started explaining to him what had happened—and said that he had a name and a connection to the Gothic assassin.

Then came the plans of revenge.

CHAPTER TWENTY

CHAPTER TWENTY

'Can you hear me now?' Harry asked, leaning towards Amber, who was still glancing around. 'Amber?' Harry asked again as Tommy remained silent.

'I can't see him,' Amber finally said.

'He's just spoken again. I take it you can't hear him?' Amber shook her head.

'This is getting weirder by the minute. How can this even be? Is there anything in there about spirits being able to talk to the living?' Tommy asked as Amber's finger began following the lines of text again.

'It's never been known before,' Harry interjected.

'It says here that spirits have been known to communicate via a Ouija board or directly via a spirit trap during their last days. Sometimes through a medium.' Amber continued to skim the page. 'It still doesn't say anything about hearing them like that. What if it's because of my brother?'

'His calling wouldn't be here, maybe not even in our day and age. It would be somewhere else,' Harry said, his face full of thought.

Tommy relayed the message. 'What if he brought us all together for some reason?' Tommy added. Again, a silence filled the abandoned warehouse.

'The wound's been stitched up,' Officer Bowden said, entering the staff room. 'She'll be fine in a few days. She'll just need some rest.' Samuels thanked him and breathed a sigh of relief. He had been sitting on the plastic chair, swirling around the now cold cup of coffee, for what seemed like hours. All he could think about was the amount of blood pouring from the wound. He'd gotten her to the emergency ward of Alterson Hospital and phoned her father, who was on his way seconds later.

All the time that was happening, Shaun sat in the backseat, giggling over her injuries, nicknaming her attacker as stabber Stu. Throughout the whole panicked trip, he asked if they thought Samuels's shots had killed stabber Stu and whether Marie had died yet. Samuels had called ahead as they pulled away from the scene, warning the emergency ward before their arrival.

When they'd reached the station later, Samuels wanted nothing more than to inflict his vengeance on Shaun as he pulled him from the car, but he knew he couldn't. If he did that, he would have handed him a get-out-of-jail-free card. After entering the station, Bowden had escorted him to the small interrogation room. Shaun had been left alone there now for nearly forty minutes. Samuels stood up, poured the cold coffee down the sink, threw the paper cup in the bin, and then headed down to the room.

In anticipation of their meeting, Shaun had been laughing and tapping the table to a tune only he could hear. With a stern face, Samuels pushed down the handle and opened the door.

'Hello, Shaun. I'm sure you'll be glad to know that Marie is fine, albeit a little sore. Her wound has been stitched up.'

'That's a relief. I was really worried about her.' He laughed, leaning his small chair back on to two legs.

'Of course. What am I saying? You love to see women physically beaten, don't you?'

Shaun shook his head, his smile still dominant. 'Officer, Officer, Officer. You don't understand. She attacked me first. She's got a lot of her dad in her, ya know! Guess that's how she had the guts to kill him.'

'That was self-defence. Did she hit you today in self-defence?'

'Anger. She feels I was unfaithful.'

'Were you?'

'Maybe I've have had a little bit extra cake, shall we say.'

'I'll take that as a yes. Do you often have your cake and eat it too? Couple of slices extra, maybe?'

'Only if the cake's well decorated, Officer. I don't buy supermarket value brands. If we're here to talk about my conquests, I've had plenty. Actually, I had three slices of cake last night, if you know what I mean,' Shaun bragged, dropping his chair back to four legs.

Samuels swallowed his anger and continued, 'Do you feel she had the right to hit you?'

'Well, she didn't like my joke, you see. I was pumping her hard, her nails diggin' in my back. She was moaning with pleasure, and just as she was about to cum all over her bed sheets, I said my ex's name. I thought it'd have been funny, and she flipped out. Same shit as normal: "I knew you loved her. I know you're fuckin' her!" It gets old, ya know?'

'So she hit you out of anger, then? Did you feel the number of hits back was justified?'

'Self-defence. She was insane. Showed all the rage of her dad, ya know?'

'No, I can't say I do. Way I see it, you provoked her, and I'm guessing you had taken some form of drugs before meeting her?'

'Officer Samuels. How could you believe such a thing? I wouldn't even know where to get hold of those nasty substances!'

Shaun's sarcasm was edging on the anger in Samuels. He took a moment to swallow his thoughts and then stood up and sighed. 'I can see this is getting us nowhere. I'll have someone see you in a moment for some blood tests. Maybe your blood knows if you could find some of those nasty substances.' Samuels left Shaun laughing to himself in the small grey room.

'Who's that?' Nathan Riley asked, watching the two coroners drop a new body on the metal trolley in his lab. Despite them lowering the body down gently, it echoed around the grey room.

'A present from the front line. He's the guy that did the stabbing on Marie earlier. Samuels popped him twice as they escaped,' one of the men stated, unzipping the body bag as Nathan walked across.

'It sounds quite a straightforward cause of death to me . . . ,' as he stood over the body of Stuart Anderton, he allowed his words to trail off. 'Oh my,' he added, looking at the wound on his neck. More importantly, the black residue along the edge of the cut.

Quickly, he stepped back to the counter and grabbed the scalpel and Petri dish and scraped off a thin layer. Without testing it, he knew it was the same ash that was on Alison Shannings' body. He glanced up to see the coroners leaving, speaking amongst themselves. Nathan heard his name mentioned . . . and something about being involved in his work. He could only assume he could fill in the blanks.

As Nathan turned back, he reached around and unzipped the rest of the bag. He glanced at the body, looking at the two bullet holes that were located towards the left shoulder and to the left side of his abdomen. Both bullets appeared to have passed through; the positioning of the flesh wounds shouldn't have been terminal. The cause of death was the cut on the neck. It was nowhere near as wide or as deep as the cut across Alison Shannings' throat, but it was just deep enough and wide enough to have punctured the jugular.

Nathan heard something and glanced around the room. The large room had grey walls and was located in the basement of the police station. He had often joked about the room being his crypt. It had been soundproofed, and the pipes that ran along the far wall were always silent, each fitted with insulation padding. There was no one in the room with him.

Again, there was a faint sound. Nathan leaned forth and tapped Stuart's pockets—a phone or pager on vibrate mode, perhaps? There was nothing on him. As he moved away, his face passed Stuart's, and that's when he felt the air from Stuart's mouth. He leaned his ear to Stuart's mouth and heard the last gasp leave him—and with it, a name: *Nemon*.

Nathan jumped back, sending another gurney rolling backwards, knocking over a tray stand. The crashing of the metal echoed around the room.

'Fuck,' Nathan exclaimed. 'Fucking hell!' Nathan glanced around. There was no one there. No one else would have heard it. He was sure he'd heard it. He approached the body slowly and lightly poked Stuart's chest like a child would a deceased animal.

There was no movement, nor was there when he poked him more firmly the second time. Hesitantly, he extended his hand, taking Stuart's wrist. He pressed his fingers against the veins. No pulse. He was dead, but he spoke. *Did he speak?* Nathan glanced around again, wishing for someone to be there. He stepped closer and poked the body with his finger yet again. No movement.

For a long moment, he leaned against the gurney holding Stuart Anderton's body, his head bowed. He had never been scared of a body before, but there was something strange about this body. Something made these murders feel different. After a moment, to compose his thoughts, he straightened his body and headed towards the door to escape his crypt. As the door closed behind him, he pulled his mobile phone from his pocket, scanned through his phone book, and then phoned Samuels.

Jones lay back on the bed, thoughts and questions running through his mind. What were these things? He had read the book on demonic possession from front to back so many times, each time finding something he'd missed previously.

No one knew where these demons originated from. They had been here since the dawn of time. Depending on what version of reality we all believe, they were here before it. The book explained it in the demons own words.

The earth was originally formed by atoms pulling together and a world evolving; like the world forming from dust and particles drawn into its core. There had always been some form of presence around this world; something that brought it together at the dawn of time. Someone controlled it, something born from darkness. We saw shapes in the stars at night and named them as our star signs. These signs could have been the first gods, the first warriors. This planet, like so many others, was created to serve a purpose. Life was created after the warriors from above were defeated. Sent down to the centre of this planet as it formed, that person became the world's first prisoner; he became the ruler of his underworld, Satan. It may have even been his form, the heat in which he fell from the heavens that started the debris being drawn to it, encasing him and his exiled warriors into their eternal prison. Satan soon tortured and forced his people—warriors and gods alike—to do his bidding, allowing the strongest to become his henchmen and the others their playthings.

While his world began to form through the layers of earth, peace began to grow above, and creatures were developed. Dinosaurs were originally peaceful, but like everything, some would soon become corrupt as Satan's minions forced their way to the surface—some in fear of the torture they were given, others to claim more souls and wreak havoc upon the gods' peace. Unknown to the gods as they watched the first volcano erupt, they began to rise. A lava so hot from the central layers of hell carried these beings through—beings that were nothing but a black dust or liquid, melted and scarred from their ascent from their damnation. These beings found their way into the dinosaurs, and soon, they turned on each other, the cursed eating the flesh of the peaceful. The heavens noticed, and the gods prepared to battle, sending down a reign of fire believing the burning meteors would eliminate even these spirits. The dinosaurs fell, and the earth burned to a crisp.

As they allowed the earth to reform with humans evolving, these beings were still there. The dust you'd see move in the corner of your eye. Maybe even that voice you think you hear behind you. There is no way to stop the demons. Some that escaped from that first eruption are still here to this day. They still have the same war raging. Many are afraid to go back for fear of what would happen. Some are warriors with missions to achieve; some are just escaped prisoners. Either way, if they go back, their punishment will be more severe than their crime.

One chapter read about how the Benovolt family had captured one man who had changed his pattern of behaviour. He had been a local sheriff and had started releasing his own brand of justice. Four people that he rumoured to have been devil worshipers had been found dead. Under their examination, they found a book called *Phuremsic*. It's the name of a type of spell that can send these beings back to hell, the same depth from which they came from.

There's a number of ways, but all the languages are now dead and gone with the people. These four religious folk were some of the last. Some spells are in Latin, but the complicatedness of the incantations is far beyond us.

There were some symbols, however, including the one they used to capture a possession demon named Sonlem. He claimed to have seen all the above. The Benovolts had lured him into a room with the symbol on every wall, the floor, and the ceiling. Once trapped like that, there was only one way the possession demons could go: back to hell. They couldn't force him out of the sheriff's body as they had hoped. The insanity that screamed from the door was beyond current wordings and languages, which led the Benovolts to believe his stories. They guarded the room for fifty-four days and then came silence. The sheriff's body was dead and the spirit gone. They doused the body with gasoline and burned his remains to be safe. This was the only possession demon they had managed to erase. Others had crossed their path and left them with scars during their escapes. It seemed they had been targeted by hell, and these demons wanted them dead. The book had remained sacred ever since.

In the book were numerous accounts of confrontations and the lists of each demon's name and the body he was in at the time. There was never a pattern. Some possessions were through law officers, single mums, criminals, politicians, homeless people . . . and even a nun on one occasion. They had been marking them for years. Sonlem had placed a bounty on their heads after arriving back to hell. The Benovolts were hunters, and a possession demon made the final kill just before the youngest brother, Raymond Benovolt, buried the books in the local cemetery.

The last passage read of a possession demon named Nemon, who was going to start the apocalypse by ringing the first bell. Raymond knew his time was up, and their warriors were circling. He could sense them at every turn. People were dying, and in one battle where he'd go out fighting, he hoped to take Nemon with him.

The possession file was by far the thickest, with pages and pages added to it. The book *Phuremsic* was inside. No matter how many times Jones read the book, he could make no sense of it. He had studied the complex symbols, though. They were circular with a pentagram drawn within. The central pentagram had a large bell within. The ten triangles that joined the central point of the pentagram to the outer circle had ten different symbols drawn within them.

Daniel glanced at the pictures once more and then placed the book on his bedside cabinet, separate from the others. He glanced at the clock. The red digital numbers came into focus, and he realised that it was nearly four in the morning. He removed his glasses and rubbed his eyes for a moment, and then closed them.

CHAPTER TWENTY-ONE

CHAPTER TWENTY-ONE

'Shaun's still up there. I left him to think about things,' Samuels said as Nathan held open the door. Samuels walked in, followed by Nathan.

'It's definitely the same substance. It's not something that you often find in knife wounds. However, I am sending some down for tests. They'll be back within the hour.'

'That's okay. That must have happened shortly after we left. So whoever killed Alison was one of those members,' Samuels concluded, looking at the wound.

'That's a very good possibility, but why would they start using ash as a trademark when they so proudly use their own crest?'

Samuels glanced at Nathan Riley. 'Do you have another theory?'

'This guy's different. I'd say a man because of the deepness of Alison's lacerations, although this quick jab motion could have easily been a female ...,' Nathan let the theory trail off, as he had more thoughts of his own. 'If I tell you something, John, you've got to promise me you won't tell anyone else. I think it's probably because of my lack of sleep, given how I've been here for'—Nathan looked at his watch, and his eyes widened—'practically thirty-one hours!'

'You've got it, Nath. It'll stay between us.'

'I think he came back!'

Samuels tried to fight back the slight smile he felt creeping on to his face. 'Sorry. He, um, came back?'

'Not like a ghost. There was a . . . I really don't know how to explain it. It must have been some air trapped in his lungs or something that got released.'

Samuels felt his smile drop; all ideas of teasing Nathan vanished. 'Did it say some weird word?' Samuels asked, his anticipation of the answer filling his face.

Nathan observed him and nodded. 'I think he said something like demon or Nemon. I couldn't be sure. It was weird and totally freaked me out.'

'It gets weirder, mate. When I leaned down to Alison on the door, I swear she said Nemon as well. What the hell does that mean?'

The two men turned their attention back to the body and watched him for a few moments just in case, just in the hope, that he would repeat that last word.

'What makes you think we can trust some old guy who burst into your bedroom? You used to think we could trust Fiona, but look where that got us,' Ben stated as Rapid and Joe Molk looked on.

'Ben, I've not let you down, okay? I haven't yet and never will. I don't know what Fiona's on about, but we'll sort it. Our problem tonight was his mate,' Squawk argued, pointing to Joe Molk, who shrugged.

'He isn't my responsibility. You sold him the gear. Christ, you sold it to him at half past two in the afternoon. What did you expect him to be like at midnight? He's an addict, duh!'

'I expected him to be gone. I didn't expect him to turn up on my doorstep and stab a cop!' Squawk stood eye to eye with Joe, who shook his head.

'Don't shift the blame on me. We both did what Tony would have wanted. We saw a chance to sell and took it. You've shifted nearly all that gear he left us, and he'll have the cash. Besides, we can't blame each other. It was Shaun who invited him back. He was off his fuckin' trolley too! How much did Shaun snort tonight?'

Ben raised a hand, grabbing their attention. 'Look, that's not our biggest concern right now. We need to find out who this Boris is and where to find this Gothic prick before he reappears.' Ben ran his hand through his blond hair. 'There is something really weird going on. I tell ya what: I'd love to speak to Tony right now and get his take. He'll be well pissed off. When Boris gives the call, we'll go in ready to kill both of 'em, Boris and the Goth.'

The streets seemed busy despite the time of morning. It was just past four o'clock, and the clubs had long closed. Michael Davies had been trying to find somewhere peaceful to lay his head for hours. All the youths screaming and running up the alleys, celebrating being out after all the weeks trapped indoors because of the floods . . . He didn't care for the kids much; they had no respect. They often spit at him or verbally abused him. In one alleyway, he had seen a young couple celebrating over some garbage cans—the girl bent over with her skirt up over her waist; the guy with his trousers round his ankles. They hadn't even noticed as he watched from a distance. He used to be like that with the girls before everything went wrong. What he'd give to be like that again, young and randy. Now all he did down these alleys was sleep and drink.

He walked down the alley next to the City Bank and took a mouthful from the bottle he'd found next to his usual bed near the river. There were some kids sitting under his bridge, swirling back bottles of cheap cider. He had seen this half bottle of vodka and grabbed it quickly. Only some supermarket value brand, but it hit the spot. He walked up the dead-end alley and sat down behind the bins, pulling his coat tight around him. It had been a gift from the homeless shelter. They'd had many clothes donated recently in preparation for the cold winter.

Michael had lived on the street for years now and had picked up a number of survival techniques. He learned the basics first. You don't want to try to place sheets of paper over you to keep warm. Roll them up and place them inside your coat, allowing them to work as insulation. He also learned quickly which people to avoid and, on nights like tonight, to always be prepared to run should any youths chase you. After twenty-plus years on the streets, he thought he was prepared for anything.

As he took another large mouthful of the vodka, he felt a drip on his cheek. He wiped it away with the palm of his hand and caught a quick glimpse of the colour. He looked up again and saw someone next to the wall just above the first level of the fire escape.

It didn't take Michael long to run up the steps. Despite knowing that he shouldn't think about it, he knew this could be a gang beating. He thought there might be money in the victim's pockets. When he stepped on to the first level, the clanging of foot to metal stopped just as Michael did. For a moment, he thought the world had stopped as well. He looked forward and then back down the ladder, then back to the victim and away again. He didn't want to look. He didn't know what to do.

The brunette was nailed upside down to the wall. One nail held her upright, as it had been hammered through both her ankles and the edge of a wooden window frame. One shoe was left on, and the other was missing. Lying side on to the wall, the body was covered in its blood. Her intestines dangled down her chest. Some had even dropped to the fire escape. One breast was nearly removed from the triangle's depth, for the Rivals symbol was dragged deeply across her. Her clothes were dangling loosely to her side. Her mouth was open, and her eyes were staring back at him. He wanted to scream; he wanted to run. After he shook the fear that was gripping him, he did both.

Michael ran down the fire escape, almost tripping on the last step. He darted out into the street, screaming for help. A couple glanced across from the other side of the street, but quickly turned their attention away from the drunk. Michael ran up the main street, hoping there would still be police cars outside the nightclub.

CHAPTER TWENTY-TWO

The police car skidded to a halt outside the alley between two other cars. Police tape now stretched the width of the alley's entrance, motionless in the still air as dawn began.

Samuels and Nathan ducked under the tape and started ascending the steel steps to the first level, where the body dangled loosely. Despite being prepared, the view still shocked them. Her body had been more damaged than Alison Shannings' had. During the time in which Michael had reported it to the police outside the Night Arts Centre and their arrival, more fragments of her intestines had seeped out. Body parts now slipped through the grating of the escape route.

Nathan and Samuels remained silent even when Nathan leaned forward and looked at the girl's face. The cut across her throat, deeper than Alison's, contained the black residue. There was black ash etched into the flesh around the carving in the breasts and stomach. She had been crucified in the same manner Alison had been. Nathan looked at the nail placed through her ankles and into the wooden window frame. He glanced at Samuels, who shook his head.

'Tell me what you know from here because there's no way you can take the window frame back to the lab,' Samuels instructed.

Nathan smiled. 'I wasn't going to ask that. The nail could be a clue. If it's the same type used to nail Alison to the church door, we could have the same killer. If that's the case, I'd guess this murder and the other happened around the same time. That means we could have two killers.' Nathan checked that his tie was tucked into his shirt as he reached towards her body and closed her eyes. There was a lot of noise coming from below them, but Nathan saw her mouth move, saw the word said. *Nemon*.

He looked back at Samuels with a look of confusion and fear. Samuels glanced around and saw the others fighting off some reporters at the bottom of the alley.

'She said it too, didn't she? Nemon.'

Nathan nodded. 'We need to get her back to the lab. I need some more tests run. We need to identify her because I think she and Stuart Anderton may have known each other. They run with the same pack.' Nathan turned her wrist to face Samuels. On the inside of her forearm, she had the engraving of the Rivals. It was in blue ink with a red lining backing it, giving it an almost three-dimensional effect.

It was Samuels's turn to nod. 'We'd best get something to ply that nail out with first.'

'I know you're going to roll your eyes about this, but can you please make sure they don't damage it.'

Samuels looked at him for a moment and then rolled his eyes as he turned towards the stairs.

Tommy awoke as the sun shone down through the shattered glass window. Everyone had left early that morning. Amber had taken a book home with her as if accepting homework from the strangest class she'd ever taken. She was working that day and had planned to return in the evening.

As expected, several new newspapers had blown into the warehouse again. Tommy got to his feet, collected them, and folded them to place on his pile. As he did so, he realised that a book was left open. After marking the page, Tommy closed it and glanced at the cover: *Rare Outcomes: The Truth about the Afterlife.* No one had even touched that book yet. They hadn't even opened the cover, so who did? Tommy reopened it to the page that it had been opened to. Glancing through some of the words, he pieced the reasons together. It explained how spirits can communicate with people of the living if given a chance.

When a spirit learned to channel its energy, objects like Ouija boards were not the only means. Newer technology could be used in the same manner. The concept of moving a cup to spell words takes the same amount of concentration as lightly pressing a key on a keyboard. Tommy looked around the room and wondered if Harry had managed to turn the pages or was there another presence placing it open so that he'd find it? The same presence, perhaps, that would blow the papers into the warehouse daily. Tommy closed the book, turned, and then sat on the steps. He then opened it once more. Skipping the prologue, he went to the first chapter, 'Seeing the Light.'

By the time they took the body down from the wall, the sun was filling the alley. She was removed from the scene in a body bag, all her body parts returned to her after she was carefully lifted to the ground.

Nathan and Samuels watched her leave. As the coroner passed them, he handed the long nail to Nathan in an evidence bag. Nathan quickly observed it and gave a nod.

The reporters clicked away as the ambulance drove off, headed back to the station, closely followed by Nathan and Samuels in their own car.

Police officers stayed to guard the entrance, preventing photographers from entering the alley. Despite the body being removed, blood clearly stained the area, and the clean-up teams would soon arrive.

CHAPTER TWENTY-THREE

'She's gone!' Officer Bowden exclaimed as Samuels entered the reception of the Alterson police station.

'What? Who's gone?'

'She was sitting here while we went to get her a drink, and when I returned, she was gone.'

'What about Shaun? Please tell me he's still sitting in that room I left him in!' Samuels's anger was showing, and Bowden nodded. 'Glad to hear it.' As Samuels walked past, Bowden tapped him on the shoulder.

'Norton's here, though.'

'Fuck's sake.' Samuels now knew his job would be harder. He knew how good Francis Norton was. He was one of the best lawyers in the city, and he was the arsehole that always got the Rivals off somehow. He was the man that proved his son's murder had nothing to do with the Rivals.

Samuels marched on towards the room, and with a calming sigh, he opened the door.

'Hello, Mr Norton. How are you?' Samuels asked through gritted teeth, forcing a smile.

'No need for pleasantries, John. We both know you dislike me. What was it you called me again?' There was a silence as Samuels released a crooked smile. 'Oh yes, that was it: a saboteur of justice.'

'Different case, different time, Francis. Can we please address this case for now?'

'For now? Meaning you're going to try to bring up a past case to . . . ,' his words trailed off as Shaun leaned back in his chair, stretching his arms behind him, a huge smile creeping across his face.

'Your client here beat his girlfriend yesterday under the influence of drugs.'

'He explains it as self-defence, and even the reports state that Fiona Roberts struck my client, Shaun Matthews, first,' Norton calmly said, turning a copy of Fiona's statement so Samuels could read it.

Samuels glanced down and then back to the two men. Norton hadn't even smiled as he showed his evidence. He simply sat there, eyes focused on Samuels, burning a hole into him.

'It also explains how he hit her several times in self-defence. Can you justify that retaliation to a slap brought on by his lying and betrayal?' Samuels challenged, and for a brief second, he thought he saw the beginnings of a smile on Norton's face.

'I told you, she was possessed. She showed all the rage of her dad. I told you she fuckin' killed 'im, didn't I?'

Norton raised a hand to silence his client as he continued to hold Samuels's stare. 'Unfortunately, Officer Samuels, neither of us was there. The law states clearly that civilians may use reasonable force when needed. How are we not to know that she didn't do more than she explained? How do we not know she was going for a weapon? No one was in that room other than Shaun and Fiona. If my client was under the influence of drugs, as you made him out to be, why would a girl willingly undress and climb into bed with him?' The silence added to the tension in the room. Samuels felt a bead of sweat form on his forehead. 'At no point did Fiona state that Shaun forced her to get into bed. At no point does it say he pulled the clothes from her body and forced himself upon her.'

'I'd never do that to her!' Shaun interrupted. Norton raised a hand again.

'My client has been honest and explained to you that he had sexual relations with another woman previous to this encounter.'

'He didn't explain, Francis,' Samuels argued. 'He boasted about his conquest, just as he did to Fiona before the incident occurred. Called her the wrong name, I believe, didn't you?'

Shaun nodded. 'I know, and I shouldn't have tried to cover up the accident by claiming I didn't care for her, because I do. I let the wrong name slip out, and she became extremely angry. I had to keep her away from me. It truly was self-defence.'

'And as you said yourself, Mr Samuels, my client's slip of the tongue enraged Fiona, and she temporarily flew into a rage that caused the self-defence actions of my client. I understand that a room-mate of the girl broke up the incident. Maybe this accusation was just another form of revenge for his infidelity?'

Samuels bit his tongue. Norton had manoeuvred him as he needed to. Samuels had even said Fiona's first attack was through rage. This case would fall to bits in the courtroom.

'I believe we need to take some more statements from both people before this matter can be ruled out completely,' Samuels stated, getting to his feet. 'This isn't Mr Matthews's first case of violence towards women.'

'Mr Samuels, may I just remind you that in those cases, Shaun was cleared of all charges. May I also remind you that you have a personal interest in this case? I don't feel you can handle this professionally. You are involved way too personally.'

Samuels felt that bead of sweat roll down his forehead. 'I understand, Francis. I will request another officer to take over, but that will also mean that Fiona and Shaun will both have to give their statements once more.'

'Very well, Mr Samuels. That is wise and honest of you.'

'Honest? Do you know the meaning of that word? You tell me about honesty when the people that ordered the murder of your son are let off due to technicalities.'

'Mr Samuels, that's slander, and I believe you know how the justice system works. My associates were not guilty. Every one of the men you accused had alibis and even CCTV footage of their whereabouts at that time. You pin the blame on the fact that they used their phones. Even your investigation couldn't link the people they called to the murder of your son, Tim Andrews.'

Samuels stared at Francis for a moment and tried to swallow the anger that he felt bubbling under the surface. His knuckles glowed white under the tightness of his fist. It was taking all his willpower to resist striking out against the man. He swallowed hard.

'How many calls did it take to water down the message to the killer? Five? Six?' Both men remained silent as Samuels's eyes became misty.

'I think you need to get the new officer for this case, Mr Samuels.'

Samuels shook his head and then walked out the door, closing it behind him. Officer Bowden was standing outside the room. Samuels wiped away a tear and then approached him.

'It's your case now. Make sure the bastard gets done for it,' Samuels stated, walking through the corridor and into the reception area. He stopped and glanced around. He then mumbled something to the two police officers behind the counter and left. He walked to the side of the station and rested his head against the wall as a few tears dropped from his face. He stepped back and then looked at the wall before throwing a couple of punches into it, feeling the pain in his hand, seeing the blood on his knuckles. Wiping the back of his hand on his black trousers, he walked across to his car.

Reverend Jones awoke dazed and confused. The sun was shining through the curtains, and he could hear the doorbell faintly as he reached for his glasses. He put them on and struggled from the bed.

'I'm coming!' he yelled as he walked the corridor to the door of his flat. He unlocked the bolt, leaving the chain on. Slowly, he opened the door to the extent the chain would allow and peered through the crack. As he saw the familiar figure, he smiled and pushed the door, undoing the chain. Opening the door fully, he greeted Boris, welcoming him in.

'How ya doing, Rev?'

'I'm not too bad. How are you? You're the one who got stabbed less than five days ago.' Boris chuckled.

'Yes, yes, I did. I'm not too bad, though. The nurse said they missed every vital organ when they stabbed me. I'm apparently very lucky. I explained to her that lucky would have been not getting stabbed in the first place.' A laugh followed, although it soon faded away. 'I was luckier than poor old Alice, though, wasn't I? I should be grateful for that. I checked myself out of there, the hospital. I needed to know I was trying to do something to help. I would be doing more if I hadn't been stabbed. It aches still when I walk, well, waddle.'

'I'm afraid there is nothing we can do, Boris. We just have to wait for Samuels to sort things through. He's a good officer. He'll capture the men who caused this. Until then, perhaps you should rest. Walking around may worsen the injuries.'

'I hope Samuels can. Boy, do I want a piece of them for what they did,' Boris said as Reverend Jones led the way through to the kitchen.

'Forgive me, Boris, I haven't been sleeping well. It was quite a horrific sight,' Jones stated, flicking on the kettle. 'Nothing a cup of tea won't fix.'

'That's what Alison used to say all the time, wasn't it? "A cuppa always makes it better."'

Jones smiled as he remembered her saying that when the first homeless people entered the church on the eve of the storm. 'Would you like one?'

Boris nodded and watched as Jones grabbed the cups from the cupboard. 'I went to the church to see you yesterday. Saw a strange man with long black hair looking over the Benovolt grave. The grave looked different. There were new cracks in it, and the angel had fallen over again. Do you know anything about that?'

Jones paused for a second, looking towards the kettle, his back to Boris.

He wondered if he could trust Boris with his finds. 'Can't say I do. I haven't been there much since . . . ,' he paused. 'Well, you know.'

Boris nodded, his eyes slightly narrowed. 'I just had a really weird feeling about the grave, that's all. Like something had been taken from it,' Boris persisted as the kettle began to rattle to a boil.

Does Boris already know? 'What do you mean?'

'I'm not too sure. You don't seem too surprised there, Daniel. Did you have that feeling too?' Boris asked as he reached behind him, feeling the top of the knife, running his finger across the engraving carved upon it.

'I've felt there was something funny about the grave since the lightening bolt hit it. Haven't you?' Jones said still with his back to Boris.

The doorbell rang, and Jones excused himself, walking out of the kitchen. Boris heard the voices and removed his hand from the blade's handle, leaving it securely tucked behind him.

'They've taken me off the case. Can you believe that?' Samuels snapped, leading the way into the kitchen. 'Oh, hello, Boris. How are you feeling now?' Samuels asked, his tone changing.

'I'm fine. They took you off Alison's case?'

'No, there's another case. It's linked to the Rivals. I nearly had something that would stick. We believe there have been two new murders linked to the Alison case. That's part of the reason I'm here; I was coming to tell Daniel about the progress. I'm glad you're here, though, because I was meaning to ask you something about that day—if I may?'

Boris nodded, taking his cup with two hands. Behind them, Jones removed another cup and filled it.

'When the attackers came into the church, did you get a look at them at all? I need to find out if they were all male or whether there was possibly a female amongst them.'

Boris appeared to be replaying the day in his mind. He then shook his head. 'Sorry, Mr Samuels, I just don't know. As they came in, I saw the masks and ran at one, pushing him, and then the next pushed me to the seat and stabbed me. I only really saw those two, and they were both male. The pain just kind of took over then. I heard Alison scream, but there was nothing I could do.'

Samuels nodded and thanked Boris for trying. They then took their tea and made their way over to the table in Reverend Jones's kitchen.

'These new cases . . . A man called Stuart Anderton and a female that we've got to identify had the same substance as we found on Alison, this ash-like stuff—'

'Ash? What . . . like fires and stuff?' Boris cut in, and Samuels nodded.

'Yeah, just like that. A few people down at the station think they had some ritual where they burned the knife first. They think that's why they wore the gloves—because the handle would have been hot. They forget the basic reason of leaving fingerprints. Sorry . . . I'm drifting off the topic. The man who's a member of the Rivals was stabbed in the throat in a different way to the others. Nathan seems to think it could have been a woman due to the shallowness of the cut.'

'What about the woman?' Boris eagerly asked, causing Jones to turn to him, his look almost asking for an apology.

Boris did so. 'Sorry. It's a bit personal. I don't mean to push your conversation.'

'Don't worry, Boris, I know all about personal. That's why I had to leave the case with Matthews. Nathan's fairly sure that Anderton's attacker was female. The puncturing was shallower, the cut nowhere near the depth of Alison's.'

'Oh, I meant the other victim—the girl in the main street.'

Jones gave a puzzled look, replaying the conversation in his head. Samuels hadn't mentioned where the girl's body had been found.

'She was murdered in the same way. Nathan believes that was the same killer as Alison, possibly even murdered around the same time as Anderton. The cuts on her, though, were deeper. It seemed to be a lot more vicious,' Samuels paused for a moment. 'She had been crucified as well. She was hung up by one nail in a window frame.' Silence filled the room until Boris broke it.

'This guy's a psycho, isn't he? What kind of man would nail a woman to a wall by her ankles?'

Again, Jones's curiosity grew. 'How did you know that?' Jones asked instantly. 'No one said she was nailed by her ankles.'

'It's been in this morning's papers, I expect,' Samuels said.

Boris quickly nodded. 'I hadn't seen it, but someone was talking about the murderer they're calling the Antichrist.'

Jones continued to observe Boris. 'The papers didn't waste any time, did they, given how this happened last night? What time was she found?' Jones asked.

Samuels shrugged as he glanced at his watch. 'About seven hours ago now. So she was found about three or four this morning.'

'The papers cut that real fine,' Jones said as Boris stood up.

'Papers always do. Bet they sold hundreds with that plastered on the front page. Poor girl hung upside down and all cut up.' Boris lifted his cup and set it on the draining board. 'I'm only doing a flying visit this morning, Daniel.

I've got a few things to do, then I'm intending to rest up a bit more. The legs already beginning to ache . . . You'll keep me posted, won't you, Officer Samuels?' Boris asked.

Samuels stood up and nodded, extending a hand, which Boris shook. 'I will, Boris. You can call me John, by the way.'

Boris smiled and thanked him before hugging Jones, who was now standing. With a goodbye, Boris left.

'Did you look at any of the books?' Samuels asked as Jones bolted the door again.

'I've looked through some. It's strange trying to get your mind around them. It's as if someone wrote a bizarre story for a strange child. On a personal level, it gives more of an insight into Revelations.'

'Revelations? The battle where the exiled angels fell?'

Jones nodded. 'They changed, John. According to these books, fallen angels, warriors, they apparently changed. It's going to take a long time for me to understand them. When I do, I'll explain more, but until then, I'm just going to talk a load of babble because I just can't bring myself to understand.'

'I understand,' Samuels replied. 'To be honest, I don't think I'd understand much now anyway. I feel like I haven't slept for a week. I'm going to head to the hospital to speak to Marie quickly. She got stabbed during Shaun's arrest last night. I'm hoping she's okay. The doctors said she will be.'

Jones reassured him, and after Samuels left, he bolted the door again and placed the chain on.

With a sigh, he headed to his phone and glanced at the time. It was about ten forty-five. He picked up the receiver and dialled his friend's number. When Patricia picked up, she recognised his voice. She had run the corner shop for about six years now with her husband, who ran the post office. After exchanging pleasantries, Jones asked her to look at any headlines linked to a murder the previous night. She glanced over them while Jones waited on the line. After going through their selection, she explained that all the headlines remarked about the quick change in the weather still. A couple of local papers honoured all the emergency service members who lost their lives. There was nothing about the murders.

Patricia then asked for more details about the murder. Jones declined, saying it was all classified, and that asking about them, was to do with a possible suspect knowing something they shouldn't have. Before terminating the call, Patricia accepted his reasons, reassured him that there were no mentions in the papers, and wished them luck in catching him. She also assured him she wouldn't mention anything about the call to anyone.

Jones hung up and made his way into the bedroom, grabbing one of the four books he had on his bedside cabinet—the one about possession. He read several pages, skimming the lines and attempting to find the part he wanted.

During his reading the previous day, he had read a small piece that explained how they could sacrifice people to send messages to their masters below. This had originally been done by animals, but soon continued with humans. He feared that that could be what happened to Alison—Boris knowing about the new cases before Samuels had told them made Jones think. Boris was the only person they knew for sure was at the church the day of Alison's death. As much as he hated to think it, he wondered if Boris had been involved . . . possessed.

Soon, Jones found the entry he was searching for. Of the tests to find out about possession, the most common way was with holy water. If a possessed person touched it, he felt fear. If he drank it and it mixed with any body liquid, it could turn it into powder or dust. *Could I chance another encounter with Boris? Possibly even try and trick him into drinking holy water?* He sat back and rubbed his face, thinking about how he could confirm his suspicions about Boris. Then the thought came to him.

Jones picked up his crucifix and walked across to the bowl in the kitchen. He rinsed it out, removing the teaspoons, and then filled it with water. As instructed by the book, he blessed the water after placing the cross inside. He then picked up Boris's cup lightly between two fingers and placed it in the water. Where Boris's lips had touched the cup, the lip marks showed up as if he'd been wearing black lipstick. He watched for a moment longer as the lip marks darkened and then slowly floated away from the cup, sinking to the bottom of the bowl—just as ash from a bonfire would have.

Unsure of what to think, Jones removed the cup and stared into the bowl. He looked at the black ash at the base with questions flooding through his mind. *How long had Boris been possessed? Did Boris know what was happening? Was Boris even alive?* He shook his head to clear the thoughts. He knew Boris, knew he would never willingly hurt someone. The demon that took his friend would have to be stopped. As he felt a rage burning inside, Jones went back to the leather book about possession and began reading once more.

CHAPTER TWENTY-FOUR

CHAPTER TWENTY-FOUR

From what Tommy had read, the book mainly focused on the spiritual afterlife. There were a number of references from ghostly encounters, but nothing to link him to the afterlife; nothing about coming back in human form. He had passed the morning reading about the effects and controls poltergeists and spirits could have on numerous items in this world. They could somehow temporarily control electrics and move items when their energy was focused. It added a more in-depth account to the book Amber had read aloud the previous evening, confirming the same. A spirit's powers matured as he did. Within the last moments on this plain, he could control nearly anything for a short time. He then crossed over.

Tommy glanced around the warehouse. He hadn't seen Harry that day, and for a brief second, he wondered if he had already crossed over, but part of him knew he hadn't. Soon, however, Tommy knew he'd lose him. It was then that he thought, *When Harry, the person who's guiding me, goes, what happens to me?*

Jones flicked the pages back and forth, trying to understand all the aspects of possession. There had been no official exorcisms for over a hundred years. Nothing indicated that one could even be performed now. The only thing that Jones could think of was trapping the demon inside the body. The more he read, the more he felt they were impossible to stop. There was no way he'd trap one in a room as the Benovolts had done with the sheriff so many years earlier. They had become wise and learned from that mistake.

During his page turning, he confirmed something he'd only touched upon in the pages before: a way demons could communicate with their masters. They'd mix the blood of the innocent with blood of their own. The two would combine, allowing images to be portrayed in the blood as it soaked through the ground to them. The demon's blood was heavier, dragging the images through. That was how the murders could be directly linked to the demon. It was also known that the victims could withhold the name of the demon in his purest form. As Jones flicked through, he saw a list of odd names on the back page. These were demons the Benovolts had faced. As he followed the list down, he began wondering which one he was facing now, which one was possessing Boris.

Fiona paced the small playground. There were children playing around her, which helped her feel a bit safer. This was where her father, Harry, had instructed her to go. When she had seen Francis Norton enter, she knew she wasn't safe; he would get Shaun out within the day. She knew what would happen. He'd find her and teach her a lesson—not to go against him and his friends again.

The words had surprised her at first when they appeared on the computer screen. They were the words of her favourite nursery rhyme when she was a young girl; her dad had read it to her every night. She then read his notes, telling her about his idea. She knew it was the only way. She would wait here until it was time to go. She knew that now it would be either Shaun's life or hers. Deep inside, she felt she had an advantage. Shaun had ordered some deaths on behalf of Ben and Tony in the past but never personally carried them out. Fiona had. She'd already taken one life. Fiona had taken her dad's.

Nemon looked around the small bungalow that Boris had called home. It was basic, but seemed homely. Well, it should have. The rains had left his home a mess. Objects lay in the centre of his front room, where the current had carried them. Paint flaked from the wall, and several strips of wallpaper lay on the floor in the hallway. He pressed down on the sofa and watched as the pressure pushed water up from the spongy surface.

By taking Boris's body, he'd taken his memories, remembered everything he had been, the pains and pleasures Boris had endured. Currently, Boris whimpered in his head while Nemon used his body. Boris had loved this home. It was his happy ending.

Nemon had never known a home, only pain and anger. He resented what humans took for granted. He was one of the first angels cast from heaven. He had never met God and doubted whether he believed. He would be punished for that. Instead of taking his punishment, he struck out, preaching to the others that they believed a lie. The angels refused to believe him and told the gods; he was then banished from heaven, sent down by the archangels, heaven's strongest warriors. The impact with which he hit earth sent him through a number of layers. The pain he felt as he struck was unimaginable. It felt as if his body was torn to pieces during the impact, as if somebody had sliced his limbs with a red-hot knife. That was the most pleasant part, though.

He found himself in a cage, his wounds healing. Then he saw the man that would become his master, his face deformed and eyes glowing red. He reached towards Nemon, and Nemon thought the man would grab him and pull him forward. He didn't. The hand reaching towards him had sharp claws that pierced through his chest. The pain surged through his whole body as he was dragged forward, the cage door being pulled off its hinges between the demon and him.

He was thrown into a pit where the ground was soft, the cage door sinking under its own weight. As Nemon felt himself slowly sticking to the substance, a set of skinny hands reached up and dragged him under. He felt the vile substance fill his mouth and then lungs. He fought back, struggling to the surface to see the creature looking down at him. This time, his master's face seemed impressed. Again, the flailing arms dragged him under. As he tried to struggle to the surface again, he saw their faces, the white bodies of the beings dragging him under. Their bodies were bold and colourless. The eyes were a glowing yellow, their teeth razor-sharp. Nemon grabbed one by the throat and repeatedly struck out, feeling the being's teeth shatter under the blows, shredding the flesh on his knuckles. He turned and struck the next one, fighting his way to the surface. As he looked at his captor, he was filled with anger. A deep breath and Nemon dived back under and struck down more of the beings, dragging one from the muddy substance, watching as they panicked in the dim red lights of hell. Nemon threw the being towards the master with all his might. The creature landed at his feet and a new glow formed in the master's eyes. The red mixed with a shade of black, and Nemon knew something was happening.

First, he felt the pain surge through his back. Then he felt his body go limp. In a terrifying second, he saw a spine form in the demon's hand, watched as ribs began to grow from it . . . , then a pelvis. Nemon's body was disappearing and reappearing. He screamed in pain and agony as his body sank to the depths. He was losing his skeleton but could remember and feel everything as the thick brown substance flowed through his body. His screams became a gargle, then silence. A silence broken as the screams were reborn as his vocal cords reformed and flesh crept over his skeleton. Then he was dropped to the floor, slipping from the demon's claws. The pain continued inside as he felt his internal organs reform—his lungs fill with air for the first time, his heart began to beat once more. Blood flowed through his veins at great speed as muscles began to reform. His torturing continued for days as muscles and nerves began to work.

As he reformed, he was chained up, and his wings were clipped to a wall on the seventh level. All around him, he heard screams, and in front of him stood a huge canyon that seemed bottomless. He looked up to see more levels. After nearly two weeks of his captivity, his master returned. Then the demon spoke, his tongue forked as he slithered out the words: 'You're ready.'

Nemon's body was still chained to the cavern on the seventh floor of hell, and he was dragged from within it. He remembered leaving it, the agony of being dragged from his own flesh. He knew he'd lost his form. It was a surreal moment when he floated, looking at his body. The next thing he remembered was the intense heat as he raised from the depths at rocket speed. Even before the islands were formed as they are today, he had been awoken and raised into a city a million miles from Alterson. He vowed never to go back. Never again would he take his form of an angel; his wings were still clipped and his body beaten. If he ever went back, the hell he endured then would be nothing in comparison. Nemon would never fail them. He couldn't. Besides, if he freed them, heaven would regret the day they threw him from their paradise.

Nemon refocused on the mirror and Boris's face. He could still hear Boris's pleas to release him, to leave his body. Boris was stronger than most. When he captured a body, the person would often give up and accept what was happening, watching as aspects of his life were destroyed. Quite often, the person would cry. Boris, however, yelled. He yelled continuously. Nemon felt like leaving, but he knew this body was his best bet; he was closest to the people that could change fate. In less than twenty-four hours, it would be over. Nemon had put everything in place. The predictions and the prophecies were correct. The first of the 666 bells of hell was here in Alterson—in that chapel. Nemon would ring that bell, and the layers would begin to break. Nemon watched with glee as Boris smiled under his control.

CHAPTER TWENTY-FIVE

It was around five o'clock when Samuels had awoken. Despite knowing he needed it, he resented having the sleep. He wanted to be doing something, working towards capturing Alison's killer, even helping in some way to gather more evidence on Shaun Matthews.

He now parked outside Koffee Korner and locked his car. As he walked in, he turned his mobile phone on. He approached the counter and ordered a takeaway black coffee, hearing his phone ring and vibrate. He pulled the phone from its case and glanced at it—three new voicemail messages. The girl handed him his coffee, and he dropped some money on the counter with a quick thank you, placing the phone to his ear.

He stood to the side and listened.

Nathan Riley had confirmed the substance as the same type of ash that was found on Alison's body. Also, on inspection, the cuts were made with the same knife; the ragged edges matched perfectly. His best guess was still a fisherman's knife. He had also identified the girl as Sonia Evans; he believed she had been recently dating Gavin Wallace, known in the Rivals as Squawk. Officers were going to notify her family that day. He added, at the end, to call him when he got the message.

The next was from Daniel Jones. He ranted and raved for a moment or two and then said he has an idea to stop the killer, but he needed some bullets first. He also warned him to stay away from Boris, as it wasn't the Boris they knew. Samuels almost smiled as he erased that message, awaiting the third.

'Officer Samuels?' a brunette standing before him said. She had a small bag over her shoulder, and her smile filled her face. It was Amber Johnson. Samuels raised a finger with a smile, listening to the third message. Amber waited patiently.

The last message was from Officer Bowden. With Fiona missing, there was no real evidence, and the time for holding Shaun Matthews without charge was up. Norton had reminded them several times. 'We've got until eight o'clock tonight,' Bowden said. That would be twenty-four hours from when the warrant had been issued. Samuels erased the message and then lowered his phone. He gave Amber another smile, unsure of whom she was.

'Did you catch Shaun?' The one line made her face come rushing back to him.

'Yes, we arrested him. My colleague got stabbed during the arrest.'

'So will he go to jail?'

Samuels shook his head. 'Fiona's gone missing, and without more information from her, the case will fall apart. This is what usually happens with these cases. It's why the gangs around here seem to get stronger and stronger, while we, the law, get weaker and weaker. Do you have any idea where she might have gone?'

'Well, she might have gone back to Tommy's place,' Amber suggested.

Samuels nodded. No one would have checked there, as no one knew anything about him or his existence. 'Might be worth checking. I think I'll head over there in a minute. Even if she's not there, he may know something,' Samuels stated, taking a sip of the coffee, which was still far too hot.

'I'm going there too. I told him I'd pop over after work. Can I catch a lift with you?'

Samuels stopped a moment to think things over in his head. He wondered if he could trust her; he had only just met her. But she had helped talk Fiona into giving evidence. If Fiona was currently running due to fear, she may be able to help again.

Samuels agreed, and the two headed off.

Jones had spent the whole day going through the possession book, making notes from the leather-bound book. He had now jotted down a brief synopsis of where the demons came from and what they were, as well as some notes on why the Benovolt family thought they were here.

Moreover, he had jotted down notes on the symbols used to trap Sonlem. Those symbols had given him an idea. Demons would expect someone to use them to trap the body within the room, forcing the demon into insanity. Jones had the idea to trap the demon inside the body itself.

He had also read in the book that a demon finds it hard to live inside a dead body and usually flees to find another. If it were trapped in a dead body, it would have nowhere to go except back to where it had come from. Then it would face its punishment.

'Tommy?' Amber called as she walked into the warehouse.

'Amber. How are you? I think I've found out something about what happened to your brother.' Amber shook her head quickly, hinting that she was not alone. As Tommy stood up, he saw Samuels walk in behind her.

'John?'

'Hi. Don't suppose you know what's happened to Fiona, do you? Has she called you or anything?' Tommy shook his head as Samuels released a sigh.

'I thought she was in protective custody.'

'She was. She left the police station of her own accord when no one was looking,' Samuels said as Tommy sat back down. 'One of my friends down there left her behind his desk to get her some coffee, and when he came back, she had gone. Another person said he saw a girl fitting the description leave as he arrived. I think she got cold feet when Tony's best lawyer turned up. How that arsehole even knew this was happening is beyond me.'

'So you have no idea where she is?' Tommy asked, glancing around the room and wondering where Harry was. He didn't believe this was a coincidence. 'I'll set out and look for her if you want. I'll ask around and see if I can find anything out. Is Shaun still under arrest?'

'Only for a short time. I've got until eight o'clock to get Fiona back in to give another statement.' Samuels ran his hand through his hair. 'I thought we had something this time.'

'We still might. She wants out from the gangs,' Tommy paused for a moment. 'She's had a change of heart.'

'Why would she have left? That's what I can't understand. She swore blind she wanted him out of her life. Surely, jail's the only way,' Amber interjected.

'What would be the longest he'd go away for?' Tommy quickly asked.

Samuels shrugged. 'Two or three years.'

'Jail's not the only way. If he went to jail, he'd be out again, and he'd be pissed off. He'd be gunning for her. That pile of papers tells us what happens when someone crosses these people. They end up dead. We heard Harry himself say he would kill the guy. That's what she was going to do. Kill him.' There was a brief silence before Tommy continued, 'Trust me, John; this is what's going on. I'm guessing there was a computer near where she went missing?' Samuels nodded, his concern turning to a more puzzled look. 'Harry spoke to her,' Tommy said, turning to Amber. 'The book was opened to a page saying all about it.'

'Harry is dead. Fiona pushed him from a window years ago,' Samuels stated, a look of concern filling his eyes.

'I know. It's a long story, but let's just say that he's what changed her mind.'

'How? I want some answers. I bet you're the one who buried all those books too, aren't you?' Samuels reached down and gripped his gun.

'I have no idea what you're talking about. What books?'

'At the Benovolt grave.'

'I read something about the graves being those of demon hunters. It was in one of the four books Amber brought here. I went there and saw an old guy called Boris and then left. There were no books there then.'

'So you looked? You opened up the grave too. I bet you were annoyed to find them gone, weren't you?'

'I never opened the grave up. Who would? What's going on here?'

Samuels shook his head and released the butt of his gun. 'Everything was so simple a few days ago. Then the angel falling and the books being found ...' Samuels forced a smile. 'Look, I'll drive around and look for Fiona. If either of you finds her or even hears from her, phone me.'

'You handled that well, John. What's going on? There's something you're not telling us. You know there's something missing, don't you?'

Samuels nodded. 'I dreamed about you, Tommy. I remembered you. You wanted revenge for what happened to Claire, just as I wanted revenge for what happened to Tim. Then you vanished and, until earlier, so had all my memories of you. I don't know why, but something tells me I have to trust you. You've already brought some luck towards our struggle. You told me back then that you'd bring the gangs to me, and you told me the same two nights ago. I sure as hell can't do it by myself.' Samuels turned to walk away.

Tommy glanced away, his mind thinking the information through, but he couldn't remember anything.

'He came back. That's why he can't remember,' Amber called after him.

Samuels turned around and observed him for a moment. 'The day I'm having, that somehow doesn't surprise me.'

'Did Claire have blonde hair?' Tommy questioned.

Samuels nodded, a slight smile returning. 'Yeah. She was also buried wearing your engagement ring. You have my number still, right?'

Amber nodded, holding her phone out. She pressed a few buttons, and then Samuel's phone danced to life. She then cancelled the call.

'Now you've got ours. If you need us, call me.'

Samuels smiled once more and left the room, glancing at his watch. He had less than an hour.

Amber reached into her bag and handed Tommy a dozen sheets of typed paper. 'It's about souls, what you thought you were. It explains things more, even lists ways of remembering,' Amber said as Tommy glanced at the pages.

'Where'd you find it all?'

'I researched it online,' Amber answered as she sat on the step, reaching into her coat and removing her cigarettes. She removed one from the case as Tommy scanned the first page.

'The book behind me explains something about the "Aurora of Role". It explains the methods Harry described that matched the equipment you found.'

'Really . . . , equipment? An egg cup and spent matches are equipment to you?' Amber laughed, lifting the book.

'It was enough to summon an angel.'

Amber smiled as she heard those words.

Samuels hadn't found Fiona, and he walked into the station at five minutes to eight. He walked up to Officer Bowden, who shook his head.

'She hasn't gone back to Squawk's nor has she gone home to her mum's,' Bowden explained. 'She's not been spotted at all.'

'Go get him. Let's get this over with.'

Bowden walked down the small corridor to the interrogation room and unlocked the door. He walked in, and within a couple of minutes, they walked back out. Shaun had a huge smile, and Norton sustained the same focus, carrying his coat folded over one arm and his briefcase in the other.

'I see you're here to see me off, Mr Samuels. Parting is such sweet sorrow.' Shaun laughed as Samuels turned the papers for him to sign. Norton watched over his shoulder, and as Shaun underlined his name, there was a slight smile.

'This didn't stick to you, Matthews, but trust me, something will. When you and your friends fall, I'll be there to watch it,' Samuels stated, staring eye to eye with Shaun.

The arrogance left Shaun. His smile faded, and he swallowed hard.

'John, you should be careful. That almost sounded like a threat,' Norton said.

'Why do you help them? Surely, they can't pay you as much as the other clients.'

'Sometimes it's in my other clients' best interests. Off the record, Mr Samuels, one day that could all change. Then you may well see these boys fall. Until then, the law is their weapon as much as it is yours. We're free to go now, so if you wouldn't mind stepping aside . . .'

Samuels stepped back and waved an arm towards the door. 'Feel free to go, Mr Matthews, Mr Norton. Please watch your step. I wouldn't want you to fall on your way out.' Samuels watched the two leave. They shook hands on the pavement and then went their separate ways. Samuels felt his anger building up. If Tommy was right and Fiona was going to kill him, he would make sure he turned up after it happened.

'John, Nathan wanted me to send you down to him right after you arrived. He said he'd be heading off soon if you wanted to catch him,' Bowden said.

Samuels exhaled. 'Screw it. I've had enough for today. The justice system doesn't work anyway.' Samuels grabbed his coat, headed down the steps to his car, slid behind the wheel, inserted the key, and started the engine.

CHAPTER TWENTY-SIX

CHAPTER TWENTY-SIX

Tony had been sitting in the bar of the Balino Hotel in London's city centre for nearly two hours. He had done so every night, making sure he spoke with the bartender and some other guests. He needed his alibi airtight in case anything went wrong. Nearly three thousand pounds' worth of drugs were circulating Alterson. If he wasn't there, no one could point fingers. He had lied to Ben and Squawk previously, saying he had meetings all weekend. He knew he could shift the blame if he wasn't there.

It was tonight that he was scheduled to meet Hayden Richards, his business associate. Hayden was the man who'd placed him in Alterson with the role he'd become known for. Hayden worked for a number of other men that Tony hadn't been told the names of. All he'd ever known them as was the syndicate. They told him what he could sell, and it was up to him how to do it. He also had to give them the cut they required or they would cut him off. That would include his protection. The syndicate had the top lawyers around the world and would always protect anyone if it was in their interests.

It was around nine o'clock when Hayden walked in with two larger men. He slipped off his coat and handed it to one, then nodded towards the bar, and the two men casually made an entrance. One of them folded Hayden's coat gently and placed it on the booth beside them.

'What's with the heavies?' Tony asked as Hayden sat down opposite him in a large leather chair.

'Can't be too careful at the minute.' Tony knew not to ask any more questions. He knew Hayden had made enemies over time. A bartender soon scurried over, carrying a small silver tray. He set down two serviettes and then the two small glasses—a single malt whiskey and two ice cubes in each. He didn't speak; he just gave a nod, which Hayden returned. The slim man quickly retreated to the bar, where he joked with one of the security people Hayden had brought in with him.

'I hear you've had quite the delivery?' Hayden remarked as he raised his glass, sipping from it.

'I've had a couple of grands' worth,' Tony replied, also lifting his glass.

'Only a couple?' Tony nodded. 'You sure?' Tony again nodded hesitantly. There was no way Hayden could have found out about his top-up supply. 'Tony, I know you've had the extra delivery from Sanders. I also know about the stuff you had driven in through fuel tanks. You should know better than to lie to me.'

Tony shook his head. He felt sweat forming under his shirt, and he placed the glass back down. 'I don't know about anything more than the deal with Kaz. You know that's the only guy we deal with.'

'Tony,' Hayden snapped, banging the glass back to the table. The couple at the table behind them jumped; Hayden raised an apologetic hand. 'I know, Tony. You've been skimming our take for a while. I've had people contacting me, saying how you've been thinning the coke with flour. You've been screwing us.'

Tony swallowed hard. The sweat now ran down his chest, and he felt his shirt absorb a few drops. He even felt beads of sweat begin to form on his forehead.

'You don't really believe that stuff?' Tony smiled. His words weren't as confident as he had hoped they'd sound. He knew that Hayden could see through him.

'You should know when to fold, Tony. You've been caught. We allowed you a good run. You've had close to twenty years pumping that city with your rats. You were always expendable. You were a test. We know the drugs will sell there. We knew we couldn't trust you. When we advised you to part ways with Wesley Curtis, it was for a reason. That reason was never what we told you.

'He was a businessman through and through. He would never associate himself with scum that would be taking the drugs, stealing from his own pocket. We've let you believe you run that city for a long time. We've bailed you out time and time again. Last night, one of your boys stabbed an on-duty officer. It went too far. You've gone too far. You're now a liability, and we wash our hands of you. Wesley Curtis will be dealing with the syndicate on behalf of Alterson.'

Tony stood up and leaned over the table towards Hayden, who remained seated. Hayden saw his bodyguards stand, and he raised a hand to them to remain seated.

'Now you listen to me, you little shit. I run Alterson. I've worked my ass off for years lining your pockets while you did nothing but order us around. Without me, you can't control anything in that city. I own everybody. And Wesley Curtis! That guy isn't a patch on me. Shady land deals and prostitution is all that guy's good for. You need me,' Tony stated as Hayden calmly stood up, straightening his suit.

'I'm sorry you're so mistaken. You've never owned Alterson. In fact, you've only had the influence we've allowed you to have. The lawyers, the councillors . . . True, some you did well to manipulate, but don't for a minute think that you're irreplaceable. Wesley has been working with us since before I approached you. He's known about this all the way along, and as of now, you and your little street rats are leaving. We own and always have owned Alterson, just like I personally own this hotel. Not bad for a little shit, hey? By the way, James?'

The bartender looked up. 'Yes, Mr Richards?'

'This man has had far too much to drink. He's becoming quite rude and agitated. I'm a bit concerned over him staying here tonight. See to it that he's removed when the bar closes.'

'Yes, Mr Richards. We will, Mr Richards.'

'You'll pay for this, Hayden, mark my words.'

'I beg to differ. Don't let me hear of you again, Boswell.' Hayden turned and walked away, his bodyguards following, leaving Tony slumped on the table. He wrapped his fingers around the side of the table and flipped it over, screaming, 'Fuckers! Doesn't he know who I am?'

Three large security men walked towards the scene, and one stepped forward, grabbing Tony Boswell's arm firmly.

'Yes, Mr Boswell. We know exactly who you are.'

CHAPTER TWENTY-SEVEN
CHAPTER TWENTY-SEVEN

Reverend Jones sat looking at the bullets. Samuels had left them there along with his gun. He reached for the small compass, checked the sharpness of the small point, and then picked up a bullet. Slowly, he began scratching the circle into the brass metal, keeping it as perfect as he could. He then followed the next circle just inside of it. Glancing at the diagram drawn in the book, he began copying it, scraping it into the metal shell.

He had been practising all afternoon. It had taken him over five hours to get the picture almost perfect. He hoped it was perfect enough. He had six bullets; he would draw the symbol on each. It had to be right. His life and thousands of others could depend on it.

Samuels sat at the table in the corner, watching the TV flicker the night away as he peeled the labels from his Budweiser. He had only been in the pub about fifteen minutes, and two had disappeared. He had chosen to leave his gun with Reverend Jones in fear for what he might do if he saw Shaun and his friends that evening.

He had joked briefly with the landlord and forced a smile, but the truth was shining through. Since his son's death, he only came to this pub to reminisce. The landlord also knew that. Samuels watched as two youths played pool, just as he and Tim had done so many times.

The Old Rope House was their weekly haunt after the marriage had broken up. He held no resentment towards Lauren, his ex-wife. He even missed her at times, but they had just grown apart during the early years of Tim's life. They had had him young, too young, really. He had been seventeen when they'd conceived. They had struggled while he went through his police training, depending on their parents to cover their bills for the run-down apartment. She was happy now, though. She had met a new man, Christian

Tyler, and they'd settled down together—never married, though. She only called him occasionally, but Samuels understood. She had a new life, and despite them both grieving, she had Christian to talk to. The last time they spoke, Lauren had even talked about having another child. Samuels fought back a tear as he lifted the bottle again, finishing his third.

Day had turned to night, and Fiona sat next to the sandpit under the glow of the streetlight. Except for a couple who pushed their daughter on the swings, the park was now empty. She smiled as she reminisced of her father and mother doing the same, sharing their plans for their lives together. Harry had just gotten the job at his office then, head of advertising. There was some irony that he died advertising the effects of alcohol and violence.

She watched as the father knelt down next to the swing, posing for his wife to take a photo. Fiona glanced at the sand and wondered what would happen to her father later. She watched as the sand began to move. She watched her father's message write itself in the sand. She read the words and then nodded heavily. Feeling nervous, she stood up and began the walk home. Shaun was released, and she now knew where he would be heading. He was predictable like that.

'Look, Ben, all I know is what Tony told me. He's seriously pissed. Hayden gave him the riot act 'cause of Anderton. He's holding us responsible. We should just be glad he gave us a heads-up.' Squawk explained this as he took a large mouthful from the can of lager.

'This is fucking bullshit!' Ben protested as he swung the car into the drive at Wilson Way. 'Why are we left to do this run? I can't stand that freak. He's like some kind of fuckin' ghost or something!' He hated everything this place stood for. He also hated the people he was dropping the gear off to.

Wesley Curtis and Ben had had fallouts before Wesley and Tony parted ways. Back then, Ben just worked as a labourer for Tony Boswell, sometimes doubling up as a waiter or bartender in the evenings. His concern now, though, was about an assassin that worked for Wesley Curtis. He was strange, dressed in white, and was never far away. The plan at this moment was to dump the excess drugs in Wesley Curtis's estate to hide all evidence linking them together; then, later, Curtis would release the drugs back to Tony in exchange for a small cut.

'He's not a ghost, Ben. The guy's albino,' Squawk stated as Rapid sniggered in the backseat. 'Besides, there's no need to stress. We don't even know if he'll be there.'

'Who cares? We won't get done. After what Anderton did, the filth'll be searching everywhere we go. This is what Hayden wanted. Tony said he set up this deal. Maybe they're going to work together again, Ben. It'll be like the good ole times!' Rapid added, rubbing Ben's shoulders. With a grunt, Ben shook off his hands.

They pulled into the boathouse entrance at the bottom of Wesley Curtis's property. He could see the collection point where Tony had instructed him to place the bag containing the four unmarked bags of cocaine, but there was nobody there.

'Where's the ghost?' Ben asked, stepping from the car.

'No suits either,' Squawk added, stepping out on the passenger side. Rapid and Joe Molk remained in the backseat. 'These guys are watching us from somewhere. Tony said to do the drop-off and run. We'd best do just that.'

'How do we know he'll get it? This is stupid. What made Tony deal with him?'

'Tony didn't choose to. Hayden implied that he needed to. If we don't, we're going to go down with it.'

Ben released a growl and threw the large bag into the boating shed. 'Fine. Trust me, though,' Ben said, spinning around looking for the cameras, 'I'm coming back for it, Curtis, when this blows over, and it better be complete.' There was no reply, no movement. Ben let out a growling noise again as he slid behind the wheel of the car, slamming the door shut. 'Fuckin' bastards. Always trying to get that little bit extra. There was some good shit in that bag too.' Ben turned the key and reversed.

'What do you say we kick back and have a few beers on the way back?' Joe suggested.

Ben shrugged. 'Well, we got fuck all else to do, have we?' Ben turned the Ford Escort and burned off down the long driveway and back on to Wilson Way.

Daniel Jones jumped as the mobile vibrated on his draining board. He stood up as the ringtone gave the dancing phone a tune. After a quick look at the face, he worked out how to answer the call.

'It's Amber. Where are you?'

'I'm afraid he's not here at the minute. This is Daniel, a friend of his. Is this work related?'

'Kind of. Do you know where John is?'

Daniel paused to think about his answer. He knew John didn't want any friends near him, but at the same time, he was concerned for John's safety.

'He's popped over to the Old Rope House. It's the pub as you enter the city. He was upset at work today. I believe he mentioned you earlier. Are you the girl who helped him get some of those hoodlums arrested?'

Amber tried her best not to laugh. *Hoodlums!* 'Yes, I believe it was us, Tommy and me. We called him to collect Fiona. We'll meet him there.'

'Okay, dear.'

The phone went dead. Jones placed it on his kitchen table and then picked up the fourth bullet. He believed two out of the first three were perfect. He had made a mistake on one. With each line he scratched upon the bullet's surface, he said a small prayer and a thank you.

Shaun had been to Squawk's place. The door had been locked. Luckily, when it came to the flats of Clements Tower, they were cheap to rent. They were also cheaply built. With one kick, the door had flung open. The lock, still attached, snapped away from the door frame.

He had marched through the apartment, checking each room. When he discovered Fiona wasn't there, anger took over, and he kicked the remaining door from her wardrobe, flipped over her bed, and then knocked over the sofa in the living room as he stormed out of Fiona's bedroom.

He had then searched the flat, looking for anything that might help him. He hadn't had a fix since his arrest nearly twenty-six hours ago. It was only now that he was really realising how much the addiction had hold of him. His skin was beginning to itch, and he was getting desperate.

He pulled out the contents of several cupboards; then, in Squawk's bedside cabinet, he found the small container he recognised. Squawk always kept his own private supply. Taking a palmful of the cocaine into his lungs, he had set off to settle his score. Fiona had made a fool of him, and she would pay.

Now he stood outside No. 23 of Wilsons Terrace. Fiona would have had to have come here. The police occasionally drove around the building, but they were leaving fifteen minutes apart during each sweep. Shaun pulled the small tub from his pocket and opened it. Pinching just a small amount of the powder between his thumb and forefinger, he raised it to his nose and inhaled deeply. With a newfound grin, he closed the box and slipped it back in his pocket. He then banged loudly on the door three times, stepping next to the door, out of sight from the spyhole.

'Who is it?' Rebecca asked, peering through. There was no reply. She checked that the chain was on and the deadbolt locked. 'I'm not opening the door until you tell me!'

She saw the shadow step in front of the peephole, but before she could focus, she felt the impact against the door. She stepped back down the corridor as the second thud came, the door shaking on its hinges. The third kick swung the door open, slamming against the wall.

Shaun ran down the corridor, grabbing Rebecca by the hair, pulling her away from the telephone. The phone dangled to the side as Rebecca struggled. With a quick motion, Shaun sent her tumbling down the hall. He lifted the receiver and heard the dialling tone. She'd never dialled the police. Shaun smiled, placing the receiver back on its cradle.

Rebecca looked up, and fear filled her. She began to scramble her way through the living room door, away from her attacker, screaming for help as she went.

'Shut the fuck up,' Shaun ordered as he reached towards her, gripping her ankle and dragging her back towards him. She screamed more as she rolled on to her back, violently kicking at Shaun. His strength was too much, and soon, he knelt across her ankles, preventing her kicks. With a heavy punch to her stomach, all her screams stopped and she gasped for breath.

Shaun stood over her and reached down, gripping her throat hard with one hand. 'Where is she?' Rebecca coughed as she reached at his hand. Shaun was losing his patience. He leaned forward and put the other hand behind her head; squeezing, he pulled Rebecca to her feet. He loosened the chokehold slightly, and the colour was allowed back in her face. As she began to breathe, Shaun asked the question again: 'Where is Fiona?'

Rebecca shook her head. 'I don't know!'

With a smile, Shaun shoved her towards the wall. Pain and fear struck Rebecca at the same time, her first tear escaping her eye.

'Squawk, what the hell happened?' Michelle asked. With a puzzled look, unsure who had phoned, Squawk asked Ben to turn down the radio. With a moan, he did so.

'What?' the reception wasn't too good on his mobile. 'What happened? Where?'

'I'm at your place, and the door's hanging off its hinges. Your sofa is upside down, and Shaun's on the war path for Fiona.'

'The fucking pigs raided me.' The anger in his tone was clear, although his statements were aimed towards his friends in the car instead of his mystery caller. 'Tony was right. They're trying to take us guys out. Why's Shaun on the warpath? Wait a minute. Who the fuck is this?'

'Michelle. Shaun said it's all Fiona's fault.'

'Oh god, I know what he's done. He thought that because she was talking to the police, she set us up. He probably thinks we're all arrested.' Squawk was thinking aloud as Rapid again laughed in the backseat.

'Bet he's going mad?' Joe joined Rapid's giggling, only for them to be silenced by Squawk.

'Phone him. Say we're on the way.'

'I would, but it keeps going to answerphone.'

'Then there's nothing we can do. He'll find out when he comes back.'

'What if he does something stupid?'

'He won't. Despite what he says, he still loves her. Sorry, love, you're just his sex toy. He said it hundreds of times.'

'Like I'd believe anything you'd say. The first thing he did when he got out was phone me. Bet he didn't phone you to see if you were all right!'

'Michelle, look, do me a favour. Get out of my flat, and don't ever come back. We'll find Shaun, and if he does something stupid, then he'll have to suffer the consequences.' Before Michelle could speak again, Squawk hung up. 'I can't stand that woman. Never have, never will,' he said.

Ben smiled. 'She is fuckable, though, ain't she? Those long dark legs, nice ass. Just about a handful of titty. Just right.'

Squawk shook his head, looking out the window. He just hoped Fiona was safe—because Shaun did have quite the temper.

The taxi pulled out of the car park as Tommy and Amber walked down the small ramp and into the pub. They saw Samuels sitting in the corner, a number of empty beer bottles in front of him. Amber smiled at one of the youths as they waited for him to take his shot in the game of pool before approaching the bar.

'Well, we can guess that John would like a bottle of Budweiser.' Amber smiled as she raised a hand to the bartender. He was in his mid-fifties and had short curly grey hair. As he came closer, his Old Rope House's logo was visible on his shirt pocket.

'Hello, what can I get you?' he greeted with a smile.

'How long's Samuels been here?'

'John? I'd say an hour, maybe a bit more. He doesn't seem himself today.'

'We're hoping to cheer him up,' Amber said. 'We'll get him another bottle of Bud, and I'll have an Archers and lemonade, please.'

Tommy felt both sets of eyes look towards him and was unsure whether to answer. The bartender smiled and then turned, grabbing the bottle of

Budweiser from the fridge and flipping the lid using a bottle opener attached to the back shelf. With a slight spin, he raised a glass to the optics and pressed up the Archers bottle, watching as the measure emptied. Tommy glanced over the rows of bottles.

Did I even drink lager? Can someone drink beer after returning? What could the side effects be?

'I'll have a bottle too, please.'

The bartender turned and opened a second bottle, placing it on the bar with the others. 'That's eight pounds, twenty pence, please.'

Amber pulled her purse from her jeans, pulled out a twenty-pound note, and handed it across.

That was something else Tommy had never considered: money. Surely, even though he'd returned, he may need some. If the Night Arts Centre were charging at the door, he would never have got in to find Fiona.

For a moment, Tommy was lost in his thoughts as he glanced at the mirror behind the bar, which showed between the rows of spirits. Amber thanked the bartender and slipped the change in her back pocket before picking up her drinks.

Tommy focused on his reflection, and for a second, he saw the blonde-haired girl again. She wore the same smile she had in the shop window. Tommy swung around so quickly that he gained the bartender's and Amber's attention.

'What?' Amber asked, glancing at the empty alcove behind Tommy.

'Nothing! I, um, I thought I saw something, that's all.'

'Stranger things have happened, you know,' the bartender said.

'Sorry? Like what?'

'This pub's haunted. We've often seen glasses fall from shelves. A cold chill will walk past you when you're in the cellar, even heard footsteps on the stairs a couple of times.'

Tommy smiled and glanced around the pub as if the ghost would appear for him.

'I bet Harry would love to get some lessons from her,' Amber joked. The bartender looked puzzled.

'There's a house near us that they believe is haunted,' Tommy said. 'The old lady calls the ghost Harry. Surprisingly, he always moves what she's looking for. Does your ghost have a name?'

'Not that we know of. She was apparently a traveller who stayed here in the 1940s. She was waiting for her husband to come home from war. He never did, and she passed away here with pneumonia. Story says she's still waiting.'

Amber made a sympathetic face.

'Don't upset her. The last thing we need is an annoyed spirit after us!' Tommy joked, and the bartender smiled once more as Amber walked across to Samuels.

Tommy followed, carrying his drink, and as Amber spoke to John, Tommy's mind wandered. He thought about the conversation he had just had. It felt normal. He realised that he was able to communicate more easily now. He had no idea how he did it. The girl had also reappeared. She fitted the description of the girl in Samuels's dream. Was she his past? Was Samuels's dream actually the reality? Was it Claire?

Tommy sat opposite Amber and John. They were talking about the evening and how he had no choice but to let them go. The two boys playing pool had moved on to the jukebox, where they were selecting some songs. A couple of local men had now entered the other end of the pub and were joking with the landlord. Soon, some music started with a fast drum beat as a guitar solo began.

'It's just proof that there's no justice,' Samuels announced, raising the bottle to his mouth.

'There is, and we'll find some. It just means that Fiona wasn't the key to start their downfall,' Amber said, placing a hand on his shoulder.

'I was the problem today,' Samuels said as he shook his head, looking down at the table. 'I lost my temper, and they had me removed from the case for personal involvement.'

'It's bound to be personal. How can it not be?' Tommy added, joining their conversation.

'You've always known about my son, haven't you?' Tommy nodded. 'He was a great kid. Wouldn't even hurt a fly. He confronted Ben and a couple of his mates in here for harassing a couple of the local girls. He was told to back off and wouldn't. They took the argument outside, and then Ben got more than he bargained for. Tim was a black belt in tae kwon do and a red belt in Judo. He made a fool of Ben and learned he shouldn't have.' Samuels placed his thumb and forefinger on the ridge of his nose as he felt the tears roll from his eyes. Amber stroked his shoulder.

Tommy and Amber exchanged a look as Samuels continued, his voice raising, 'If I were here, I could have stopped him. I could have confronted them, threatened to arrest them. Something . . . anything.' Samuels slammed his fist down on the table as he tried to gain control of his emotions. The two youths glanced across from the jukebox as the barman walked down the length of the bar. He looked and then gave Tommy a nod, which Tommy returned. The bartender then went back to his conversation at the other end of the bar.

'So what should we do tonight?' Joe asked as they sat around a picnic bench in the beer garden of Quest Club. Ben chugged on his bottle as he looked at the neon sign above the pub's entrance.

'Well, leave here for a start. The Eighties are fuckin' over!' Ben exclaimed, looking back towards the pub's inside. Quest Club was a small resort close to a holiday park on the outskirts of Alterson. It was also the closest place to Wilson Way, which sold alcohol. Inside the resort were rows of computer games and a restaurant that sold basket meals, mainly to tourists. There was also a small bowling alley at the back, which was mainly used by children while their parents relaxed at the long bar. Just buying their drinks, they'd received some dirty looks from holidaymakers.

'What about a pub crawl? Get absolutely sloshed?' Rapid suggested.

Ben gave an agreeing nod. 'Could do? You in, Squawk?' Squawk forced a smile and nodded.

'Wonder why Shaun isn't answering?'

'I wouldn't worry. It's like you told Michelle—he's probably looking for us. Or he may not be answering her calls!' Joe said, watching as a couple of girls walked towards the bar. One glanced back at him, and he smiled. She quickly turned, giggling.

'She's not even old enough to drink, mate,' Rapid remarked, noticing Joe's wandering eyes.

'I wasn't lookin' to drink with her. She had a really nice-looking ass!' There was a pause as Joe seemed to think his statement through. 'She'd be legal, right?'

'Okay, let's do this pub crawl,' Squawk announced, swirling down the last contents of his glass. 'We'll try Shaun again when we enter the city. Last thing we need is you getting done for doing some school kid!'

'She was at least sixteen or seventeen, right?' Joe asked, standing up, as the others laughed.

'Just make sure you tell the arresting officer that she said she was okay.' The four men left, laughing as they jumped back in the Escort, heading to the city's limits. There they would leave the car ready for collection in the morning.

It had taken a few moments for Samuels to get himself back together, and despite some looks from the youths, no one had seemed to notice.

'So how come his surname was Andrews and yours is Samuels?' Amber asked as Samuels finished the drink that she had bought him. Tommy still hadn't touched his, unsure of what would happen if he did so.

'After his mother, Lauren, and I divorced, she changed her name back to Andrews, her maiden name. We talked about it and decided to raise Tim with that surname to continue her family line. I have a brother who's already got two great kids. Lauren was an only daughter, and her parents had no brothers or sisters. It turned out, though, that it never really saved her family's name.' An awkward silence followed before Samuels broke it. 'I need another drink, I think.' He stood up and looked at his friends. 'Either of you?' Amber glanced at her glass, which was half-full. She shook her head.

'Have this one,' Tommy stated, handing him the bottle he'd been watching for the previous twenty minutes. 'I don't think I should drink it anyway.'

Samuels pondered for a moment and then accepted, sitting back down.

'I don't mean to pry, but you said you had a weird dream that made you remember me. What can you tell me about it?' Tommy didn't want to drag the conversation away from Samuels's son, but he needed to know. That dream may hold the answers to who he was, who he is.

'How don't you know? What happened to you?'

'I'm not sure, and if I told you, you'd just think I was making it up.'

Amber looked around, checking that there was no one trying to listen in.

'Why don't you try me? I've heard a lot of whacky stories lately. Amber said you came back?'

'In the alleyway outside the Night Arts Centre. The day of the rain. I couldn't remember anything. It was agony beyond anything human.'

Amber watched as the two boys played pool, oblivious to the conversation.

'I was beaten and freezing, and as I walked towards a recycling bin, a lightning bolt hit and scattered some clothes towards me.'

'The same night the angel was hit at Alterson chapel.'

Tommy nodded as Samuels combined their stories. 'I ended up in the warehouse, trying to keep warm, and that's when I saw Harry. He asked me to help Fiona.'

Samuels nodded. 'Things started getting strange for us that night too. Well, I say *us*, but I actually mean for Daniel Jones. He's the reverend of that chapel. He had a strange dream, much stranger than mine. He dreamed of a number of books in the Benovolt grave. When he checked, they were there. He's been studying them ever since.'

As the conversation continued, comparing the strange events, the Ford Escort pulled into a space in the Old Rope House's car park. The headlights went out, and the engine ticked to a stop as the four men climbed out. Squawk checked that the four doors were locked, slipped the keys into his pocket, and then followed Ben and the others into the pub.

Shaun slapped Rebecca across the face once more. Blood ran down her face from her right eyebrow. Her eye was now blackened and her lip split in several places. She was crying for him to stop. Her head was pounding, and she felt sick through the pain. Shaun was looking more and more annoyed, as he was getting no closer to his goal. He needed to know where Rebecca's daughter was. He removed a hand from her throat and grabbed the back of her head. He took a step forward and threw her into the front room table. The three-foot high table buckled under the impact, one of its legs snapping. Rebecca rolled around holding her ribs, crying out for him to stop.

In the doorway of the house, Fiona entered, lifting her leather coat from one of the hooks behind the door after pushing it shut, silently slipping it on as she continued up the hallway towards the front room.

Shaun knelt down, his back to the door, and pressed Rebecca's cheeks together. 'I'm only going to ask you once more, then I'll snap your fucking neck. Where's your daughter?'

'Right here!' Fiona's voice was cold and firm.

Shaun released her mum and turned to face her. He chuckled as he saw her appearance: the light blue jeans, grey T-shirt, and heavy-looking black leather coat.

'A bit avenging angel, aren't we?' Shaun sniped.

'If only you knew, lover boy.' It was then that the lights began to flicker. Shaun's smile faded.

CHAPTER TWENTY-EIGHT

CHAPTER TWENTY-EIGHT

CHAPTER TWENTY-EIGHT

The four men entered the pub with a confidence about them. The two youths playing pool seemed to sense that they needed to step aside. Even as they did so, Joe cast them a look that made them step back farther. The bartender looked up and slowly approached them. He knew them; he hated them as much as Samuels did.

'Four lagers,' Ben stated as the bartender locked stares with him. 'They ain't gonna pour themselves, you know!' The bartender glanced at them and then back to the table where Samuels was seated. He saw the look Samuels was casting them. He knew how angry Samuels was. He knew this was a disaster waiting to happen.

'I can't serve you. Not tonight. I want you to go.'

Ben looked at his friends and then back to the bartender. 'Four lagers now.' Ben leaned closer to the bartender, who, despite the intimidation, stood his ground.

'Sorry, not today!'

It was then that Squawk tapped Ben on the shoulder. He tilted his head in the direction of Samuels's table. 'Come on, guys, not now. Not with the shit Tony's in,' Joe added, stepping towards the entrance.

'That's exactly the reason, Joe, my boy. Exactly the reason.' Ben walked towards the table, and Amber looked down to her drink. Tommy continued to look at Samuels, ignoring them.

'I hear you've been causing me some problems,' Ben said, waving a finger towards Samuels, who grunted in his direction.

'Haven't yet. Give me time.'

'So you aren't the one who raided Squawk's earlier? Sounds like the kind of shit you'd do.'

'Probably one of your fucked-up friends.' Samuels laughed loudly. The bartender hovered next to the phone in case he needed to call the police. He knew Samuels was too drunk to do much. 'Fuck off, Ben. I'm having a quiet drink, okay? I can't be dealing with your shit right now.'

'My heart bleeds. Sorry, I interrupted your night out.' Ben leaned down level with Tommy. 'What about you, Gothic boy, am I ruining your night out?' Tommy remained silent. 'Thought as much. You're not so mouthy when it's a fully grown man, eh?' Ben slapped Tommy around the back of the head.

'Oy!' Samuels cried as Ben looked at him with a smug grin.

'Yes, Officer Samuels. Are you going to arrest me?'

Samuels got up and walked around the edge of the table. 'Don't be stupid. I can't arrest you. I'm off duty.' Before Ben could reply, Samuels threw the punch into the side of his head, sending him crashing into Tommy and then rolling to the floor. There was a moment's shock, and no one moved. Tommy gave Amber a smile and then swung to his feet, looking at the other three men.

'Care to play?' Tommy asked as Samuels dropped to his knees, punching Ben in the back of the head repeatedly. Amber stood up and glanced at the brawl, looking unsure what to do. The bartender lifted the phone.

The two youths ran from the pub as Joe Molk walked towards Tommy, his fists clenched. He swung a right hook, which Tommy dodged, throwing a knee into his stomach, followed by a heavy punch to the back of his head. Joe stumbled forward to the floor as Tommy walked towards Rapid, who was standing aside, awaiting the encounter.

Squawk stepped back to the door, looking on, his anger simmering as he wondered if Tommy had killed Sonia; she still hadn't returned his messages.

Rapid stepped in with a jab so quickly that Tommy didn't even see it. It connected with his jaw and was followed by a second, hitting Tommy's nose. He felt the blood run down to his lips almost instantly, its coppery taste filling his mouth. He stepped back, causing Rapid to miss the next jab before throwing a kick that Rapid sidestepped, reaching forward and shoving Tommy to the floor. Rapid stopped and smiled before watching Tommy struggle up.

'Thought you were tough?' Tommy smiled, his chin now dripping blood. On the floor behind him, Ben had gained the upper hand and was holding Samuels to the floor, threatening to punch him. Rapid went to throw a punch, which Tommy dodged, grabbing his wrist, yanking it forward, and pulling Rapid towards him. 'Allowed you a fighting chance!' Tommy said as Rapid threw a punch at him with his free hand, which Tommy caught, holding Rapid's arms across each other by the wrists.

'Look out!' Amber's warning came too late. The snooker cue wielded by Joe Molk snapped over Tommy's back, but his grip never weakened. If anything, it grew stronger. Tommy grinned through his bloodstained face as he saw the concern in Rapid's eyes. He threw four headbutts into Rapid's face, shattering his nose. Rapid dropped to the floor, and Tommy swung around.

Blood, his own and Rapid's, was covering him. His smile still showing, although there was a sinister glee to it. Molk glanced at the broken pool cue in his hand and then back to Ben, who was now standing up, with Samuels's blood on his knuckles. They both stared at Tommy.

'Well?' Tommy asked as Squawk pulled Rapid back from the brawl. Rapid was barely conscious when Squawk helped him to his feet.

'The police are coming; I've called them!' the bartender shouted. Ben and Joe quickly ran from the pub, catching up with Squawk, who was helping Rapid limp towards the car. Squawk threw Ben the keys, and he unlocked it. Rapid and Squawk clambered into the back and pulled the door shut as Ben pulled out of the space. The car was gone before Tommy had even finished helping Samuels to his feet. The bartender had run round and was trying to help Samuels.

'Are you okay?' he asked, trying to place a cloth against Samuels's cheek, which he pushed away.

'That wasn't the way to have gone about it,' Tommy said, wiping the blood from his forehead.

'I did all right. You didn't have to jump up and help.'

'What was I going to do—leave you to fight four men alone?'

'Tommy, now's not the time for this conversation,' Amber interjected as Samuels shot her a glance.

'When is, then?' Samuels said. 'When they've won? You don't even know what you're fighting them for, Tommy. You can't even remember who you are! Look at you. You win a fight and think you're a hero, but you're not! You're just a ghost of who you think you are, and until you've figured it out, you're no use to me.' Samuels was yelling now, and the locals were watching. They almost seemed to be getting some entertainment out of it.

'You're right,' Tommy agreed, turning to Amber. 'Can I have your phone?' Amber nodded and passed it to him. 'Take care of him. Get him to his phone and wait. I think I know a way to find out what really happened. I'll phone you tomorrow.'

'Do you know how to use it?' she asked, and the bartender looked at her as if the question amazed him. *Who didn't know how to use a mobile?* 'He's not very good with technology,' she added involuntarily. Tommy glanced at the face of the phone and realised that he knew what everything meant. He nodded and then left the pub.

'We've got to go too since you called the police,' Amber stated.

The bartender's face glowed proudly. 'I didn't ... wouldn't. I just thought it would make them flee, and I was right. Place this on your cut, and I'll phone you a taxi,' he suggested as Amber took the cloth from him and pressed it against Samuels's cheek. He didn't argue this time; he just thanked her. Amber glanced up, giving the bartender a smile as he dialled for the taxi.

Shaun spun round, looking at the room. The lights had flickered for a few moments. Even Rebecca had gone silent except for the occasional whimper.

'What? You think some sketchy wiring would scare me?' Shaun asked, his voice slightly uneasy. Fiona smiled, stepping towards him.

'Oh, I've learned lots, Shaun. I can do things now that you could never imagine.' Shaun watched Fiona as she paced around him towards her mum. Fiona knelt down and began to help her mum, and Shaun shoved her sideways. Fiona tripped on the broken table, and both stumbled to the floor, turning as Shaun walked towards her.

'Squawk ain't here to stop me now.' Behind them, a picture dropped from the wall. Shaun stopped in his tracks and glanced behind him. As he turned back, he felt the heavy blow between his legs. The impact of Fiona's kick caused his knees to buckle as he dropped down. Seated in front of him, Fiona threw another kick to his chest, the heavy boot pushing him backwards. Fiona struggled up and grabbed her mum, taking her from the front room to the hall, closing the thin door behind them. Coughing, Shaun pulled himself back to his feet.

'Mum, go tell the neighbours what's happening. Get them to call the cops.'

'But you?'

'Mum, do it. Do it now! I'll handle him.' Rebecca shook her head. 'Mum, I'm not alone.' Again, the lights flickered. 'Dad's come home!'

Rebecca looked at the flickering lights and then her daughter. Behind them, they saw a foot break through the door of the living room. Rebecca nodded and fled the house; Fiona ran into the kitchen and pulled open the drawer. She had enough time to pull out a bread knife and turn before Shaun burst into the room. Fiona didn't have time to raise the knife in defence, for Shaun immediately charged at her, slamming her back against the sink. She yelped out as her back bent over before she tumbled forward, dropping the knife. She rolled on her side, holding her back, trying to ignore the pain. The impact of Shaun's kick followed. She curled up as the second hit her stomach.

In the corner of the room, Harry frantically tried to grab an open bottle of wine but couldn't. He panicked as he watched Shaun kneel down, slapping his daughter across the face.

Tommy grabbed the sheets of paper and glanced over them. Amongst the notes Amber had printed was something about remembering. He found the page and skimmed it before slowing on the centre of the page. It explained how sometimes a lost soul can regain his conscious memory by touching that which he became. Tommy glanced around the room. *What does that even mean?*

He read the same line again and then thought back to the first book he'd read: *Myths, Legends, and the Afterlife.* He found the page he'd folded back and looked over it again. It listed some ways and again mentioned that he could access knowledge of his life through something that pulled him back. *What did? What made him give up salvation for vengeance?*

Then he thought about Samuels's dream, the newspapers, the people he'd met. None of it was coincidence. It had been placed in that order so he'd know. She was buried with his engagement ring on her finger. She was the reason. Claire! The images around him were of her. The blonde hair . . . , her smile. Tommy checked her surname and read the paper dedicated to the memories of the victims of the drive-by shooting. They were buried in Alterson cemetery seven days after. That's where his answers would lie.

Harry focused. He stopped panicking and slowly reached out, feeling for the bottle. Wrapping his fingers around its neck, he felt his grip upon it and turned the bottle upside down, the wine pouring from the bottle and splashing to the floor. Shaun was still kneeling next to Fiona as she struggled against his strength. Shaun turned round and froze in disbelief as he saw the bottle float towards him at great speed. The bottle hit the ridge of his head and shattered; blood poured from the laceration in his cranium. He fell forward, reaching the deep gash to cup the blood that spilt.

Fiona, despite the pain, moved quickly. She grabbed the knife on the floor and stuck it in Shaun's side, and with a loud grunt, she pulled it out quickly. Blood ran from the wound, spreading across the kitchen tiles. She looked around the room, hoping to see Harry, but she couldn't. She watched as Shaun's body straightened out and he lay flat on the floor, unable to move, life oozing out of him.

Fiona walked out of the room and into the hallway, stopping to look at herself in the mirror. Her face was bruised, and the cut from earlier had been reopened. It was accompanied now by two or three other small cuts, and blood flowed down her face with the blood from the first. She was a bloody mess, and her back felt as if it was on fire because of the pain, but still she smiled. Unlike Shaun, she was alive. She was a survivor.

Tommy walked through the dark cemetery, reading the headstones from the previous year. Seven rows from the path and the fifth headstone in, he saw it.

Claire Hearst
Trusted friend
Beloved daughter
Devoted partner
1996-2018

The drive-by had occurred on 14 December. Tommy looked around the empty graveyard and then at the palms of his hands.

Tommy swallowed hard with his dry throat and then placed his hands upon the headstone.

The memory hit him like a bullet to the brain.

Rebecca was out on the balcony with Sally Whiteman from next door. 'The police are on their way,' Sally said as Fiona nodded, smearing the blood down the side of her face, attempting to remove it. 'I'll get you a towel.' She scuttled off into her home. Watching her disappear from their view, Rebecca turned to her daughter.

'Is he . . . ?' She didn't need to finish the sentence. Fiona nodded. Before anything else was said, Sally, the sixty-five-year-old neighbour passed her a towel, saying how she needed to apply pressure to stop the bleeding. Fiona smiled as her substitute nurse tried to help bandage the wounds.

'What happened to him then? How'd you get out?' she asked, pushing Fiona's hand away in an attempt to hold the cloth there for her.

'I think I knocked him out with a wine bottle,' Fiona said, glancing behind her and into the family home. 'I didn't know what to do. He had a knife. I just had to react.' She was wondering where Harry was.

'Well, that was mighty brave of you, bursting in to save your mum like that. We always told you he was bad news. Fancy trying to steal from your, would be, mother-in-law.'

'Trust me, he would never have been my son-in-law!' Rebecca said.

From inside the house, there was a crash. Fiona pushed away Sally's hand and glanced back into the kitchen through the window. Shaun, blood pouring from him, was trying to pull himself up.

Sally looked around quickly. 'Where are those boys in blue?' she remarked. She pointed towards her house, ordering Fiona and Rebecca inside.

'What if he smashes down your door too?' Fiona asked, watching her mother go in.

'That's what home insurance is for. Get in there. Don't be any braver than you've been!'

Fiona saw the bloody Shaun standing on his feet with the help of the kitchen sink. The blood had covered his face completely. As he turned to look directly into Fiona's eyes, she watched the blood run from his chin. His eyes were peering out of his crimson mask. How on earth was he still alive?

'What were you thinking?' Jones asked, running the towel under the cold tap again.

'I wasn't. That was the problem,' Samuels said, running a finger across the large gash above his right eye. 'That prick was looking for a reason to fight. I just thought I'd have a better chance if I threw the first punch!'

'You're not a spring chicken now. You'd stand no chance against those youths.' Jones passed the damp towel back as Amber sat sipping her tea, laughing at the two older men.

'Do you really need to remind me about that?'

'You're forty-five now, and he's what . . . twenty-two, twenty-three?'

'Look, I lost it, okay? It doesn't matter anyway. Nothing will come of it. You can't pin anything on them, no matter what happens, because they always seem to be a couple of steps ahead.' A silence followed as Samuels glanced at the towel to see if his wounds were still bleeding. 'It did feel good, though,' Samuels said, smiling.

Amber laughed again. 'You did get him a beauty with that first punch.' Samuels joined in with her giggling as Jones shook his head.

'What the hell is going on?' Wesley Curtis yelled, walking down the garden path to the boathouse. Three police cars had pulled up about twenty minutes before, and now several officers stood looking around the boathouse. On the bonnet of the car sat a large bag, now unzipped. Inside it were several packages of cocaine.

'Mr Curtis, we're placing you under arrest for possession of class A narcotics with the intent to supply,' Officer Bowden announced, walking towards him and removing a pair of handcuffs. The two large security men accompanying Wesley started making their way towards the unravelling situation as Curtis raised a hand to stop any confrontations. Above them, in the top window of the mansion, a white figure looked down. Bowden glanced up and swore he saw something, but he shook the thoughts away as he turned back to Wesley Curtis.

'I've never seen that bag before in my life, but I will come with you to help sort this out. This whole area is under surveillance. Whoever dumped that there will be on camera,' he said, pointing to the surveillance cameras around his property. Bowden nodded and opened the car door.

'Calvin, do me a favour. Remove tonight's footage and pass it on to Norton. Let him know I've been taken down to the station. The quicker we get this cleaned up, the better. I don't want this hanging over my reputation.' Calvin nodded and jogged up the pathway back to the house.

Curtis sat in the seat and nodded for Officer Bowden to close the door.

CHAPTER TWENTY-NINE

The ring was gleaming in the sun as he showed it to his friends. The small diamond was all he could afford, but he knew she would love it. Despite the cold day, he felt all the excitement of a summer afternoon when he proposed to her on the bridge at the park. Claire didn't answer; she smiled and leaped into his arms, throwing hers around him. They were standing like that, in each others arms, the same evening. The Christmas lights twinkling above them as they kissed so passionately. Still in each other's arms, they heard the car screech around the corner, and they watched as a man leaned from the backseat window, with gun in hand. The bullets echoed down the street. A child further up the street had a bullet tear through his chest, sending him to the ground with blood spraying from the wound.

Tommy swallowed hard.

Between the shops was the old county hall. The police chief walked out; he was the target, and the bullets showered down on him. Tommy and Claire never saw the attack coming. Even before Claire could turn, the bullets tore through her back. The sound of glass shattering was heard as Tommy felt the pain burn through his stomach.

Even now, pain etched its way through his body, causing him to scream aloud in the empty cemetery. That night he had lain on the broken glass of the shop window—the window in which he had seen her reflection three days ago. She had landed on top of him, her mouth opening and closing as she tried to speak. Blood dribbled uncontrolled from her mouth. Tommy wanted to hug her, but he could only move one hand. He glanced to the side and saw the glass through his forearm. The pain still burned now. Blood pumped from the bullet holes in his stomach, the bullets that had torn right through Claire's body. Her mouth was still opening and closing like a fish thrown from the water and gasping for air. Her eyes seemed to dim as she lowered her head, placing her cheek against Tommy's. Tommy's cries went unheard with the pandemonium in the street that night, and now they went unheard in a graveyard. Within a matter of minutes, seven lives had been stolen that night. Then there was silence.

He saw flickering lights as he was being rushed at a great speed. The lights were long tubes between the ceiling tiles, and voices assured him that everything would be okay. He was being rushed through a hospital ward, and he saw a plastic mask lower over his face—and again, nothing. Tommy lowered a hand from the gravestone and felt his stomach. There was a pain there. He felt he was bleeding all over again. He glanced at his hand, unsure if it was reality or a memory, and he saw the bloody palm. He looked at Claire's name and then slapped the bloody hand against the cold stone.

He was lying there in a grey room with one picture on a wall, a vase of flowers, and the accompanying beep of his machines. He lifted his arm to see the bandages around it. People came, but Claire did not. When he asked for her, he was told to concentrate on getting better. After the questioning, an officer sat with him alone and expressed how sorry he was. It was Officer John Samuels. He assured him that he'd do everything in his power to get them.

The graveyard was white with frost the morning of the funeral. All the people huddled together as they wept, pulling their black coats tightly around them. After they left, Tommy stood looking at the loose soil that now filled the hole. He needed revenge. There was no evidence linking the Rivals to the crime. The car used had been reported stolen the same day from a home on the east side of the city, and it was found two days after the assassination, burning in a field outside Alterson. As always, everyone had alibis. Tommy knelt down on the cold floor and scooped up a handful of the soil, gently sprinkling it back down. He spoke to her, saying how much he loved her, and after some time, he slowly walked away.

The doctors had tried everything to help Tommy. They had given him antidepressants, anti-anxiety pills, and countless other drugs. His friends had distanced themselves in concerns of his actions; revenge seemed to fill him. No one could help Tommy. No one could mend a broken heart. No one could calm his anger or console his hatred. His parents were concerned, and he reassured them that he was fine. He spent hours standing at her grave, and when everything was silent, he could almost hear her voice. Sometimes, he even felt she was there watching him.

It was 14 February when they announced that the case had been closed. No evidence had ever arisen, and there was no way forward. Samuels had promised to keep trying, but now the case had officially been closed. Tommy refused to accept it, swearing he'd get the evidence. Samuels said to let it go, but Tommy swore he wouldn't. He couldn't.

It was a windy Valentine's night when Tommy headed into the Night Arts Centre in search of justice. He confronted Ben Williams, saying how he knew he'd arranged the drive-by. Ben originally ignored his accusations and laughed at Tommy's threats. His laughs turned to anger and concern when Tommy said he had evidence. Ben had grabbed him, and Tommy shook his grip off and left the club.

Outside, three of Ben's friends had grabbed him and dragged him up an alleyway next to the club. They beat him to the ground and demanded the evidence. Eventually, Tommy said that this was the evidence. He had tape-recorded the whole conversation. Ben went for him again and repeatedly punched him. Tommy's face became a crimson waterfall under Ben's onslaught. He was thrown to the wall as Ben spoke to Rapid. No one watched Tommy as he slid the small Dictaphone tape into a crack in the wall. Ben swung around with the gun Rapid had handed him, demanding the recording. Tommy threw the Dictaphone at him, and it landed on the ground next to his feet, breaking into three pieces. Tommy said they got away with it. With Ben's words of 'not yet', Tommy saw the trigger squeezed and felt a bullet tear through his chest. He gripped the wound, blood squirting between his fingers. His heart beat erratically at the memory. He watched as he saw Rapid kneel down and scratch the Rivals symbol into his chest with a large penknife.

Tommy was suddenly standing next to a light. A voice kept calling him, saying it was his time. Tommy stood watching their moves, their habits. He kept thinking of Claire. He asked the voice if she had entered the light, and it refused to answer. Tommy refused to go. For months, he'd watched others drift by and enter the light. Every time they did so, it shone brighter for a moment. 'You can't wait forever,' the voice said to him, and the rain began to fall. For the first time, Tommy answered with the words 'I refuse to go.' That was when the pain started, the light expanded, and he was in the alleyway again. That was when he came back.

Tommy slid down the headstone, and for a moment, he felt a presence and heard a voice. 'She said you'd never leave. She assured me you cared too much.' Tommy struggled to open his eyes as he felt his chest compacting again. There was some form of light standing before him. It looked human but was so bright that he couldn't focus on it or even open his eyes widely. 'We'll meet again,' the light announced, and with those words, the image faded. Tommy forced open his eyes, adjusting them to the darkness. He glanced at the headstone in front of him. It wasn't Claire's; it was Oliver Johnson's.

Tommy stood up and felt his chest. The pain was easing, and just like before, the wounds were healing over.

'We need you,' a voice stated. Tommy glanced around him. He saw more than fifty hollow forms looking on. 'We can help.' Her voice was dignified, and as he focused more, he recognised the councillor's face. It was Mary Watson.

'How? How can I help you?'

She smiled and walked towards him. Tommy felt a white light shine over him, and more images flushed through him. He saw the car coming towards him, and then it was gone. A security guard handed Squawk a brown envelope in a nightclub for an exchange of money. Squawk had placed the video in a vault, in remembrance of Rapid's first kill.

As the images sunk in, Tommy watched as another man walked through him. There was an image of flames engulfing them. Tommy stepped back, and as the flames died down, he saw through them, saw the man cowering on the floor. There was a metal case he was protecting under its boards; he dropped it there as the flames grew closer. He was in the Alterson fire.

Tommy felt the heat die away, along with the form. He saw the feet of another being and looked up at a younger man standing in front of him.

'My dad used to say you'd be the answer. He said you had that love that no one could take. Take care of him.'

'Tim?'

The spirit smiled with a wink and then stepped into Tommy. Again, the light shone. Tommy watched as the other spirits walked towards him. Each stepped through as the light grew brighter, just as it had before he returned. As the last person walked through, Tommy turned round and looked at the light. It gradually faded, and Tommy was left in darkness again. A gentle breeze blew across the waves of grass, and silence filled the air. Tommy had no idea that he was being watched from a distance. The shadow observing him gripped the knife's engraved handle.

Shaun struggled to stay on his feet. Blood was pumping from the wound in his stomach. He felt the flow as it ran down his leg. He gripped the knife Fiona had used and now slowly limped his way along the hallway to the front door. There had been the sound of police sirens as he leaned on the broken door. It didn't matter now. He would kill her and then bleed out. He knew it was over, but she'd done this to him, and now she had to pay. He leaned in the doorway, his arm limp at his side, holding the knife. He pulled the small pot from his pocket, and using his thumb, he pushed the lid open. Raising the pot to his nose, he inhaled deeply, coughing as he did so. Feeling a brief moment of painlessness, he dropped the pot and stood on his feet.

Fiona saw the police car at the bottom of the road, and she saw Shaun on the balcony. She could push him just like her father. He would fall, probably dying at the bottom. She looked at her mum and Sally seated in the kitchen. They were full of fear. Fiona watched as his bloody form stood level with the window. He placed a bloody hand on the window, peering in. He saw them and leaned back, making a fist. He hit the window, causing a crack to form from corner to corner. Sally screamed, and Rebecca began to cry. Fiona coldly stared at him. The second punch shattered the glass.

'I'm gonna gut you like a fish!' he exclaimed, pointing the bread knife at her.

The police started to ascend the steps to the third level as Shaun started climbing into the window, pulling himself on to the draining board, in the kitchen. Blood dripped from his face, over the plates and sink, as he did so. The broken glass still in the frame sliced against his stomach.

Fiona grabbed a saucepan from the unlit stove. 'I'm warning you, Shaun,' she threatened, wielding the pan.

There was a cold chill in the room, and Shaun stopped. His eyes bulged. He looked around and mumbled something, throwing the knife to the side. It echoed as it spun around the steel sink. Everything seemed silent as Shaun pulled himself back out on to the balcony and leaned against the railing.

Fiona lowered the saucepan, smiling. She mouthed the word 'Dad' at Shaun, with her mum and Sally behind her. Shaun involuntarily nodded. Fiona knew it was him.

'Freeze!' The first policeman was taking the last of the stairs. The officer's breathing heavy. Shaun's body seemed to be out of control as he stepped forth and then back to the railing. With a struggle, Shaun looked towards the policeman. Fear filled his eyes.

'What's the stupid son of a bitch doing?' Rebecca asked as he leaned further back on the balcony, his upper body towards the drop. Sally stood up and stepped closer to the window, watching as Shaun shook his head violently from side to side, blood spraying from his chin.

'Why? Why are you here?' he shouted, his eyes darting from side to side. The police looked at each other.

'We answered the disturbance call, and now we're placing you under arrest.' One of the officers stated walking towards Shaun with his handcuffs at the ready while the other held his gun out, marking them.

'No!' Shaun screeched as his body tilted further back. His feet struggled to touch the floor. 'Please. Have mercy. How are you doing this!' Shaun continued screaming as he fought against his own body. A moment later, his weight shifted, and he rolled back, falling from the balcony. The two officers quickly ran down the steps, almost as if to race the falling body. The loud thud echoed through the forecourt.

Fiona, Rebecca, and Sally all ran to the balcony and peered over as the officer approached Shaun's body. Blood was pooling around him. Despite a sigh of relief, Fiona also felt a moment of remorse. She had loved him no matter what he'd done. She looked at her mother, who stepped forward and hugged her. Feeling her mother's embrace, she began to weep.

'The videotape showed three known drug dealers dropping off the bag with an unknown assailant,' Inspector Dibble stated as he entered the room. 'Ben Williams, Gavin Wallace, Joe Molk, and a fourth person. He can't be identified from the videotape because he was on the far side of the car and didn't get out. We were told that one of these men was delivering these drugs to your premises this evening as a tip-off.'

'May we ask who made that contact?' Wesley asked, returning Inspector Dibble's glare.

'I've respectably represented each of those three men at various times under the instructions of Tony Boswell. I believe we can all do the mathematics and work out who made this call to you. Would it have happened to have been from a businessman currently at a meeting in London?' The inspector nodded before Francis Norton continued. 'I thought as much. I can actually explain to you the reasoning for this, as my client here, Mr Curtis, has since begun working with some business clients of mine instead of Tony Boswell. They, like myself earlier today, discovered that Tony Boswell is a very fraudulent man. He has been passing money through his business accounts, money made on the black market, including from drugs sales, all of which were sold on his behalf by those individuals in that car. If you watch the videotape again, you'll clearly see that this was a dump and run case. They discovered that I was mounting a case to expose the individuals for these crimes after misleading me all this time. They disposed of their merchandise in an attempt to frame Mr Curtis.' Francis Norton opened his briefcase and removed several sheets of paper. 'These photos, taken this weekend by a private investigator I hired will give you some evidence. Ask around. I know there's a number of other people waiting to give some more.'

Dibble took the pictures and started scanning through them. He nodded as he looked at the crates being offloaded into a container at the marina. He saw Ben Williams handing a security man an envelope. Another photo showed the clothes in a pile and Ben Williams holding a small white bag identical to the ones found in the boathouse at Wesley Curtis's place. Dibble nodded and thanked him, opening the door and allowing them to go free.

'Oh, and when you're officers arrest them, Boswell especially, remind them to get a good lawyer because my client here has got the best.'

'This place is a wreck!' Squawk announced, looking around his bedroom. He couldn't help but find it strange, the manner in which things had been moved. The door hadn't been neatly forced open like the police usually would. He'd been raided before, and the door was forced open to avoid some damage; this time, it was only standing by one hinge. The sofa and Fiona's bed had been tipped over, and in his room, a number of shelves were emptied. Squawk went straight to his bedside cabinet. His private stash was gone.

'This wasn't the pigs. This was Shaun. He stole my gear. That's what he was looking for.'

Ben screwed his face up. 'He smashed up your house for a couple of lines?' Squawk shrugged off the question.

'You got a message!' Joe stated, standing next to the answerphone.

'Play it. Probably Tony checking up!'

Joe pressed PLAY, and the message started. There was some sobbing, and the four men looked at each other before the woman started talking.

'Gavin? Gavin, are you there?' There was a pause as the person waited for him to pick up. 'I guess you're not . . . , and I didn't want to tell you this over the phone. Sonia never came home last night. We had a phone call from the police this morning . . . , and she's been killed. They wouldn't even let us see her. They said it was under suspicious circumstances. Please call us when you hear this. I want to explain more, talk to you about it. Please call.' Again she sobbed, until she was cut off by the beep.

Silence filled the room. The four men looked at each other. Rapid lowered the red towel from his broken nose.

'Man, I'm sorry,' Joe said as Squawk raised a hand.

'I'm gonna kill this fucker,' Squawk ranted, grabbing his mobile. 'I thought it was some prank, like you said, Ben, but it's not. It's just like that bloke said. He's the answer to all this. He knows more about this fucker than we do.' He glanced at the two messages flashing at him and ignored them. He scrolled down to Boris's number and dialled. Impatiently, he waited as Boris answered on the third ring to Squawk's anger.

'You knew he killed her, didn't you?'

'Hello, Gavin,' Boris said, 'let's say I had my suspicions.'

'Where is he? I'm going to kill him.' Boris looked across the graveyard and smiled.

'It's funny you should mention that.'

Chapter Thirty

Daniel Jones sat bolt upright. His breathing was heavy, and cold sweat clung to him. Something was happening. The red lights of his alarm clock danced to 3.05. He swallowed hard and stood up from the chair. He looked at the bullets and then the gun. He could almost sense the presence approaching his door as he slipped the bullets into his pocket. Then came the loud tapping against his door. Jones walked towards it and prepared himself.

The cars' wheels spun as Squawk slammed down the accelerator. He sped down the city centre, ignoring several people that screamed abuse at him as they drunkenly danced through the street. Even Ben seemed worried as Squawk appeared possessed with revenge. Ben glanced back, and it was clear that Joe and Rapid shared his concern.

As the car bounced over a speed bump, Squawk felt against his ribs the reassuring knock of the gun in his jacket pocket. He had phoned some friends as he ran down the steps to the car, calling in everyone who owed him favours. He had sworn Sonia vengeance; he would kill Tommy Atkins that morning.

Tommy now lay on the grave, his back resting against the headstone. His body still ached, but the wounds were closing. He could still feel the ridges of the Rivals symbol against his chest as he ran his fingers along it underneath the T-shirt. Slowly, he knelt and cautiously got to his feet.

Boris stood in the cemetery gateway, readjusting the grip against his knife. There was only one way this fight could go down, one place in which he could kill Tommy to fulfil his mission. He glanced at the street, worrying that his manipulated minions wouldn't make it in time as he watched Tommy pace around Oliver's grave. He prepared to confront him, maybe even delay him. He couldn't fail his mission. He wouldn't go back to hell's prison.

'You knew I'd follow you when you came here, didn't you?' Jones said, following Samuels down the steps. 'Look at you—you're still under the influence!'

'Look, I've got one crazy person on this ride. I don't need another,' Samuels stated as he walked out the main entrance from Daniel Jones's building. Buckled in the backseat was Amber. Jones gave a slight smile as he saw her, and he jumped into the passenger seat. Samuels glanced at the two of them as he dropped some bullets into his gun. Locking on the safety catch, he swung behind the wheel.

'I know you'd want to hear this. They've been spotted on the CCTV, heading through town at high speeds. I also answered your phone. My guess is they're going to the church. I think they're after Tommy. He rang, and there's more evidence,' Amber explained, raising her eyebrows as Jones turned to her. Before he had a chance to ask anything, the car jumped to life and the blue lights danced through the darkness.

Amber's smile showed her excitement as she glanced out of the window as the images blurred into the distance. Samuels's foot was as heavy on the accelerator as it could be.

'Finally . . . evidence and warrant. It's about fucking time!' Samuels said through gritted teeth.

CHAPTER THIRTY-ONE

CHAPTER THIRTY-ONE

The car burst through the closed gates, causing a spark to come from the hinges as they broke from the concrete pillars. The commotion caused Tommy to look up. He saw the car crash into several headstones as it came to a halt. The four men jumped out, and Tommy smiled involuntarily. He hit the redial button and dropped the phone to the ground.

'Hello, boys. Are we having a pleasant evening?' Tommy's words were more confident than their previous encounters. He now knew everything.

Boris had some growing concerns as Squawk ran towards him, pulling the gun from his jacket. Boris knew he couldn't let him bleed out here, not in the graveyard. He would fail.

'Wait!' Boris shouted, running from the back of the cemetery. 'He's phoned someone! He has evidence on you!'

Squawk briefly turned; Tommy didn't. He ran at Squawk and pounced forward, sending him crashing to the ground, the gun sliding across the grass. Tommy threw some punches at Squawk's face as Ben grabbed him and pulled him off by the back of his jacket. Tommy quickly readjusted himself to face Ben and gripped his shoulders, tossing Ben over his hip and on to the ground with a judo-like throw.

Rapid shoved Tommy back, seeming shocked at Tommy's actions. Tommy remained standing, briefly smiled, and then threw a kick towards him, connecting with his stomach and causing Rapid to buckle over as Tommy stepped towards Molk, throwing several quick punches to his face and knocking him to the ground. He swung back round with a kick to the side of Rapid's head, sending him down. With a menacing smile, he watched Ben get back to his feet. Tommy was enjoying his revenge.

'They're there already. I heard them,' Amber stated, switching Samuels's mobile to speakerphone. The muffled noises from the cemetery filled the police car. 'I think there's someone helping Tommy too. He hollered something before it went like this.' Samuels nodded. The speed of the car increased slightly as they entered the main street.

'How do we know he's a friend?' Jones asked, his hand still placed over his pocket, holding his bullets steady. He didn't want the artwork on them scratched if the bullets rubbed together.

'It doesn't matter. They're there, and we will be soon,' Samuels answered, trying to press his foot down harder on the accelerator.

Two more friends of Squawk's had turned up, and still, Tommy dominated the scene. He had been punched and kicked, and he fought the six men continuously, but still retreated no ground. Joe Molk lay against the headstone, holding his head where it had been lacerated. With his tongue, he felt where three of his teeth had been knocked out.

Boris stood nearby, looking at the scene. He'd seen these warriors before—the men given power by the gods, power his kind could take.

Tommy swung one of the newer men round, releasing him in time to go stumbling head first into another headstone. Tommy glanced back and had a heavy punch thrown against his cheek, the impact barely affecting him. He threw several punches of his own. Tommy watched the man stumble to the floor as he felt the pain burn through his shoulder.

Tommy swung around and stared the man in the eyes. He could see the man's fear. With two hands, he shoved him back to the gravestone, the impact winding him. Tommy reached behind and pulled the butterfly knife from his shoulder; blood ran from the wound. Tommy glanced at the blade and then threw it away. He swung back and looked at the men struggling to mount an offence as another of their cars arrived at the cemetery gates.

Three men got out and looked at the situation. They saw six men struggling to get to their feet, three of whom were now unable to. Hesitantly, they walked forward, talking amongst themselves, planning a route of attack.

Tommy had seen them, and a bloody smile spread across his face. Fists clenched, Tommy marched towards them.

Boris knew this was his chance, and he gripped the blade tightly as he ran across to the fallen men, assuring Tommy was a good distance away from him. He dropped to his knees next to Squawk.

'I can help you. You can be strong enough to beat him!' Boris said, placing a hand under Squawk's head. Squawk shook his hand free and knelt up again. His mouth was full of the coppery taste of his own blood, and he spat twice, attempting to get rid of it. Squawk turned to Boris.

'I'll kill 'im. I guarantee it!'

'Oh yes, of course you will. You're doing such a good job so far. You need my help. I can give you the strength you need. I can give you strength even beyond his dreams. All you got to do, Gavin, is accept it,' Boris paused as he glanced at the scene ahead of them. 'That's all you need to do!'

Squawk looked and shook his head as he got slowly to his feet. 'What on earth can you do to make me stronger?'

'Just accept the deal, and I'll show you!' Boris's tone had changed.

'Fine. I accept!' Squawk laughed as he went to walk past Boris, towards Tommy, who had now subdued the new adversaries. Boris quickly dragged the knife across his hand, coating it with his own blood before slicing it across the back of Squawk's neck.

Squawk screamed as he turned round and looked at Boris. 'What? You fuckin' traitor!' Squawk's punch knocked Boris from his feet. He turned to see Tommy walking towards him.

'Ready for another round?' Tommy asked, reaching towards him.

Before Tommy could grab him, Squawk kicked him in the stomach, the impact buckling Tommy over. Quickly Squawk followed it with a knee to Tommy's face. Blood erupted from his nose as he fell to the ground. Squawk quickly capitalised, throwing several kicks at him as Ben began to stand up.

Ben reached to the side of his face, felt the deep cut, and wiped away some blood as he watched his friend stamping down the man responsible.

He smiled as he walked up behind him, and it was then he saw the black bubbles sizzling from the neck wound. Black soot danced above the red blood that flowed from the cut.

'What the fuck?' Ben's words and hesitation caused Squawk to turn towards his friend. The colour drained from Ben's face as he looked into Squawk's eyes. His eyes were blackened. It appeared the pupils were melting. There was a moment of stillness as the two looked eye to eye. 'Squawk, your eyes, man ... W ... wh ... what happened?'

Squawk tilted his head and looked at Ben. He tilted his head back the other way. A twitch danced over his body, and a smile slid over his face. 'Squawk?' Ben was taking a step back as he saw that his friend had changed. He'd thought before that there was something strange about him, and now he could see it.

He glanced at Boris, who stood with his arms crossed and knife pointing to the side. 'What the fuck did you do to him?' Boris shrugged.

'Pure? He purified me. I have no guilt. No remorse. That soul took everything from me. He will die.' Squawk was pointing at Tommy, who still lay on the ground. Squawk's voice was different; there was an angry calmness tone to it. His intentions were so severe, yet they seemed justified.

'He didn't, man,' Ben said. 'Listen to me. We're friends, you and me. We have been for years. I'll help you. You need a doctor.' Ben stepped towards Squawk, reaching a hand out to his shoulder. Squawk reached towards it, and in a quick motion, he flicked his hand back so Ben's fingers touched his own forearm. The cracking of Ben's wrist echoed moments before Ben's screams filled the cemetery. Several men looked on as Squawk pushed his friend to the ground. He glanced back at Boris and slowly tilted his head again before nodding to him.

Chapter Thirty-two

The police car crashed into the back of the second car. The sound echoed through the churchyard as it became engulfed with a sea of blue. Samuels swung from the driver's seat, pulling his gun ready, flicking off the safety catch.

Amber quickly followed him, grabbing some things from the backseat. Jones stood beside the car, holding the engraved bullets in his hand so tightly that they dug into his palm. Samuels looked at the three men who lay on the ground at the entrance and then continued walking. Amber dropped to her knees, handcuffing one of the men who lay on his front, unconscious, with a pair of handcuffs she had gotten from the backseat. As Samuels heard them locking, he turned back to see Amber kneeling there.

'What are you doing? Get back to the car!'

'I'm trying to help. You can't do it alone.'

'You're right. I can't. But it's too dangerous for you. Use the CB in the car. Call for backup!'

Amber nodded and ran back, stopping to look at Jones as she did so. He seemed distant as he looked across the graveyard. 'Are you okay?' she asked.

Jones nodded. 'For now.' Jones could see Boris in the distance; he was watching how things were moving along. He watched as Squawk kicked his friend in the chest so he was lying on his back. Squawk then raised his foot and stamped on Ben's face.

Tommy was getting to his feet as he saw Squawk remove his foot from the Ben's face. Ben's face had caved in under the blow, and it was no longer recognisable. His body lay there twitching as Squawk's friends began to walk or crawl away from the scene.

Squawk ran at Tommy, throwing a number of wild punches that Tommy dodged by stepping back. When he saw an opportunity, he stepped forth, throwing several of his own. Several connected with Squawk's face, but none seemed to make a dent. Squawk shook them off just as Tommy had previously.

The three bullets tore through Squawk like a hot knife through butter. He turned to face Samuels as he fell to his knees. Blood pumped from his wounds, but he remained on his knees.

Samuels froze as he looked at Squawk. His eyes had burnt from his face, and the empty sockets were all that remained. A black goo seeped down his cheeks. Fear filled him.

Before anyone moved, Boris grabbed Samuels and swung him to the ground, pulling the knife from its sheathe. He raised the knife up above him, and Tommy quickly grabbed Boris's wrist, pulling him backwards to the ground.

'What are you doing?' Tommy hollered as Boris lay on his back, looking up at Tommy. The question was unnecessary. In Boris's eyes, Tommy saw a white spark in his pupils. Something wasn't right. Boris tilted his head with a slight smile as he pointed to his left.

Tommy turned and caught a glimpse as Squawk dived towards him, shoving him to the ground. Several of the fallen men now stood on the sidelines, clearly unsure of what they were watching.

Amber and Daniel Jones stood next to the car; Daniel had stopped Amber from calling the police station. She was puzzled, but Jones had explained that this wasn't just the gang's fight. He had showed her one of the bullets with the symbol and said the police couldn't stop the fight. It was then that Squawk had thrown Tommy to the ground.

Boris got to his feet first, and he moved over to Samuels. With a firm kick to the side of his temple, Boris knocked Samuels unconscious.

CHAPTER THIRTY-THREE
CHAPTER THIRTY-THREE

CHAPTER THIRTY-THREE

Samuels began to stir as he watched Squawk, or at least what was once Squawk, dominating the fight. He grabbed Tommy and threw him head first at a headstone. The granite cross crumbled under the impact. Still, Tommy somehow struggled to move, his body beaten and bloody. Flesh was dangling from his cheek as he pushed his weight up on all fours. Squawk grabbed him by his long hair and tilted his head back, clenching his fist as he raised it high above him as if to hit the last destructive blow.

'Stop!' Boris ordered. With a tilt of his head, Squawk released Tommy's hair, allowing his motionless body to drop to the ground. Boris pointed to Tommy and raised an open hand, symbolising for Tommy to be lifted. With a nod, Squawk followed the instruction and lifted Tommy's lifeless body up and over his shoulder. Boris pointed towards the church, and Squawk carried Tommy as instructed.

Samuels had gotten to his knees, and as Boris went past him, he delivered another kick to the side of his head, knocking him unconscious again. Boris led the way into the church, leaving all the fallen men in fear. They left one door slightly ajar as they entered, not expecting anyone to follow.

Jones released Amber's wrist. She turned to him as he stepped forward. 'Wait here, and don't let anyone follow me,' Jones instructed as he started walking towards Samuels, who lay motionless on the grass. He picked up the gun and opened the chamber, releasing the plain bullets before inserting the ones from his pocket, the ones with the symbol. Amber had followed him, and she dropped to her knees next to Samuels. She watched as Jones changed the bullets.

'What are you doing? He was unstoppable,' she said as she placed a hand on Samuels's back.

Jones looked at her, his face a mix of fear and confidence. 'There's a way. I think I know what I'm doing, but please don't follow.' Amber nodded as she began rubbing Samuels's face, trying to bring him round. Jones glanced around the cemetery at members of the Rivals. None could make a quick escape; their injuries prevented it.

'Make sure they all get collected,' Jones stated, tapping Amber on the shoulder. Amber gave another nod and then watched as Jones approached the church doors, reaching in his pocket as he entered.

He gripped the church key in his hand, and as he peered in, he saw that no one was in the hall's entrance. Cautiously, he entered, closing the large wooden doors as silently as he could, turned the key, removed it, and then slipped it back in his pocket. As he peered into the empty church, he gripped the gun's trigger tighter.

Chapter Thirty-Four

Tommy could see the long shaft of the church tower above him. At the top, the single bell stood silently. He struggled as he came to, realising his body was stretched out. His eyes followed down his right arm and saw the tight leather looped around his wrist and nailed into the floor with several inches of the large nail showing. He glanced to his other arm; it was tied the same. As he struggled to move his legs, he felt the same restraints. Tommy had been strapped up in a star shape. Somehow though he could feel cold air all around him. He knew his coat and T-shirt had been pulled off, but he felt like he was floating. He struggled to see, but in the corner of his eye, he noticed the thin dip that led to a circle below him, no more than a brick's depth, but he was suspended above it. He could even feel the blood dripping from his face. Pain still surged through his body.

'Hello, Tommy. Before we continue, I hope you understand that this was nothing personal. You see, you're one of his warriors,'—Boris pointed upwards—'and I'm . . . well, let's just say that I'm not one of his any more. He made the mistake of sending me down below for rebelling.' Boris was now walking around the circle that Tommy was held over. 'You just became some little pawn in a much bigger game. But you chose to be, and if it's any consolation, you've managed to get the revenge you desired. All the Rivals—well, the main influences—will go to jail. Whoever you did this for would be proud. However, you'll become the first key to the gates.'

'Who are you?' Tommy asked.

'I'm Nemon. That won't mean shit to you, so why ask?'

'I want to know your name for when I free myself and tear your head off!'

'I can see why they allowed you back; you've got a bit of character about you. I like that. If you haven't realised, you're actually tied with leather straps to a thin circle underneath the bell tower. You've got nowhere to go. You see, that bell is like a lock.' Nemon pointed upwards again, and Tommy's eyes followed the tower to the top. 'There are six hundred and sixty-six of these locks around—every one a remote church with a tower and the thin brickwork along the base just like this.' Nemon knelt down and ran his fingers along the edge of the circle. 'Now as your heart bleeds out and your blood drips down, it'll slowly fill this circle. With your heart's final beat and its final drop, this circle will be covered, and that bell will ring. That'll then expose the other churches, and after the first one has rung, bad things will start to happen here on earth. It means some of my friends will be coming up. This world banished them, and they're a little annoyed about that. Well, I don't need to prolong your death with my idle chit-chat. You can see where this is going. I'm only telling you this because after you bleed out for me, you may want that info as a bargaining chip down below. Sorry, kid.'

With those words, Boris stepped forward, raising the engraved dagger above him with his grip tightened. 'Oh, I should have just added that the reason my friends didn't come to the party when they rang that bell every Sunday morning. It had to be a set thing. Your blood, my knife! Once again, good luck below!' With those words, the knife plummeted down into Tommy's chest, straight through his heart. Tommy's screams travelled up the bell tower as the blood began to drip from his body.

Tommy struggled, but to no avail. He couldn't free himself. Boris's form laughed as he stepped back to the curtain that camouflaged them from the church hall, which Jones was now pacing his way through.

'Boris, I thought we should have a couple of words!' Jones yelled.

Boris smiled as he watched the blood drip down to the circle below Tommy. 'I'm glad you owned a pure heart like that. When it empties and stops beating, it's party time! But first I've got to have a chat with Mr Jones! Don't die before I get back!' Nemon sniggered as he straightened up. He glanced at Squawk and ordered him to watch Tommy.

The body of Squawk nodded. His eyes were gone, and the black goo slid down his cheeks, some of it beginning to exit through his nose. It seemed Squawk's insides were changing into it. Even the few cuts on his face turned black as they healed.

'Daniel, how have you been?' Nemon asked as he appeared through the curtains like a magician entering the stage. 'I must apologise for not phoning, but I've been busy!' Boris stated as he looked up to see the gun pointed at him. He tilted his head to one side and raised his arms. 'Don't be like that. We can be friends.'

'So what's your real name?'

'Have you been drinking? My name's Boris. Can't you remember?'

'I've known Boris for years, and I know he wouldn't do what you've done,' Jones said, holding his pose steady and casting an eye through the sight of the gun. 'I can also guess you got to that body by possessing Bethel. It's the only way I can explain her death before she died.'

'So you know I'm a possession demon. I guess you may as well know I'm called Nemon.'

'I just wanted to check before I kill you.' Jones's words were cold, making Nemon laugh.

'I'm sorry. I shouldn't laugh. You look so demon huntery and all, but despite you being all the fun of the fair, you need to do some more research 'cause that gun won't harm me.' Nemon's tone had changed; a more sinister voice now spoke to the reverend.

'What makes you so sure?'

'Because this is a vessel! It's just skin and bone! What I am is much greater, and the ways to kill me died out many years ago. Being a man of the cloth, I'd like you to know that the church you—yes, you in particular—hold so dearly is what brings forth your world's demise.' Nemon waved an arm towards the curtain, lifting it aside to show Tommy lying on the floor.

'You really believe that, don't you! What did you say to me a minute ago? I'm all the fun of the fair?'

Nemon nodded, laughing. 'All you humans are, 'cause to us, that's what you represent: a funfair! The fairground rides, to be precise. We can pick and choose which meat puppets we ride.'

'I never did like the fairground.' Jones squeezed the trigger, and the bullets ploughed into Boris's body. The first passed straight through his shoulder, the second lodged in his chest, the third in his head. The recoil of the gun sent Jones towards the floor as Nemon screamed in pain. Jones's ears were ringing. Despite expecting the gun to be louder than in the movies, he'd never expected it to be that loud.

Tommy had stopped struggling. He was growing weak. The blood was dripping at a fast pace as it ran down the point of the knife and on to the brickwork below him. It flowed through its cracks, forming a symbol that was engraved at the top of the knife's handle. He looked up the long tower, forcing himself to keep his eyes open as he saw the bell begin to sway.

He closed his eyes briefly as he felt his head drop back. The jolt made his eyes open instantly, and he mustered up some strength, but he struggled against his restraints unsuccessfully, the leather cutting into his wrist as he did so.

Tommy turned and took a long look at Squawk. His eyes were hollow and black, the stains running over his cheeks from the sockets. He was standing in one spot, staring at the wall ahead of him. Tommy could hear the voices in the church's main room, but couldn't make them out. He looked to his hands and then up at the long tower. He tried raising his hands once more but couldn't even tighten the strap because his arms hung limply downwards. His eyes closed.

'Tommy?' the female voice sounded soft and caring.

Tommy slowly opened his eyes to a white glow. He turned his head and saw her lying next to him. Her blonde hair was trailing over her shoulder as she lay on her side, looking at him. For a moment, Tommy became lost in her bright green eyes; he remembered being lost there before, and he warm from the memory. He studied her face, watching as the smile spread across her red lips. 'You know you can't let it end like this.' Tommy felt a flutter inside him as if his heart had skipped a beat. 'They need your heart to beat its final beat. It never will.'

'Claire?' She nodded. 'I thought I lost you!'

'We've got to stop this, Tommy. You know how much I loved you?' Tommy nodded. 'Can you remember what you said at my graveside that day? Can you remember why your heart can't beat its final beat?' Another memory was released inside him. Nothing other than Claire seemed real. For a moment, he felt the knife push upwards in his chest as he felt the scar try to close. He looked up to the bell that swung back and forth.

'I have no heart,' Tommy said, turning back to Claire with a smile. 'I gave my heart to you forever more.' Tommy clenched his fists. He looked beyond Claire to his right arm and, with one sudden movement, yanked the restraint, snapping the leather. Claire smiled as she floated to her feet.

Squawk had instantly sprung to life as Tommy snapped the restraint. He stepped forward, raising a foot above Tommy's stomach as Tommy snapped the second strap. Before Squawk dropped the foot, Claire had placed a hand over his face. He had frozen, his foot hovering over Tommy, as if someone had paused the scene on a video.

Tommy raised his legs, snapped the remaining straps, and slid back to the edge of the circle, away from Squawk's boot. He pulled the knife from his chest, feeling the pain briefly as the flesh moulded itself back together. Tommy glanced at the pattern on the floor; it was identical to the symbol on the top point of the knife handle.

The tower began glowing white as Claire raised her left hand towards the bell. Amongst the light, the faintest chime sounded. Then, as the light dimmed, the bell hung central and motionless at the top. Tommy looked back to Claire, who was still holding a hand to Squawk, keeping him in the position.

'Gavin, I know you're in there still. All these years, they manipulated your path for this moment, prevented you from making your decisions. Let me show you your past; let me show you your future, the path they choose for you. You can then decide,' Claire said, placing a hand to each side of his face, her thumbs over his eyes. As she began to glow, she pushed both fingers into Squawk's eye sockets.

Gavin 'Squawk' Wallace saw his past. He saw Tommy walk into the apartment and lean forward, grabbing him in the chair and shaking him as he ordered a friend to call for an ambulance. Saw the concern of Claire and Tommy in the waiting room that night. Watched them leave when they found out he was okay.

The alleyway was cold, and Sonia was scared. He had been chasing her after she had left the flats, calling after her, saying it was destiny. He had eventually caught her after chasing her through two housing estates. She had taken what she'd thought was a shortcut but was actually a dead end. Boris's form grabbed her by the hair and then slammed her to the floor. Nemon's eyes were shining as he swung the knife down, stabbing her in the chest. Sonia was still alive but barely conscious as Nemon dragged her up the steel steps to the second level of the fire escape. In a quick motion, he dragged the knife across her throat. He carved the symbol deep into her body and then smiled as he took several more swipes across her throat, deepening the cut. He saw him pick up her phone and taste her blood before speaking. For a moment, he had stolen her voice.

He saw the body of Stuart Anderton lying in the street outside his apartment while the ambulance sped to his aid. Stuart was rolling in pain as they had rushed off to phone the ambulance and save themselves. He saw Boris smile, and he pulled the knife across his throat and then ascended the fire escape and went into Squawk's bedroom, where they first met. Then the light shone brighter, almost engulfing the tower.

Squawk screamed out as he saw the images: creatures with scales crawling from holes in the earth, humans with teeth that could penetrate skin with just a touch, a wolf-like creature tearing people limb from limb, black dust floating towards a young couple. The fire escaping the bell tower, he himself standing amongst the flames, changing, growing as his flesh burned into hardened charcoal. Then he saw the outcome. He saw the Twelve before him, worshipping him. The death and destruction they caused.

The light was dimming in the tower, and it took Tommy's eyes time to adjust as he looked at Claire and Squawk. Claire had stepped away from him, and Squawk's eyes were glowing white. It appeared that all the light from the tower had retreated inside him. The glow had removed the stains across his cheeks and seemed to be overflowing his eyes. He looked to Claire and then Tommy, a smile creeping across his face as he looked to the curtains.

'I will not be their monster. I shall not allow the demons and spirits to arise because of him. The Twelve will not destroy us all,' Squawk announced as he paced to the curtain. Outside the tower, there were several gunshots, which caused Squawk to take flight through the curtain as the voices continued.

'Why do all you humans insist on shooting me? Have you not realised that it doesn't kill me!' Nemon said, standing back up. His anger looked intense as he towered over Jones.

'That body is going to die on you, and when you leave it, you'll have to go back to hell.'

'Naive fool. I explained to you before that this is a vessel, a shell for me. Yours will do just fine.'

Jones closed his eyes and prayed the diagrams were right, hoped everything went well. He opened them as he heard Nemon mumble.

'What the . . . ? What have you done?'

'Sometimes, bullets can work,' Jones stated, struggling to his feet. Before Nemon could move, there was a crash from behind. He swung around to see Squawk running forward. He gripped Nemon by his jacket, lifted him from the floor, and ploughed him into the wall. The impact echoed around the hall of the church. Before releasing the hold, Squawk swung around, throwing Nemon into the pulpit, shattering the wooden structure as Nemon, in Boris's body, rolled along the floor. Blood pumped from several of the deep wounds as Squawk walked over, glancing towards Reverend Jones before looking down at the beaten body of Boris. Nemon reached to the wounds, and gripped them, watching as the blood pumped up between his fingers as several arteries became severed. He knew there was a large piece of varnished wood still puncturing his right side.

'You've used me, manipulated my life.' The white light from his eyes seemed to rage more powerful. 'You killed Sonia!'

Nemon looked up from the floor and raised his bloodied hands as if pleading for mercy.

Squawk showed none as he reached down and grabbed Boris's wrists, dragging him to his feet and swinging him around, releasing him in the air. Boris's body was thrown into the wooden seating, sending several of the benches tumbling back.

As Nemon rolled out of the capsized seats, he felt the piece of wood slide from his wound. The blood poured from it. Every time Nemon moved Boris's body, it threatened to fall apart. Blood was pumping from several large gashes.

Nemon struggled up, feeling scared and trapped in a body that was failing. He turned around to see his challenger standing ready. Squawk reached forward, grabbing Boris's beaten body, and threw him back to the floor.

As he glanced around his church, Reverend Jones watched Boris's body be thrown like a rag doll. He had been teaching here for years, spent happy times with friends, and sheltered others in times of need. Further back, he even held his family within these walls. No one would have predicted the horrors this church hid. Not even Jones would of believed, if he hadn't heard Nemon exposing them to Tommy previously. All those memories would have to be destroyed, along with the church he loved so dearly. As he was collecting his thoughts, the combatants' yells became louder, and he remembered the scene unravelling before him.

Boris was throwing some punches back now in an attempt to stop Squawk's power. He landed a number of punches that did manage to faze Squawk's rage, although soon he reached out and grabbed Boris, slamming him to the floor and holding him by the throat. Boris was reaching up, clawing and pushing at Squawk, who refused to let go. Soon, Boris's body went limp. It was only then that Squawk released his hold. He stood up and looked down at Boris, motionless. As Squawk looked to the skies, Nemon forced Boris's body into life and swung his legs round, sweeping out Squawk's, sending him crashing to the floor.

Tommy stood face-to-face with Claire's form. She was fainter than a real person but not as translucent as Harry. 'Are you going?' Tommy asked.

Claire smiled, holding a hand out before her, the palm upright in front of Tommy. She nodded. 'Yes. The world doesn't need me. I have loved ones that are waiting, but I knew you wouldn't go. I waited for this moment, to be the one who'd show you what you were born to achieve. You can make the difference.'

Claire motioned to her hand, which Tommy reached up and touched, a coldness crossing over them. Images like that which ran through Squawk's mind entered Tommy's. He saw the glowing eyes of beasts that he couldn't even imagine. Cloaked beings that hid their identity stared down on him. Then the image of shadows; the Twelve, flowed into him. The coldness stopped, and he looked at Claire to find her still smiling.

'They're all coming, and I told the powers you could stop them. You've been given your heart back, and I've taken back my pain. I had watched all those people. I'm sorry I sent their emotions to you, but I knew you'd help them. You always helped everybody. I love you, Tommy.' As she said the words, she leaned forward and softly placed her lips on Tommy's. He expected them to be cold like her palm, but they were as soft and warm as the kisses they'd shared when she was alive. Then his eyes closed, and he tasted and smelt her once more. He smiled as he opened his eyes. The tower was alive with light. Then there was none; Claire had crossed over.

Jones was rummaging through the small cupboard in the corner of the kitchen. The paint tins rolled across the floor as he threw them out of his way. He had several old rags placed next to him and had finally grabbed what he needed. He placed the bottle of white spirit upright on the draining board as he heard another loud crash coming from the church hall. He wrapped the old rags around the mop head and dowsed them with the bottle after opening it.

Jones stopped and glanced around the room for a moment, then built up his courage with a tight squeeze of his eyes. Picking up the fire lighter used to spark up the grill, he pressed the button and watched the small flame dance to life. The flame barely touched the fabric before the blaze engulfed the cloths covered in white spirit.

Tommy pushed the curtains out of his way and stood in the entrance, with Nemon's knife griped tightly in one hand. His body was still aching, and he felt weak as he watched the two men trade blows as they slammed each other into the wall.

Tommy struggled to follow the wall towards the entrance. It was as he grew level with the kitchen that he saw the flames appear first, followed by Reverend Jones gripping the long pole.

'I know what the tower is going to be used for. Please wait outside,' Jones exclaimed, his intentions obvious.

Tommy shook his head. 'Don't be foolish. Let me do it. We know I can heal quickly. If I'm trapped, I can probably recover. The smoke wouldn't affect me.' Tommy was pleading as Jones held his grip on the pole, shaking his head.

'This is my church, Tommy. I'm not leaving it like this. Besides, you're in no shape to do this. It has to be done right. You want to help me? Keep them away from me.' Jones pointed to Boris and Squawk. Boris was now holding his own; his face was bloody, but he was kneeling on Squawk's chest, raining down blow after blow into his face.

Tommy accepted the terms, walked to the centre aisle of the church, and raised the knife.

'Hey, I think you need this.'

Nemon stood up, staring at Tommy and then the knife. 'How did you do this?' he demanded, walking up the aisle. He hadn't noticed Reverend Jones, who ran down the left side of the church. Jones kept glancing back over his shoulder as he watched the flame slowly begin to creep along the base of the long tapestry that hung the length of the wall at the far end. He watched as the fabric depicting the last supper burned; before he lit the next, the flames danced level with the table. Soon, the supper would cook.

'I didn't. The person who owned my heart returned it. And now I'm going to remove yours!' Tommy's voice was calmer and more confident than before as he paced towards Nemon, the knife held out in front of him.

It was as they grew closer that Nemon smelt the burning. The tapestries had flames billowing up them, reaching the ceiling. The walls were lined with them, and several were now ablaze. As Nemon was turning towards Jones, Tommy pounced, stabbing Nemon in the shoulder with his own knife. Both men stumbled to the floor. Nemon quickly turned and threw several punches at Tommy before reaching back and pulling the knife from his own shoulder with a yell. The black blood dripped from the blade to the floor. Tommy watched as it absorbed into the carpet that lined the centre, leaving no trace on the top.

Nemon quickly threw a kick to Tommy's face with the hiking boots that Boris wore. He turned to see Squawk standing up and looking at him. Blood ran from his face, but the eyes still glowed. He reached towards him, gripping his throat with one hand. With the vice-like grip, he lifted Boris from the floor, and in the struggle, Nemon dropped the knife. As Nemon struggled hand over hand to break the hold, he watched the flames begin to creep through the church as Jones set fire to the bookshelves containing the hymn books. Soon, the blaze was getting out of control.

Squawk swung around and threw Nemon towards the pulpit again. This time, Boris hit the thick central stand. He quickly shook off the impact, feeling the release of the pressure around his throat. He grabbed the wooden cross that he had smirked at a couple of days previously and swung it from left to right at Squawk, who kept stepping back towards the burning walls of the church. On one of the swings, Nemon caught the flaming tapestry with the cross, flicking it across on to the wooden benches. Oblivious to the feuding men, the wood sparked to life, and the flames slowly crawled their way along the varnished surface.

In one quick motion, Squawk swung an arm forward, snapping the cross at its centre. He followed through and grabbed Nemon by the throat, punching him back into another of the flaming tapestries. The artwork dropped down, engulfing the two in flames as they continued to battle. With a kick, Squawk stumbled backwards, out of the flaming fabric. Boris flicked his body back, and the tapestry fell to the floor. As he glanced at his shirt, he saw the small flames flickering, and he began to pat them out. As he did so, Squawk charged at him, flames burning from his jacket, and he lifted Boris's form and dropped him down on the flames. The flames soon gripped their clothes and climbed around their flesh. Despite the pain and the smell of burning flesh filling the church, the two men struggled to fight. Their skin blistered in the intense heat and burst almost instantly.

Jones saw Tommy struggling up with the help of the wooden bench, with Nemon's knife back in his grip as he did so. Jones glanced at the fire and threw the burning mop to one side as he ran towards Tommy. Hoisting Tommy's arm over his shoulders while flinging his own around Tommy's waist, he helped support Tommy on his feet as they left the church.

Next to the large wooden doors, Jones reached into his pocket and searched for the key. Outside, several voices were calling for them, and he heard the door being kicked in an attempt to break it open. Reverend Jones panicked slightly, as he couldn't find the key at first. He reached deeper, and the second he felt it between his fingers, he felt relief flow through him. Quickly, he unlocked the door.

Instantly, as the door edged open, Samuels pounced in, and he quickly grabbed Tommy, hoisting the weight on to his shoulders, relieving the weight from Reverend Jones, who glanced back over his shoulder at the burning church. Tearing up slightly, Jones turned and left.

Once outside, Jones swung the wooden door shut, quickly locking it. All three men stumbled away from the church and sat on the grass, grasping the reality of what had just happened. As they felt some energy return to them, they stood up and made their way to Amber, who stood in the cemetery gateway, watching the smoke escape from the bell tower.

Samuels already had his mobile in his hand, ready to call the station. As he went to dial, Jones placed his hand on his wrist and shook his head. 'Not yet, John. Let's give it just a little more time.'

Samuels observed Jones and then Tommy, lowering his phone as they watched the fire grow. Soon, several flames escaped the bell tower in the same way the smoke had previously. Without any warning, the large circular stained glass window at the front of the church shattered as flames erupted through it. All the men jumped, including the gang members that were handcuffed along the wall, as the coloured glass fragments fell to the ground.

'I think that could be considered a sign that it's time to call it in,' Jones said as Amber giggled behind them. She was now seated on the car bonnet, with one leg tucked under herself and a smile across her face.

Jones couldn't help but return it. The city was now safe.

Chapter Thirty-Five

'The church had burned for most of the day. When fire brigades arrived, the flames had engulfed the entire building. It had been late in the evening when the fire was brought under control. Some people believe, however, that the faith of this church's worshippers was rewarded on this day because, by some miracle, the structure had not been damaged at all, despite everything inside being reduced to charcoal. No one could understand or explain this. It's also believed that due to a recent police investigation causing the back door to be removed, the two remaining people feared to have been killed in the blaze may well have escaped. Forensics are still working through the debris, but no bodies have been discovered so far.

'Also today, in the early hours of this morning, came the fall of the street gang known as the Rivals. This happened during a showdown with police at the church, where several key members were arrested. Since then, evidence has been found linking the fire, an attempt to hide drugs at a local businessman's house, and the drug culture of Alterson to not only these gang members but Alterson socialite and businessman, Tony Boswell, who is believed to have been financing them. Local business tycoon Tony Boswell was arrested in the early hours of this morning in a low-budget London hotel chain . . .'

Jones turned off the TV, interrupting the news reporter, and sat back in his chair, holding his coffee in both hands.

'You know they're going to keep coming here now, don't you? They're going to want to open that gate,' Jones said, looking to Amber and Samuels. 'Everything I've read means that small chime may have been enough to raise some demons and spirits. It's weakened. We're the only four people who know of this. We need to work together. We need to protect it.'

'Yeah. We will just give Tommy time,' Amber added. 'We've just dealt with defeating a demon—well, winning a war anyway.'

'A battle. The war's not even begun yet!' Samuels cut in, placing several marked bullets on the table. 'We'll need a lot more of them and whatever other weapons exist.'

Jones looked at the bullets and nodded. 'That knife is one of the best weapons we have. It hurt Nemon, not just Boris's body. When that knife went in, the blood that left was black. If we find out how it works, that could possibly be used to kill the demons.' Jones's eyes fell upon Nemon's knife, which sat in the centre of the kitchen table. 'Well, possession demons anyway!' Jones quickly corrected.

'What do you think Tommy is doing?' Amber asked.

'Don't know, but I know what I promised him.' Samuels stood up, pulling his coat from the back of the chair. 'He wanted me to speak to his parents, said they knew me and trusted me.'

'What are you going to say to them?' Amber asked, turning the mug in circles on the table in front of her.

'The truth. I'll explain that Tommy stopped the Rivals.' Samuels pulled his coat on and nodded to Jones. 'We collected the evidence from the places Tommy said. It was all there—even the box on Vauxhem Street, where the fire occurred. I don't think the new homeowners were to impressed as we pulled up their patio, but buried under it, just a few feet down, they found the box. They also found a box of videos in the attic of Squawk's flat, death of Mary, as Tommy said, plus a few others. Can't understand why he kept them. You'd think they'd destroy evidence like that!'

'What do you think happened to Squawk and Nemon?' Amber asked.

Samuels shrugged, and Daniel looked at the knife. 'I don't know, but I feel that if they're alive, they'll want that. They'll probably come for it too.'

'And we'll be prepared. Don't you worry!' Samuels added.

'Of course, we will. Look how well we've done this time without any practice,' Amber boasted.

'I expect we will,' Jones said. 'I just hope Tommy can cope knowing everything he lost.'

His footsteps were heavy, and with each one, the water splashed up and into the top of his boots. Water had soaked what remained of his trousers as he stumbled through the ankle-deep water along the edge of the sewer. He stepped on to a ledge against a storm drain and ran his fingers along his cheek. The skin was ragged and solid. In some areas, he even felt what he believed to be bone. His vision was slightly impaired in one eye, and he felt the flames touch it before he managed to escape the church. He had barely escaped Squawk's clutches as he dived from the door. He had seen the flames engulf his enemy's face.

Even now, though, he had no idea what gave Squawk the images, but he needed to know. He needed to communicate with his master below; he didn't want to go back, having failed his mission. He knew what pain and torment would follow. The body he had become trapped in was already beginning to smell inside, and the shape outside made it impossible to blend in. He needed his knife back; he needed to allow another message through. Then with what things were rising from the depths, he'd prepare for revenge. The reverend would die for his interference; Nemon would make sure of that.

Tommy stood at the end of the street and watched as his father left the car in the driveway. He was more frail now than Tommy remembered. His face had a few more lines, and his black hair was now faded grey. As always, he'd get to the front door and glance over at his garden and then double-check that the car was still there before entering. This time, however, his routine was changed, and he watched the police car roll up at the end of the lawn.

His fathers jaw dropped as he saw Samuels swing out of the driver's seat, holding up an evidence bag with a Dictaphone tape in it. Tommy watched as Samuels was greeted with a handshake. As Tommy saw the two men smile, he felt a tear roll down his cheek. As they entered the house and closed the door, Tommy turned away and walked out of the housing estate, removing the hat, his hair flowing behind him.

'It was this tape that led to the gang's downfall. I know that doesn't explain much to you, but if your son hadn't recorded this evidence, we wouldn't have leads to the other evidence.' Samuels felt a slight warmth inside him as he saw Tommy's parents' smiles mix with tears, their upset mix with pride. 'Somehow, he had hidden this in the church that caught fire last night. He left it there with the reverend, never explaining what was on it. Tommy had told him that when the time came, he'd understand. That time came three days ago, the day after the floods, when a woman there was murdered and tortured as they questioned the tape's whereabouts. Reverend Jones then played it back and gave it to me.'

'Is that why they killed him?' Tommy's mum had tears in her eyes, her bottom lip curled in under her upper teeth as she fought against her emotions. Samuels nodded. 'Tommy did it so he knew you'd be safe. He knew the gangs wouldn't stop hunting for it. He gave his life so everyone else could be safe. That's the kind of son you raised.' Samuels's words conveyed his feelings, the way he was grateful for Tommy bringing the murderers of his son to justice. As Samuels saw a tear run down Tommy's mum's cheek, he wiped away one of his own.

Tommy stood overlooking Claire's grave as he had done so many times before his death. He couldn't sense her presence any more and knew she was gone. He could still replay the kiss in the bell tower and taste her lips and smell her scent. He'd hold on to that for as long as he could. She believed in him.

Several stars shone in the clear night sky, and there was some dew forming on the grass. He had been there since the sun began its daily retreat to the night but couldn't seem to pull away. The church had been quarantined, but the churchyard was open.

As Tommy glanced up to the heavens, wondering if Claire now lived there, he heard soft footsteps on the grass behind him.

'Thought you'd be here!' Amber stated as Tommy turned. There was a slight twinkle in his eye as he saw that Fiona stood with her.

'Hey,' Fiona greeted, seeming unsure of what else to say.

'I just wondered if she'd be here. I know how strange it sounds,' Tommy said as he walked towards the path where the girls waited. 'I hear Harry managed to communicate with you?'

'Have you seen him?'

Tommy shook his head, and the smile faded from Fiona's face.

'I think he saved me,' Fiona said. 'When Shaun was trying to kill us, he stopped and smiled. I asked if it was him, and I'm sure I saw Shaun nod. He then dropped the weapon and fell from the balcony.'

'The most important thing he had was you. Making sure you were safe was all he cared about. My guess is that he's with Claire now. Maybe they're comparing notes about us!' Tommy joked as he led the way down the path, pausing at the end of the row to glance back once more at Claire's headstone.

Claire had believed in me. Now I have to honour her memory. They had no idea what was coming, but they'd need to be ready. The Twelve were coming.

Lightning Source UK Ltd.
Milton Keynes UK
UKOW050933151011

180342UK00002B/128/P